The Stones
of Mourning Creek

The Stones
of Mourning Creek

Diane Les Becquets

Marshall Cavendish

Grateful acknowledgment is made for permission to reprint the following song lyrics:

"There Will Be Peace In The Valley For Me"
By Thomas A. Dorsey
© 1939 (Renewed) Warner-Tamerlane Publishing Corp. and Unichappell Music Inc.
All Rights Reserved   Used By Permission
Warner Bros. Publications U.S. Inc.,
Miami, FL 33014

Marshall Cavendish Corporation, 99 White Plains Road, Tarrytown, NY 10591
www.marshallcavendish.us

Library of Congress Cataloging-in-Publication Data
Les Becquets, Diane.
The stones of Mourning Creek / by Diane Les Becquets.
p. cm.
Summary: In Alabama in the 1960s, fourteen-year-old Francie develops a controversial
and dangerous friendship with a "colored girl" her own age.
ISBN 0-7614-5238-9
[Prejudices—Fiction. 2. Race relations—Fiction. 3. Friendship—Fiction.
4. Country life—Fiction. 5. Alabama—History—20th century—Fiction.] I. Title.
PZ7.L56245St 2005
2004064953

Printed in the United States of America

First Marshall Cavendish paperback edition, 2005
Reprinted by arrangement with WinslowHouse International, Inc. and Diane Les Becquets

2 4 6 8 10 9 7 5 3 1

 Marshall Cavendish

Acknowledgments

Many thanks to: my first readers Deb Lundberg, Bev Steinman, Ceanna Ryndfleisz, Rita, Byron, Rick, and Mom; Lynn Cooley, my literary warrior and faithful encourager; Dolly, my writing comrade, who cared for these girls as much as me; Gus and Christine for all the snacks and steel; Judy for her guidance; my neighbor Libby, who rises as early as me and whose wonderful library of books and CDs remains at my disposal; Avis and her bookshop for the music and breaks; Gary, my laptop physician; Tom and Jeannie Kilduff, Lorraine Taylor, Lorenzo Holcey, Linda LeMaitre, Mike Bartlett, and Angie Harris, who provided answers to my endless questions; Eveline for the vision; all those wonderful families who were the soil of my Southern roots, you know who you are; Mom and Dad, who fostered my earliest imaginings; and my brothers who helped glue them together; Mamaw and Papa Joe, who gave me the 'Southern' voice; Grandma, who never quit; my mentor, Taylor Littleton, who saved me in the midst of my confusion way back when; Nancy Stauffer for pointing me in the right direction; Ken and Rachel Parlin and all my fellow Stonecoasters for the uproariously good times; my big little sister, Carol Houck Smith, for telling me to 'slow down'; my amazingly warm-hearted and discerning editor, Francesca—thanks for believing; Mary Frances and Anne, in whose lives the story was born—friendship never ends; Tim, Nate, Seth, and Jake for all their patience, hugs, and notes on napkins; and to my muse, as always, be well.

For Mom and Mary Frances
and in memory of Anne

Table of Contents

" 'O sun, stand still over Gibeon,
   O moon, over the Valley of Aijalon.'
   So the sun stood still,
   and the moon stopped,
   till the nation avenged itself
   on its enemies."

                    Joshua 10:12–13

Prologue

THE CLOCK TICKS TOO LOUDLY. Francie has long been in bed. She kissed me good-night before she turned in, her silky red hair brushing against my face, the smell of the wind and the grass still on her skin.

I sit at the kitchen table, a cup of coffee held to my face, the liquid now lukewarm. Sometimes I iron, sometimes I watch TV. Most of the time I just sit, an ache down my neck and across my spine. I set the cup in the sink, then open the back door. It's a cold night for April, the cool air hitting my face. I stare out at the black sky. No moon, no stars. From the kitchen light, I can see the outline of the woods behind the house. Time slips through my fingers. Maybe a few minutes, maybe a half hour. I go back inside, walk through the living room, and down the hallway to Francie's bedroom. She is asleep, the covers gently rising and falling as she breathes. I kneel beside her, lay a palm over her hair and kiss her forehead, her face lightly freckled, her eyelashes the color of copper.

The floor creaks underneath my feet as I leave the room. Hank's cap and flannel shirt hang on a hook by the back door. I put them on, and step out of the house. At the edge of the woods, I stop for a moment and look back, the light from the kitchen falling over Francie's face in her bedroom window. She's awake, and I wonder if she sees me. *I'm going to find your daddy*, I think to myself, and turn again toward the woods.

About a mile or so away is Mansfield's place, a brown-sided building that looks like a barn. I recognize some of the cars, hear the familiar chatter and hollers. Not too far away is Hank's truck. I edge my way closer to the window. I see Hank across the room. I've found him this way before: a bottle of whiskey in one hand, a cigarette in the other. A noise startles me from behind, the crying of a child, a voice much like my Francie's.

I make my way to the back side of the building. A man yells out. A girl is struggling on the ground, the man sprawled on top of her.

"No!" I scream.

He jumps off the girl, stands quickly, facing me.

Not you, I think. *How could you?*

His belt is undone, his face in a sweat.

"Run!" I scream to the girl. "Run!"

He comes toward me. I open my mouth to scream again, but he is too quick. He knocks me to the ground, my face in the dirt. I try to get up, but he is on top of me. A sharp pain bores into my back. Deeper, deeper. *Oh, Francie.*

Chapter 1

Mama Rae and Ruthie

MAMA USED TO SAY some folks do their crying on the inside. I suppose she was talking about herself, only I didn't know it at the time. After she died, I was doing my share of crying on the inside, too. Mama left us in April. Two months later, I still felt like a chunk of my heart had been swallowed up, and what remained was nothing but a raw knot twisting itself around in my chest. I thought I had to be strong for Daddy, had to take care of him. So every time that knot would start to work itself up in my throat, I'd push it down with all my might. Sometimes I'd wash the dishes, or change the sheets, or take a long walk until I'd end up at the bank of Mourning Creek.

Summer in Alabama can feel like a roaster oven, full of steam. The day I got bit by the devil was no exception. I was sitting by the creek. June heat clung to my skin so thick and damp, I could feel the sweat on the back of my knees and down my neck. A handful of cool stones lay in my left palm. One by one I tossed them into the water, listening to their *kerplunks* and waiting for the breeze that I was sure would never come.

I edged my way down the bank to scoop up more stones. Crouching along the creek's shallow fringes, I dipped my hands into the cold water, then splashed it over my face. Cupping my fingers together like a ladle, I dipped my hands once more, when a sudden pain, sharp and fierce, grabbed hold of my right ankle. My body swung around fast. Stretched out in front of me was a cottonmouth, its fangs deep in my skin. I fell backwards into the water, screaming and kicking, driving my left heel against the serpent's head. The snake released my ankle and slithered a couple of feet from me into the water. I bounded up, landing on the bank, shrieking so loudly I could hear the sounds ricocheting inside my head. My ankle throbbed like a bullet of fire. Grabbing fistfuls of grass, I pulled myself to a level spot on the bank, the pain quickly shooting up my leg.

"Anybody, help!" I yelled. "Help!" But I knew no one was around. A fever-ache began to crawl over every part of my skin. Even the hairs on my head hurt. I lay my face on the grass. "Help," I said, my voice not much more than a whisper. My clothes were wet, my skin cold. I held my arms over my chest. The smell of the earth filled my mouth. "Don't let me die, Mama. Please don't let me die."

Splatters of light blinded my eyes. *So tired*, I thought. *If only I could sleep.*

When I awoke, I was lying on a cot pushed up against a wall. Sitting beside me was a big colored woman laying a cool washcloth over my forehead. She wore a sleeveless house dress with a bright orange-and-gold floral print, stretched tight across her generous bosom. Her hands and face were as black as coffee.

"Where am I?" I asked, the words thick and heavy and hard to get out.

"Hush now, child," she said. "The good Lord and Mama Rae gonna make everything all right."

I remembered the snake, the creek. So tired. My body weak. Again, sleep came upon me in a wave. My mind floated out at sea, the sky a powder blue. Mama called my name, from a distance at first, then closer. She was coming for me, walking on the water. Her red hair blew around her head and shimmered under the sun in a beautiful halo. Her face and bare feet were the color of porcelain. She stretched out her arms for me, her pink satin gown flowing over her body. "Mama!" I cried. I tried to run for her, but instead began to sink into the dark water. "Don't leave! Come back!" My body shivered to the bone.

When I opened my eyes, a tall colored girl about my age stood beside me in a pair of faded overalls about two sizes too big. She pulled a quilt up onto my shoulders and tucked it around me.

"She's awake," she said, looking over her shoulder at the woman who was now sitting in a rocking chair at the other end of the cot.

Again I thought of the snake. "How did I get here?"

"Got angels watchin' out for you," came the woman's voice. She swooped her eyes up at the girl.

I sat up partway, noticing the room: a small living area with a kitchen space attached. Next to the cot was a black leather trunk with a pipe and a pouch of tobacco on top. At the front of the room was a long picnic table covered with a red-and-white checkered oilcloth. My jeans were laying over one of the benches. I remembered falling into the creek.

"There was a snake," I said, my voice raspy like I'd been asleep a century.

"And he took a fine likin' to that ankle of yours." The rocking chair creaked loudly as Mama Rae stood. "I got one of my boys out lookin' for your daddy. He'll be comin' 'round soon." She laid a hand over my forehead.

I thought I might have seen the woman and the girl before, but I couldn't recall for sure.

"What time is it?" I asked, looking around.

"After seven," the girl told me. "You slept straight through supper, even while all of us were in here eatin'."

I closed my eyes slowly, then opened them wide like I couldn't believe I'd been asleep that long. I wondered where Daddy was, wanting more than anything to be in my own bed.

"Is there a bathroom?" I asked.

"It's outside. Can't have you walkin' just yet. You'll have to let me carry you." Mama Rae slid one arm underneath my shoulders and the other beneath my knees, tucking the quilt around me. Her skin smelled of onions and bacon. She brought me down a narrow hallway decorated with photographs of smiling black faces. Off the hallway were three bedrooms, two small ones on my right and a larger one to my left with a big iron bed. She opened the back door, then carried me across the porch and down a worn-out path to an outhouse situated under the shade of two enormous oak trees. I'd never known anyone with an outhouse before, and wasn't real happy with the thought of it.

Mama Rae unwrapped me from the quilt and set me down. "You holler when you're done," she said.

She closed the door behind her, leaving me in the dark. The only light came from the cracks in the wood, allowing me to see the picture of Jesus stapled to the wall. I cast my eyes down at the black hole where I was supposed to sit, and couldn't help but wonder what kind of things might be crawling around inside. Getting bit on my ankle was one thing; getting bit on my privates was another.

When I was finished, I tried to stand, but a pain like a sliver of lightning shot through my leg, making me wince. "Ready," I said, loud enough for Mama Rae to hear.

She opened the door and wrapped me back in the quilt, lifting me in her arms. "Give it time, child. Give it time."

As she carried me to the house, I noticed how small it was. It looked like a perfectly shaped box with a triangle on top. Like the walls inside, it was white, and shone against the evening sky despite the peeling paint and bare spots where the wood peeked through. On the covered back porch was a cistern, a fair-sized stack of wood, and a large metal tub hanging from the wall beside the door.

Most of the colored folks' houses were in a small community

just outside of town, about a mile from where Daddy and I lived. I'd never been to that part of town before. Never even touched a colored person's hand before, either.

Mama Rae brought me back inside to the largest of the three bedrooms. She set me down on the big iron bed and propped a couple of pillows up behind me. Then she struck a match and lit a hurricane lamp on the nightstand. *They don't have electricity, don't have running water*, I thought. And at that moment I counted myself very lucky.

Just as she'd gotten me settled in, a young boy appeared in the doorway. His big, black eyes with long, curly lashes stared back at me. He was wearing brown trousers that fell just above his ankles, his feet and chest bare.

"Alby, whatch you doin'? You get on out of here!" Mama Rae snapped sternly. His face darted quickly behind the doorway. Mama Rae patted my arm. "I'll get you something to eat."

The girl came into the room shortly after with a bowl of chicken broth and a plate full of biscuits. She handed me the food, and crawled up on the bed beside me.

"What's your name?" she asked.

"Francie."

"My name's Ruthie. Mama says your daddy owns the grocery store."

I nodded, then bit into one of the warm biscuits.

"My daddy's the pastor at the Baptist church. He's over there tonight. Got a prayer meetin' goin' on.

"You go down to the creek much?" she asked.

I stopped chewing for just a minute, thinking about Mama and the creek. Thinking about the snake and the way his teeth felt in my skin.

"Sometimes," I said.

"I like to stroll off every once in a while," Ruthie told me. "Sometimes I take myself along the creek. Never come up on anyone down there before, until today, when I saw you layin' out on the bank. At first I thought you was dead, but when I got down close to you I could tell you were breathin'."

I looked at my plate, not feeling very hungry anymore. "So you're the one who found me," I said.

"I ran back to the house. Told Mama to come quick, that a white girl was layin' by the creek hurt. Most of the folks around here call Mama Dr. Rae. She stitches people up, delivers babies, gets rid of all sorts of fevers.

"When she got to you, she tied her handkerchief real tight around your leg and started suckin' and spittin'. Before she carried you back to the house, she put somethin' under your tongue. Supposed to make you sweat all the poison out."

"I coulda died," I whispered.

"Yeah, but you're all right now."

Ruthie looked over at the door, then back at me, like she was making sure nobody was listening.

"I almost died before," she said quietly.

I looked into her brown eyes, big and wide with what she was saying. "What happened?"

"I guess it wasn't my appointed time neither, 'cause a beautiful angel came and saved me."

I stared down at my plate, thinking Ruthie was crazy in the head for making up such a story.

"Whatch you two girls talkin' so quiet about?" Mama Rae walked into the room with one of Ruthie's gowns that smelled of cedar and cotton. She checked the bite on my ankle. "Looks like the swellin's gone down."

"I should get home. My daddy'll want to know where I am."

"My boy Tom's still lookin' for him," she told me.

I looked away, not wanting to meet their eyes. *How could Tom know where my daddy had gone off drinking?* I thought of Daddy stumbling into the house in the middle of the night, and I wondered when he'd realize I wasn't there. Wondered when he'd come for me. Sometimes I wished it was me who had died, just so I could find out how sad Daddy would be.

Mama Rae sat on the edge of the bed, causing my body to roll towards her. "I was real sorry to hear about your Mama." She lay her hand over mine.

Everyone knew Mama, I thought, and for a split second that knot inside my chest started to feel like molten wax. I couldn't make myself busy. I couldn't get up and run away or take a long walk to the creek. All I could do was lay on this strange bed in this strange house, and hope all those feelings tying up my throat would soon go away.

It was late the next morning before Daddy finally came for me. He stood in the doorway of the room where I'd been sleeping, talking to Mama Rae in a somber kind of voice, the same kind of voice people used when they came visiting after Mama passed away. He'd been drinking—I could tell, which embarrassed me to no end. His trousers were dirty and his jaw and eyes swollen.

He walked over to the iron bed in which I lay, the floor creaking underneath his heavy steps.

"How ya feelin', Bean?"

I stared at the white wall in front of me. "Okay," I finally said.

He slipped one of his arms behind my back, the other beneath my knees.

"Thank ya, Rae," he said, his voice hoarse.

As he carried me through the front room, I noticed a white boy sitting at the long table drinking coffee. He had thick, wavy hair the color of chestnuts, and eyes so dark they looked like two pieces of charcoal. *What's a white boy doing out here?* I thought. I knew I'd never seen him before, and wondered if he might be from out of town.

Ruthie followed Daddy and me out to the truck, carrying a brown paper bag with my clothes inside.

Daddy slid me into the passenger seat, shut the door, and walked around to the other side.

I leaned over the rolled-down window as Ruthie handed me the bag.

"Who's the boy?" I asked her.

She looked back at the house as if she wasn't real sure who I was talking about. "Earnest? He's just somebody helps Mama out once in a while."

"Hey, Ruthie . . ." I glanced at Daddy, then back at her. "Thanks."

"It was nothin'." She smiled.

You saved my life, I wanted to say, but the words never came.

Ruthie lifted her hand in a small gesture of a wave. Daddy started the truck and pulled away.

Chapter 2
Pure Grief

WHEN WE GOT TO THE HOUSE, a dark blue pickup truck with a large silver brush plate was parked out front. Leaning against the truck, facing us, was Harvey Mansfield. He'd retired from county sheriff almost eight years before. His back was pressed up against the door, his long legs crossed in front of him. A cigarette dangled from his mouth, sending smoke around his face.

Daddy slowed the truck. Instead of driving around back, he stopped in front of Mansfield and got out. I stayed in my seat.

Mansfield pulled in on the cigarette, then let the smoke escape from his nostrils in two long trails. "I'm real sorry 'bout May," he said.

"I bet you are." Daddy's neck was pulled back, stiff and erect.

My eyes and ears opened big at the way Daddy was talkin'. Lots of folks were sorry about Mama dying, always offering their condolences, which Daddy accepted politely.

Mansfield uncrossed his legs and stood up straight. Then he tossed his cigarette to the ground and put it out with the toe of his black boot. "I just came to pay my respects, Hank. I didn't come to stir up no trouble."

"I don't want your respects," Daddy said.

"Suit yourself." Mansfield turned to leave, his left hand on the door of the truck. "Maybe some other time."

Daddy's shoulders instantly flared back, like a thick rubber band about to snap. "I know how May died," he yelled.

His words stabbed through me like a hot poker. Mama fell into a ravine, Sheriff McGee had said. She hit her head.

Mansfield dropped his hand from the truck door. His body quickly wheeled around. "What the hell are you sayin'?"

Then Daddy stepped closer, pointing a finger into Mansfield's chest. "She didn't fall and hit her head. I saw the body, Harvey, before the wake."

My body lurched forward, my hands gripping the dashboard in front of me.

Mansfield knocked Daddy's arm away. "You better think real hard 'bout what you're sayin'." He turned and reached for the handle of his truck.

"You son of a bitch!" Daddy lunged forward, knocking Mansfield to the ground, then toppled over him. I opened the door, ready to jump out, when a terrible pain shooting up from my ankle stopped me short. Mansfield, sprawled out in the dirt, wiped his face with his sleeve as though his jaw had been knocked loose. He stood up slowly, brushing the dirt from his clothes.

"Your wife hit her head, Hank. She hit her head 'cause she was married to a no-good drunk." He staggered back to his truck, got in, and drove away.

Daddy stayed on the ground. He drew his big legs up to his chest, hugging them with his thickset arms, his body rocking forward.

I climbed out of the truck, limped over to him, and knelt beside him. He was wearing a white undershirt, soiled with dirt and sweat, the same shirt he'd worn for the past two days.

"What did you see?" I asked him.

His brow scrunched up in the middle like he wasn't sure what I was talking about.

"You said you saw Mama's body before the wake."

He stared off toward the road. "You shouldn't have heard all that."

I wanted to grab him and shake him till he told me what was going on. "Why were you so mad at Mr. Mansfield? What about Mom?" My voice was growing louder.

"Your mama hit her head, just like everybody said."

Daddy's eyes were still on the road. I tried to stare him down. Tried to make him look at me. "That's not what you told Mr. Mansfield."

"Doesn't matter what I told Mansfield."

He propped his chin on his knees, then reached his hand over and patted my arm. "I'm gonna start takin' better care of ya, Bean," he finally said.

It was then that I looked away. "Like last night?" My voice, barely audible, ached inside my throat.

Daddy wrapped his arm around my shoulders. "I'm sorry," he said, pulling me against him.

"I need to check on some things at the store. How 'bout you go rest and I bring us home some sandwiches from the diner?"

He stood before I could say anything, then reached his hand down to help me up. I leaned my weight on him as he walked me toward the house.

"You gonna be all right?" he asked.

"I'm okay," I said, my voice as sullen as a hole in the ground.

Once we got inside, Daddy picked me up in his arms and carried me back to my bedroom.

"Good thing you don't weigh a ton," he said, forcing a laugh.

He set me down on the mattress. "Anything I can get you before I leave?"

I just shrugged my shoulders, avoiding his eyes. *Mama wouldn't have left me*, I thought. *Mama Rae wouldn't have left me, either.*

Daddy leaned down and kissed me on my head and messed up my hair with his hand. "Everything's gonna be okay, Bean."

I glanced at him just long enough to see his mouth twitch, like he wasn't real sure about what he was saying.

After he left, I lay in bed and listened as his truck pulled away, my eyes burning clear through the ceiling. Daddy could be like a stone when he didn't want to talk, smoothing things over so you couldn't find out what was under the surface.

I thought about what Daddy had said to Mr. Mansfield. Thought about the early morning in April when Sheriff McGee drove out to the house. I was still in bed when I heard him knocking. I looked out the window in the living room and saw his car. Then I opened the front door for him, thinking Mama and Daddy were still asleep. He asked if he could come in, said he needed to talk to me. I told him I'd go get my parents, but he said there wasn't any need. He showed me how to make a pot of coffee, and sat with me at the kitchen table, his elbows propped up in front of him, the cup of coffee held close to his face.

"Fact is, your daddy ain't home, Francie. Got him down at the jail now, sobering up."

I knew my daddy had been drinking and staying out late, and Mama had said he'd been doing his share of gambling, too, but he'd always be home by morning. I thought about waking my mom, feeling real uncomfortable with what the sheriff was saying. That's when he told me.

"Your mama ain't home neither, Francie. Been an accident. Been a real bad accident. She's dead, Francie. I'm real sorry."

Then he told me about her falling down and hitting her head. Now my daddy was saying something else. I'd seen Mama's body at the wake. She looked peaceful, her hair combed back pretty from her face. Different people around me were saying how Mr. Cochran, the mortician, had done a good job. She was wearing the pink satin nightgown I'd chosen for her. Daddy had asked me to pick out something she might wear to church. But I figured Mama wasn't going to church. I figured she was going to sleep. When I gave Daddy the nightgown to take to Mr. Cochran, he held it to his face for a long time, his eyes closing in a lot of pain, then said that would be fine.

I remembered standing in front of Mama's body at the funeral home. Pastor Johnson from the Methodist church where our family attended came up behind me and told me I could hold Mama's hand if I liked. But I didn't want to hold her hand. I was afraid it would feel cold, and I wanted to remember how her body had always felt warm.

Now, still lying on the bed, I looked at all the pictures Mama and I had colored along the walls. One day, before I was old enough to start school, I'd gotten hold of a box of crayons and drawn a bunch of faces on the plaster. When Mama saw what I'd done, instead of scolding me she picked up the crayons and drew flowers next to all those faces. Over the years, whenever I'd have a bad day, she and I would add new pictures around the room. One day when I was home sick from school, she set up a ladder next to my bed and drew a giant sun on my ceiling. "This ought to cheer you up," she said.

Staring up at the ceiling, I must have dozed off, because when I checked the clock on my nightstand it was nearly four o'clock. The house was as still as a pond. "Daddy!" I yelled. He didn't answer. I got out of bed and limped to the back door to look for his truck, but it wasn't there. I couldn't find any sign of the sandwiches he'd promised to bring home, either.

Daddy could be off drinking again, for all I knew. The phone hung on the wall next to the kitchen table. I called down at the store. Mr. Tucker, who works for Daddy, answered.

"Your dad came by here just before lunch. Said you'd gotten bit by a snake. Told me he was gonna take the rest of the day off."

"Did he tell you if he was going anywhere else?"

Mr. Tucker was ringing up a customer. I could hear the cash register and voices in the background. "Didn't say, Francie."

I took the phone book out of one of the cabinet drawers and looked up the number for the diner. When I called, a man answered. I asked to speak with Sylvia, who had worked tables there for as long as I could remember.

"Sylvia, it's Francie. Has my daddy been in today?" I asked.

She was popping her gum. "I haven't seen him. No, wait a minute, one of the girls said something about him stopping in for coffee early this morning. Said one of the colored boys came in asking for him. Had your daddy all shook up. Everything okay, Francie?"

I nodded into the receiver. "If he comes in, will you tell him I'm looking for him?"

As I hung up the phone, I wasn't sure whether to be madder than a bull or worried sick. I left the phone book on the counter, not sure who else to call, then opened the cabinet by the sink to get down a glass. Toward the back of one of the shelves was the coffee mug Mama had always used. I took it down and held it out in front of me, running my finger over the white nick in the rim, back and forth. I thought about all the nights Mama had sat up drinking coffee while she waited for Daddy to come home. "Go on to bed," she'd tell me. I remembered the last night I saw her. She wore Daddy's John Deere cap on her head and the flannel shirt Daddy always wore when he went hunting in the fall. It hung down to her knees and flapped in the night air over her blue cotton dress—the same dress she had on when I hugged her good-night, smelling mildly of sweet powder and the chicken she and I had eaten earlier. Standing there with her mug in my hand, I could still see the buttons at the neck of that dress, could still feel its texture under my skin.

"Your wife hit her head," Mansfield had said. "'Cause she was married to a no-good drunk." That knot in my chest started to lodge itself in my throat again. Sometimes I felt like I was just as drunk as Daddy. Drunk on the pure grief that Mama was gone.

I placed the mug back on the shelf and closed the cabinet door.

Again Daddy's words ricocheted in my head. I saw the body, Harvey, before the wake. Thunder sounded in the distance. Mama used to say God's heart was breaking when the clouds would rumble like that. I went back to my bedroom and put on a pair of jeans and a short-sleeved blouse, then folded Ruthie's gown and slid it underneath my pillow.

I wasn't going to be like my mama, I told myself. I wasn't going to wait up for Daddy to come home and look after him like I didn't have a life of my own.

The house was so quiet, I could count every breath I took. I put on my sneakers, loosely tying the one on my left foot where my ankle was still tender, and left out the back door. The air was pine-heavy, like that before a storm. Our closest neighbor, Mr. Lampley, lived by himself on a small farm that backed up to the side of our yard. He had all kinds of things growing on his land, from pole beans to corn to cabbage, though he made the better part of his living from the filling station he owned in town. He'd been growing beans for as long as I could remember. I used to hide between the rows of stalks when I was small till my daddy would finally come and find me. That's when he started calling me "Bean," and the name stuck. At fourteen, I'd long since stopped playing on Mr. Lampley's property, though I still liked to visit and see how his hogs were doing.

I quickened my steps across the parched soil, limping only slightly, then began to climb the hill in front of me that led to Mr. Lampley's house. A painful sensation shot through my ankle, making me stop for a second to catch my breath.

I looked back toward home. Still no sign of Daddy's truck. On the other side of the hill, honeysuckle sloped toward Mr. Lampley's barn and house. I broke off a branch and, pinching off the buds, sucked their juices one by one, aware of my empty stomach and longing for the sandwich Daddy had promised to bring me.

Mr. Lampley was standing in his yard at the bottom of the hill behind the pen where he kept his hogs. He held a metal pail in one hand and a white envelope in the other. He stood with his head tilted toward the ground as if his mind was heavy. After a few seconds, he placed the envelope in the pail, and, stooping over, set the pail upside down on the ground, next to the fence. As he turned and began to walk toward his house, he saw me and waved.

He lay his hand over my head and smoothed down my long red hair like he always did when he saw me.

"Hey, Francie. How come you got a limp?"

"Was down at the creek yesterday," I told him. "Got bit by a cottonmouth." I showed him my ankle.

"Dear child." He was a slim-framed man with baggy trousers and a baggy shirt, always smelling of dirt and sweat and the outdoors and a trace of gasoline. He reminded me somewhat of a walking cane, though his shoulders slumped over only slightly. His hair was shorn white and his face craggy, tinted by the sun and wind. I looked into his blue eyes, the color of a perfect blue sky. He cupped his hands over my shoulders and shook his head.

Then he frowned. "Come here. Let me show ya somethin'." He motioned me toward the pen.

We walked back to where he kept the hogs. Matilda, his oldest, was lying on the ground, looking fatter and bigger and more tired than I'd ever seen her look before.

"She's got a sickness," he said. "Come down with it a couple a days ago."

I remembered the week-old leftovers I'd fed her on my last visit, when Mr. Lampley wasn't home.

"I came to see ya day before yesterday," I said. "I fed Matilda some old food from the fridge."

By now, Mr. Lampley had his arms folded on top of one of the pen posts with his weight shifted on one leg. He let out a chuckle.

"Your leftovers ain't what's ailin' that woman, Francie." He leaned over to spit.

"Feels like we might be goin' to get us some rain," he said. "Could use some."

"Yessir."

He looked over at me. "What's on your mind, Francie? Got them gears of yours turnin' something over in your head."

I kept staring down at the pigs, trying to find the right words for what it was I wanted to say.

"The night Mama left, I saw her take off for the woods. You reckon she was going to look for my dad?"

"I reckon so."

"I figured she was taking a back cut to town. That maybe my daddy was at the bar across from the diner, and him having the truck and all, she would have had to walk."

Mr. Lampley just listened, and though I was still staring at Matilda, I could feel his eyes watching me.

"The sheriff said Mama fell in a wash in those woods and hit her head."

"So I heard."

"But Daddy seems to have some other ideas inside of him. Maybe it's those other ideas that have him drinking so much."

"What kind of ideas?"

"I'm not sure."

Mr. Lampley still had his arms folded over one of the posts on the pen. He leaned his head down, supporting his chin on his arms, then turned his head kind of sideways so he could see me better.

"I've known your daddy a long time, Francie. Think maybe you ought not go worryin' yourself with his ideas. Let him work them out himself. Seems to me your daddy's drinkin' so much 'cause he misses your mom. He's got a heavy heart, not unlike someone else I know," he said, raising his eyebrows slightly.

"I remember your Mama when she was just a girl, 'bout your age. She and one of my boys used to be friends," he told me.

Mama had told me about Mr. Lampley's boys. She said both of them had died in the Second World War. She hadn't told me she was friends with one of them.

"Both my boys got drafted," he went on. "Wade and Maurice. One of 'em ain't never comin' home. The other one shouldn't have."

I thought they had both died. That's what Mama said. "What happened to them?"

"Wade got shot down," he said. "He was only eighteen."

"What happened to the other one?"

He spat again. "I wish I knew."

I wondered if his son was missing in action. World War II seemed like a century ago, and yet I knew for Mr. Lampley it must feel close.

I thought about the war going on in Vietnam. A couple of the kids at school had brothers who had gone over to fight. I hoped they would make it back home.

We both stood there quiet for a moment, then I remembered the pail Mr. Lampley had turned over on the ground when I'd first walked up.

"What were you setting out in the pail?" I asked him.

He lifted his eyebrows slightly, hesitating before answering.

"That's where I keep a whole bunch of money." He smiled.

I thought he was pulling my leg. "Kind of like your bank?"

"Mmm-hmm."

He laid a hand over my head, smoothing down my hair again. "It's just about suppertime," he said. "Why don't you let me fix ya up somethin' to eat?"

I shrugged my shoulders. "It's okay. Daddy's gonna be waitin'."

His eyes looked toward the hill from where I'd come, as if he could see right through it that Daddy wasn't there.

"Your ankle feelin' all right?"

"It's okay," I told him.

   🌰 🌰 🌰

I made it home, pain shooting through my leg. The house echoed with an eerie quiet. I found a bottle of aspirin next to Daddy's unmade bed, took one of the tablets, then ate the last can of tuna fish in the cupboard. The phone book was still out on the table. I looked up Bud's Palace, the bar across from the diner. The phone rang about ten times before someone finally answered.

"Yeah." The man's voice was low and gruff.

"Is Hank Grove there?" I asked, trying to make my voice sound older than it was.

The man started laughing, then hollered out into the room. "Some kid's on the phone, looking for her daddy."

I hung up, my hand shaking. "This is what he did to you, didn't he, Mama," I said out loud. "Had you worrying the life right out of you. I can't do it, Mama. I just can't."

Back in my bedroom, I lay on top of the covers. Rain began to fall, slapping the tin sheet roof above me. Folding an arm under my pillow, I touched Ruthie's nightgown, then slid it out and held it up to my nose. It smelled of cedar and the biscuits I had eaten at the Taylors'. The rain poured down, hitting the roof like pellets. I closed my eyes.

Dear God, bring Daddy home.

Chapter 3
The Man in the Garage

AN EARLY MORNING GLOW filled the house. I rose from my bed, my ankle stiff, and padded down the hall in my bare feet to Daddy's bedroom. His sheets were still untouched. "Daddy!" I called out as I headed toward the kitchen. He didn't answer.

I sat at the table, propping my elbows up in front of me. The coffee pot was sitting where I had left it two days before, a sure sign he hadn't come back. *He's okay, he'll be home*, I reassured myself over and over in my head.

Twenty more minutes passed. I was still sitting in the kitchen chair, staring at the back door, the clock on the wall ticking like a time bomb.

I would go to town, I decided. I would find my daddy and bring him home.

I washed down a couple of aspirin, then left the house, the sun climbing the sky in front of me. It would be a hot day, I was sure. The ground was already dry and looking thirsty again. I walked to the end of the driveway and took a left toward town. Just before the bend in the road was a shortcut, a path through backyards with a steep pitch, but because of my ankle I stayed on the road. The mile to town seemed long, each second taking an eternity.

"He's just having a cup of coffee. He had too much to drink."

I whispered these things to myself as I approached the diner, not paying any mind to the few people I passed. Daddy's truck wasn't out front. Through the window, I scanned the different clusters of people. He wasn't there. I looked around the room again to be sure, my heart feeling like a lead weight falling in slow motion. Another block down Main Street was Daddy's store. The sign on the door said "CLOSED." The door was locked. I limped down the alley to the back of the brick building where Daddy always parked his truck. As I turned the corner, I wasn't sure whether I felt panic or relief. Daddy's brown Ford was pulled in caddy-cornered to the back door, as if he'd parked it in a hurry. I thought I heard a voice. I stopped, then heard it again.

"Bean, over here."

I saw what looked like a shadow behind a trash bin. I walked toward it with queasy legs.

"Daddy?"

His body was slouched over against the brick wall of the building, his right arm bent strangely over his legs, which sprawled out in the bloody gravel. His shirt was also smeared with blood. His head slumped over his chest. My stomach almost heaved at the sight of him.

"Get me a cigarette," he mumbled. "Out of my truck."

I didn't move. "Where's Mr. Tucker?"

Daddy slowly shook his head. His eyes closed. It was still early. Too early for the store to be open.

"I'll get help," I said, taking giant steps backwards. I turned and took off down the alley, despite the pain in my ankle. *Oh, God, not Daddy. Not Daddy, too.* As I crossed the street, I wanted to yell, but everything inside me felt trapped. Suddenly the town seemed strangely unfamiliar—the sidewalks, the people, the shops. And all I could do was run, fear and mistrust pumping through me with each breath I took. Faces passed before me. I pushed harder, then took the shortcut to my right. The sun was in my eyes. I would soon be at the crest of the hill, where the land opened up to backyards.

"I say, what's wrong with you?"

A voice echoed out, strong and familiar.

I looked across a fresh-cut mowed lawn. A brick house sat back about twenty yards on the other side. It had a driveway that curved around to an open garage. I took a few steps toward the voice, my lungs grabbing for air.

Then I saw Mansfield sitting inside the garage in a lawn chair, a cigarette dangling from between two fingers.

"I gotta be goin'," I told him.

He slowly raised the cigarette to his mouth. I could feel his stare as though it had a grip on me, a magnetic force.

"Whatcha scared of? I ain't gonna bite ya."

I pulled away.

"You just go on then. Go on and take care of your business. And tell your daddy I hope he gets to feelin' better real soon," he hollered after me.

Hearing those words was like swallowing a flame. Everything inside of me burned. Daddy was hurt. Daddy was bleeding bad.

As I turned to go, Mansfield started laughing.

I took off running again, forgetting my sore ankle. I passed the turnoff for my house and could soon hear the chanting of the creek from the rain the night before. Hours seemed to fly by, though the sun was still low. A couple of colored folks' shanties appeared on either side of me. Then the whitewashed Baptist church. Out of breath, I made it to Ruthie's. A long, sodden driveway with tire paths led up to the house. I stopped and leaned over, grabbing my knees. A dog barked. I looked behind me, but no one was there.

"Hey!" I yelled, pushing the air out of me as hard as I could.

Mama Rae appeared behind the screen. I could see her red apron and the contour of her bosom through the wire mesh. As she opened the door, she raised a hand to her forehead, shielding her eyes from the sun.

"Francie? Dear Lord! Whatch you doin' all the way over here with that ankle of yours?" She hurried toward me. "Ain't got sense, I tell you. Children ain't got any sense."

I thought I would collapse with relief when she got to me. My breathing was raspy; I realized I was crying.

"What is it, child?" She drew me against her.

"It's Daddy," I gasped. "He's hurt. He's hurt bad."

"Where is he?"

"In town. At the store."

She hurried back to the house, pulling me behind her. Inside, I saw Ruthie and Alby and two younger children sitting at a long table with plates of food in front of them.

"Tom, start your daddy's truck," Mama Rae yelled toward the bedrooms. "And hurry."

Footsteps sounded from down the hall, bare feet shuffling against the floor. Then the back door banged shut. Within seconds, Mama Rae and I were behind Tom. He climbed into the driver's side of an old yellow Chevy. I sat in the middle between him and Mama Rae. He was tall, his head clear up to the roof of the truck.

"He's at the store," I told Tom as the engine chugged to a start. "Around back."

Mama Rae wrapped an arm around me and pressed my head against her side. "Gonna be all right, Francie. Gonna be all right," she said as Tom held the steering wheel steady between his hands and the dust kicked up around us.

The shade from the town's trees soon spread over us. Tom turned down the alley beside the store, gravel spinning beneath the tires. As soon as he stopped the truck, the three of us climbed out, the engine still running. I led them behind the bin where Daddy lay.

His body was so still I thought he was dead. And all that blood. My stomach went weak. I held my arms over myself, my body like cold liquid. Mama Rae leaned over Daddy, working her hands on his wounds. He let out a slow, guttural moan from his throat and stirred.

"I'll kill 'em," he said. "I swear I'll kill 'em." His voice went high, cracking at the end. He was panting, his breath shallow and uneven.

Mama Rae told him his arm was broken and she was sure some of his ribs. She wiped his face gently with a handkerchief, then gave it to him to hold on his head where he'd been cut and was losing blood.

"Ya done good, Bean." As Daddy tried to reach for me, his face twisted in a spasm of pain.

"We're gonna have to get your daddy to a hospital," Mama Rae said.

She placed her hands under Daddy's shoulders, being careful with his right arm, and instructed Tom and me to hold Daddy's legs. He yelled out in a terrible way as the three of us carefully hoisted him into the back of the truck. I was quick to recognize just how strong Mama Rae and Tom must be to lift my dad, and wondered fearfully how anyone could break such a big man's arm. I thought of Mansfield, could still hear his laughter in my head, could still feel the fire from his words burning inside me. But Mansfield wasn't as strong as my daddy.

With his head in my lap, I pressed my hands over Daddy's fine brown hair, matted together in patches with the crust of his blood.

"Who done it?" I asked.

He just closed his eyes and wouldn't say. I wished he could sleep, but knew the pain and the sharp bumps and jolts of the county road would keep him awake.

"I promised to come home," he struggled to say. "I promised to bring you lunch." His mouth winced with each breath he took, as if the air was a knife going into his chest.

"It's okay, Daddy." I leaned my head down close to his, pressing my face upon his cheek, and prayed he would be all right.

Mama Rae was right. Daddy's arm was broken and also four of his ribs. He stayed at the hospital for the next few days. I stayed with the Taylors.

The Taylors had five children, including Ruthie. Tom was the oldest. His face looked a lot like Ruthie's, though it showed no expression. His body was long and lean, his arms like two stiff cords of muscle.

Ruthie was the next to the oldest. Then Alby, who slept in the same room as Tom. Alby drifted through the house as if he were a ghost.

I slept with Ruthie in the same room as Rachel, one of the twins. Rachel and Willie were nine, with sweet smiles and faces as round as full moons.

On my first evening with the Taylors, a tabby wandered up to the house. Mama Rae told us not to feed her, that if we did she would start hanging around. Ruthie told me she'd always wanted a cat, so we snuck some food out from the kitchen and fed her anyway.

"You'll have to think up a name for her," I said, stroking the cat behind the ears. "She looks like a pumpkin, with all that orange on her."

"That's it!" Ruthie smiled. "Punkin."

As we crouched in the dirt next to the cat, I saw Alby about twenty feet away, just standing there watching us. "Ya want to pet her?" I asked him, but he just kept standing there looking at us.

"How come he never says anything?" I asked Ruthie.

"Nobody knows. He wasn't born that way. He used to talk a lot. Then all of a sudden, one day this past spring he just shut up. Wouldn't answer anybody. Just stays quiet all the time. Daddy took him to a doctor over in Birmingham. The doctor couldn't find anything wrong. Says Alby can hear all right, just doesn't want to talk. He told Daddy not to worry. Thinks it's just a phase Alby's goin' through. That he'll outgrow it."

We were still crouched next to Punkin when we heard Reverend Taylor whistling. He walked down the driveway toward the house, one hand in his pocket and the other hitched onto the jacket that was slung over his shoulder. He wore a crisp white shirt and a navy tie, loosened around his neck.

"Since when did we get a cat?" he asked, kneeling next to Ruthie and me.

"Since Ruthie decided to feed her," Willie said, coming up behind us.

The Reverend reached up, grabbing Willie, and pulled him over in a playful tackle. Then Rachel, who had been playing near us, came running up and jumped on top of both of them. The Reverend wrapped her in his arms, hugging her tight. He smelled of aftershave, clean sweat, and starch, and I found myself wanting to be as close to him as the rest of them, as if he was sweet sap, easy to stick to.

I hadn't seen him when I'd stayed at Ruthie's two nights before, and I realized he and Mama Rae must have slept in the front room, letting me have their bed. By the next morning, when I'd left, he was already gone.

Once the ruckus between him and the twins had settled down, Ruthie introduced us. We were all still crouched on the ground next to the cat, who was busy eating up the food Ruthie and I had brought her. The Reverend shook my hand. "Your ankle healing up all right?"

"It's feelin' fine," I told him.

He stood, nodding his head slightly. "Mama got her ways, don't she."

His face wore a wide grin and his cheeks were as round as his eyes—large, happy eyes with flecks of sun in them. He was tall and sturdy and handsome in every way, and immediately I thought I might be looking at a grown-up Ruthie, their faces were so much alike.

Mama Rae greeted him at the door. He bent over, kissing her big, then slid an arm around her thick waist and rocked her to and fro. They laughed easily together for no reason at all.

"Mmm, mmm. Somethin' smellin' good, Mama. Whatch you got cookin'?"

He swung her in his arms to the kitchen area, the door banging shut behind them, and I soon found myself standing on the front steps, peering through the screen at the two of them. Red beans and rice and sausage were simmering on the stove. The Reverend lifted the lid and inhaled deeply, his lips stretching across his face in a contented smile, and the two of them started passing conversation back and forth as if it was butter, sliding gently and easily between them.

Soon Mama Rae called us to the kitchen. She asked Ruthie and me to set the table for supper. While we were laying out plates, Mama Rae gave a loud whoop, swinging her voice high, which started me giggling.

Ruthie smiled back at me. "That means it's time to eat."

As we gathered around the table for supper, the questions began.

"Is your daddy gonna be all right?" Rachel asked.

"Her daddy's gonna be just fine," Mama Rae answered for me while passing the food.

"Who done it, Mama?" Ruthie wanted to know.

"We don't know."

"Why would somebody beat him up so bad?"

Again, I thought of Mansfield. I thought of him sitting in his garage, his long legs stretched out in front of him.

"Today, when I came runnin' to get help, I saw Mr. Mansfield," I said.

Reverend Taylor looked at Mama Rae. "What do you know about Harvey Mansfield?" he asked me.

"I know he knew about my daddy gettin' beat up. He said so.

Said he hoped my daddy would get to feelin' better real soon."

"I bet he does," Tom said under his breath.

"You keep yourself quiet," the Reverend shot back. "Ain't your business to be speakin' about."

Tom's fist clenched around the fork he held in his hand. Then he set it down and got up from the table. Within seconds the back door slammed shut.

"Children, eat your supper," Mama Rae said.

Suddenly I felt like a giant outsider. Tom's bitterness and the way Mama Rae and the Reverend kept everyone quiet over the whole thing lingered like a bad taste in the mouth.

"Why's Tom so upset?" I asked, wishing the words back in my mouth as soon as I'd said them. I saw the pulsing in the Reverend's tight jaw. His eyes shifted back and forth over the table while he weighed his words carefully before letting them out.

"Let's just say some folks don't think the world of Harvey Mansfield."

I wanted to say my daddy didn't seem to think the world of Harvey Mansfield either, but I kept those thoughts to myself.

'Bout that time, Willie broke the uneasiness that was clinging all over us. "I don't like the way he's always got smoke coming out his nostrils. Me and Rachel call him the dragon."

Rachel raised her hands up in the air like claws, then scrunched her nose and mouth together, letting out a growl.

Suddenly I wanted to laugh. Daddy liked his cigarettes, but he always blew the smoke out of his mouth.

"All right, that's enough," Mama Rae said.

I tilted my face to my plate, hiding the makings of a smile, then looked at Ruthie. She had her right elbow on the table and her hand pressed against her forehead like a shield. I thought she must be smiling too, though I couldn't tell.

                        ⁂

As soon as all the dishes were cleaned and put away, the twins raced in their bare feet down the hall to the backyard. "Don't slam the door!" Mama Rae hollered behind them, but she was too late.

Ruthie grabbed my hand. "Let's go," she said.

I limped idly behind her, my ankle feeling more stiff and sore than it had all day.

"Been on your feet too much," Mama Rae said, catching a glimpse of me from the side of her eyes.

"I'll make her sit down outside," Ruthie told her.

Ruthie led me behind the barn near a cluster of raspberry bushes. One by one we pulled the tart berries off the branches and popped them into our mouths.

"Willie and Rachel really call Mansfield the dragon?" I asked her.

"Mmm-hmm."

"Your folks sure sound like they don't care for him much."

She put her hands on her hips and turned her back to me. "No one around here does," she said. There was something edgy about her voice.

"How come?"

Ruthie was facing the woods that spread out past the barn. "He's mean," she said. "He's always using the word *nigger*. He hawks his spit back in his throat, then chucks it real close to colored folks' feet." She was speaking rapidly.

"Your mom and dad like Sheriff McGee?" I asked.

"He uses the word *nigger*, too, but I don't think he's as mean as Mansfield."

Someone hollered from around front. "It's Earnest," Ruthie said, turning back toward me.

I followed her to the other side of the barn. Earnest was helping a colored boy to the house. Blood was oozing from the boy's nose and lips, and one of his eyes was all swollen shut.

"Mrs. Taylor!" Earnest hollered again.

Within seconds, the Reverend bounded out the door with Mama Rae right behind him. He took hold of one of the colored boy's arms and wrapped it around his neck, then he and Earnest led the boy the rest of the way inside.

"Who is he?" I asked Ruthie.

"Jonas Whitlow," she told me. "One a Tom's friends."

"What happened to him?"

She shrugged her shoulders real uneasy-like. "Mama says there's some fightin' goin' on. Every week or so, Earnest or Tom come bringin' somebody up to the house for Mama to look after."

"Fightin' over what?" I asked her.

"They won't tell me nothin' about it. Just tell me to stay away."

"Anybody ever end up in the hospital?"

Again, Ruthie shrugged her shoulders. "Mama thought one of 'em might have a concussion once. She kept him at the house a couple a days till she decided he was all right."

Earnest was standing at the screen door, saying something back to Mama Rae. As he stepped outside, I saw the blood down the front of his shirt, reminding me of Daddy.

"Jonas gonna be okay?" Ruthie hollered at him.

He stopped a few feet from the house and looked over at us, those dark eyes of his staring up from beneath a thick wisp of his hair.

"Couple of his teeth got knocked loose, but yeah, he's gonna be all right."

"How come you never get beat up?" Ruthie asked.

"I'm not the one doin' the fightin.'"

His eyes fixed on me for a split second. I stared back at him, waiting for him to say something else, but he didn't. Just meeting his eyes made my face tinge and my heart thud loudly. He walked on up the driveway. Then he turned right at the road and disappeared into the thick trees.

       ᶲ   ᶲ   ᶲ

Each of us visited the outhouse one last time before turning in for the night. "Dear Jesus," I said, while staring at the dark picture of him on the wall. "Be with Daddy. Make him all right." I thought about how mad I'd felt at Daddy that morning. My feelings seemed to be riding inside of me like a giant seesaw.

On the way back from the hospital, Tom and Mama Rae had taken me by my house to gather some of my things. I brought the nightgown of Ruthie's I had worn only two nights before.

Ruthie and I dressed for bed, me wearing the soft cotton gown.

"Ruthie?"

"Hmm?"

"Me and Daddy, that's all there is. I mean, he's all I got."

It didn't take long for Ruthie to answer. "You got me now."

Soon after, we were both asleep, but sometime in the night a dream came, shaking me so that Mama Rae had to hold one hand till I fell back to sleep while Ruthie held onto the other.

It was Mama. She slipped into the woods, her red hair flashing through the dense thicket. She was running fast and breathing in loud gulps of air. The sky was black. She looked like a wraith weaving her way between the trees. I opened my mouth to yell to her, but no sound came out. Shadows loomed over her. She fell to the ground.

"No!" I cried out.

Someone took my hand. I thought it was God.

"Hush, child."

It was the Reverend. My body shivered from the sweat beginning to dry on my skin. Ruthie pulled the blanket over me and took my other hand. Mama Rae appeared in the doorway. She walked over to the bed, then knelt next to the Reverend. Said she would stay with me. Ruthie was still close. The big woman hummed sweetly. Ruthie did the same before slipping off to sleep, her hand still holding mine.

Chapter 4
Lonesome

MR. TUCKER DROVE DADDY HOME from the hospital one evening just before suppertime. I met them at the house with a chicken casserole and a pot of black-eyed peas Mama Rae had sent home with me. Daddy had a bandage over his forehead where the gash above his eyes had been stitched shut, and he wore a cast on his right arm clear up to his shoulder.

"Looks like somebody went after you with a two-by-four," I told him when he got out of Mr. Tucker's truck.

He tried to force a laugh, but then his face grimaced in pain and he grabbed hold of his right side with his free hand. "Got my ribs all wrapped up, too," he told me.

Mr. Tucker walked around the truck to help Daddy into the house, but Daddy slung his free arm away from him. "Don't need anyone's help," he said.

Once inside, he sank heavily into his chair at the kitchen table. "Might as well start eatin' in here. Can't go holdin' a tray steady in my lap with my arm all broke."

Ever since Mama died, Daddy and I had stopped eating at the table. Neither one of us wanted to look at her empty chair. We'd put our plates on trays and eat in the living room in front of the TV. I wasn't sure I wanted to start eating at the table again, but on account of Daddy being hurt, I didn't say anything.

I fixed up our plates and poured us each a glass of milk.

Daddy had one of his legs raised up under the table, his heavy boot supported on Mama's chair. I wanted to knock his foot onto the floor.

"Why'd someone go beatin' you up?" I asked him. "Who was it?"

A spoonful of peas was suspended in front of his mouth. "Ain't your business to go worryin' about," he said.

"What about Mr. Mansfield? I saw him the day you were hurt. He knew."

Daddy dropped his heavy foot onto the floor and scooped up another spoonful of peas. "There won't be any more trouble," he said, his voice sharp and final.

I gulped a big mouthful of milk, then thunked my glass on the table. I tapped my foot on the linoleum. It made a slapping sound. I could feel the blood steaming in my cheeks. Daddy just kept eating. No matter how much noise I made, I could tell he wasn't going to look at me. He had no right to shut me out. Since Mama died, I was the one doing his laundry and fixing his meals and cleaning his house.

"If I'm old enough to be takin' care of you, I'm old enough to know just who it was that beat you up." I was staring forward at nothing, my fingers gripped so tight around the glass of milk I thought it might shatter in my hand.

Daddy dropped his fork on his plate. He reached for my face, turning my head toward him, making me meet his eyes. "Like I said, there won't be any more trouble."

After the dishes were put away and Daddy was settled in his recliner in front of the TV, I told him I was going for a walk.

"Your ankle feelin' up to it?" he asked me, his eyes still on the television.

"It's feelin' fine," I said, tasting the anger that was still in my voice.

The screen door banged behind me as I left the house. The air was still warm and thick, the sun a couple of feet above the trees. Mama always said humidity was good for a woman. Kept her skin looking young. I took a right at the road, and walked a couple hundred yards to the open field on my left, just before the creek. Already I could hear the lapping of the water over the rocks. Mama and I used to walk down to the creek after supper, dusk settling upon us like a cloak of fine silk. She'd pick clover from the field and tie it together, then lay it like a crown on my head. Ever so often she'd trace the freckles on the back of my hand as if they were cities and towns on a map. "You have your whole life before you, Francie," she'd say in a long, deep breath. We'd sit and watch the sunset, the sky turning the colors of crimson and blue marble, the evening stars appearing like fireflies on an oil canvas.

I walked through the field to the bank of the creek. The sun, now behind the trees, cast dancing shadows across the water's surface. I thought about the snake, but decided I was safe as long as I stayed on the bank. Sitting back in the grass, I laid my palm on the warm ground beside me where Mama used to sit and tilted my face to all that open sky.

"Mama, why did you have to go and leave us?" A burning ache started up behind my eyes, and it didn't take long for the tears to come. I buried my face in my knees, all that pain inside of me rising to the surface like great, tearing claws. Then the breeze came, stirring the grasses and gently lifting the strands of my hair. I breathed in, catching the sweet scent of Mama's skin mixed with the pungent fragrance of the earth. "Is that you, Mama?" I demanded of the trees, of the open sky above me. "If that's you, why don't you talk to me?" I stood quickly, whirling around, trying to catch the wind in my face, trying to catch her scent. "Why don't you tell me what to do with Daddy? Or where you put the flour sieve? Or how to defrost the icebox without getting water all over the floor?"

The air went still. "Don't leave me," I cried.

❧   ❧   ❧

When I got back to the house, Daddy was snoring in the recliner with three empty beer bottles on the floor beside him. A rerun of *Perry Mason* was on the television. I brought the bottles to the trash can in the kitchen, then turned off the TV and the lights. Daddy's snoring stopped. I froze in the doorway to the hall, waiting to see if he was still asleep, listening to all that silence around me. About a minute later, his snoring started up again, long and deep.

I lay in bed that night, staring out the window, the covers kicked back and my cotton gown sticking to me. I thought of all the nights Mama would come in my room and crawl in bed beside me. "You're my miracle," she once told me, stroking my hair away from my face. "Doctors had told me I couldn't have any children. Said certain parts of me didn't work just right, and here you come along."

Lying in bed, I tried to remember every detail of Mama's face. *If only I had a picture*, I thought. Daddy had gotten rid of all her pictures. One morning, just a couple of weeks after Mama died, I found him in the living room taping up a bunch of boxes.

"What are you doing?" I asked him.

He wouldn't answer, just kept going about taping those boxes, his face in a sweat, his body moving in a frantic way. There was an empty bottle of Jack Daniels whiskey on the floor beside his recliner. The whole room smelled of his drunk stench. Then it struck me. All the family pictures that Mama used to keep out on the bookshelves were gone. I ran back to Mama and Daddy's bedroom. The picture of Mama that used to sit on top of Daddy's bureau was gone, too. The room was a mess, drawers open, clothes everywhere.

"No!" I screamed.

I ran back into the living room and grabbed Daddy's arm. He slung my hand away. "Stay out of the way," he said.

Across the top of one of the boxes, Daddy had written my uncle's name, one of Mama's brothers who lived somewhere in Georgia.

Again, I grabbed Daddy's arm. "You have no right!" I screamed. Again, he pushed me aside. He lifted the box in his arms and carried it out to his truck. I knew all the pictures of Mama and us together were inside that box. Daddy must have worked all night while I was asleep. I dug my fingernails into the tape on one of the other boxes. Inside were Mama's dresses and scarves. I took out one of the scarves, then hurried to my bedroom and slid it between the box springs and mattress. In one day, Daddy had tried to get rid of everything that belonged to Mama. All that was left behind was her powder on the bathroom shelf, the gold coffee mug with the nick in the rim, and her purple-and-yellow scarf that I kept hidden away.

Now, I knelt down on the side of the bed and pulled Mama's scarf out from under the mattress. Climbing back onto the covers, I held it to my face. It still bore a trace of the powder she wore. I stared out the window at the woods behind the house, remembering the night Mama disappeared. Something in the trees moved. I pressed my face closer to the screen. I could swear I saw the shadow of a man at the edge of the woods. I squinted, trying to peer into the dark, then saw the outline of a beard in the moonlight. The air escaped from my mouth in a loud gasp. I jerked away from the window, fear slapping inside my chest like a couple of windshield wipers. After a minute or two passed, I edged my face in front of the window again. The shadow was gone. I thought about waking Daddy, yet suddenly I wasn't sure what I had seen. It had appeared and disappeared so quickly. I shut the window and turned the latch. *Wasn't anything. Just a shadow. Just a tree or a limb,* I told myself. I tucked Mama's scarf back under the mattress, as if it was her spirit keeping me safe.

Sometime in the night, a dream like the one I'd had at Ruthie's came stirring up my sleep and giving me such a fright it took Daddy's heavy arms and a whole lot of praying to settle me back down.

Mama disappeared into the trees again. I could see the tail of her dress catching the branches as she ran. Trees were everywhere, like a wall surrounding her that I couldn't get through. She fell to the ground, leaves and dirt covering her face. Blackness swallowed her.

I screamed, waking myself. Daddy heard me and came running.

"Bean," he called. "You okay?" He hurried over to the bed and knelt on the floor.

"You were dreaming," he said. "It was only a dream." He rubbed my hair back with the big palm of his hand.

I was still for a minute, trying to steady myself. Then I sat up and told him, "I had the dream before, when I was at the Taylors'." I paused. "It was Mama. I couldn't get to her. I couldn't help her."

Daddy put his hand on my back and rubbed it in circles like he did when I was a little girl. "It's gonna take some time,

Francie." He sighed. " It's just gonna take some time."

*   *   *

One night, Daddy gave me some money and asked me to pick us up dinner at the diner. When I got there, Sylvia was wiping tables.

"Why, hey, Francie. Whatcha know?" Sylvia is a small woman with long pink fingernails and peroxided hair. A couple of people sitting at the counter drinking coffee turned their heads to see who had come in. A television was suspended from the ceiling above them with white static and voices from the news out of Montgomery blaring from the speakers.

Sylvia had gum in her mouth that she popped when she chewed. Once when I was there with Daddy and she didn't have any customers, she tried to show me how she popped it like that, but I could never do it.

I sat in a booth where she was setting out salt and pepper shakers and rearranging a vase of silk flowers.

"Don't know nothin'," I said.

She planted her fists on her waist, with a dishrag wadded up in one hand and her right hip cocked out to the side, then popped her gum big. "Why, Francie May, I reckon you know a whole bunch, you just can't remember it right now." She laughed at herself and, leaning forward, poked me in the side. "How's your daddy gettin' along?" she said, moving on to the next table.

"All right," I told her.

"Did he ever tell ya who it was he got into that fight with?" she asked.

I shrugged my shoulders. "Doesn't wanna say." I laid the money in front of me and slumped down in the booth. "I'm supposed to bring home some supper," I said.

"Now, if that don't beat all," she said, her arms doing circles on the table. "Francie bringin' home the bacon. How old you be anyway, Francie?"

"Fourteen."

She swung her head to the side, pursing her lips. "Gettin' all grown up," she said. She took out the order pad from her shirt pocket and the pen from behind her ear. "What'll you and your daddy have?"

"A couple of sandwiches," I told her. "A reuben and a roast beef."

The bell above the door rang. "Hey, Sylvia," came a man's voice. It was the sheriff. He walked up to the counter, his stocky body rocking from side to side, and took a seat on one of the stools.

"Hey there, Clem. What can I getcha?"

He rubbed a hand over his face like he was tired. "Let me have some coffee," he said. "I'm waitin' on Harvey."

I wondered what the sheriff wanted with someone like Mansfield. I imagined Mansfield walking in, sitting up high and mighty next to Sheriff McGee. Remembered him saying he wanted to talk to me.

Sylvia poured the sheriff a cup of coffee and slid it out in front of him. I stared up at the TV footage of helicopters in Vietnam. More young men were being drafted. "To boost U.S. military strength," the newsman said. I wondered if more boys from Spring Gap would go over. So far, no one from our town had died. The war seemed like something unreal.

Sylvia brought me two white bags with the top edges rolled over. "I put some doughnuts in there for in the mornin'," she said. Then she winked, picked up the money I'd laid on the table, and walked over to the cash register.

The sheriff turned around and smiled at me kindly. "How you gettin' along, Francie?" he asked, holding the coffee cup in front of him.

"All right," I said, scooting myself out of the booth.

"That was some brawl your Daddy got himself into."

Yeah, tell that to Mansfield, I thought, but I didn't say anything.

Sylvia walked over, handing me my change. "You tell your daddy to come see me, now," she said.

＊　　＊　　＊

When I turned the corner for the driveway, I saw Daddy on the front stoop.

"Bean, hurry up. I got somethin' to show ya," he hollered.

As I walked up to him, I saw he was holding a hound puppy in the crook of his unbroken arm.

"I've been thinkin' a lot about those bad dreams you've been having," he said. "The neighbor's dawg down the ways had babies. Been thinkin' a puppy like this might do those dreams of yours some good."

He looked down at the puppy and stroked its brown head. The skin above the dog's eyes was all rumpled like an old man's. "Why don't you come hold this little fella in your lap?"

I set the bags down and sat next to Daddy. He shifted the puppy onto my lap. Both its front and back paws hung off my legs. I laid my hand on top of the puppy's scrunched-up head and dragged my fingers back and forth over his silky fur.

"How old is he?" I asked.

"Eight weeks," Daddy told me.

"He's gonna be big."

"Mmm-hmm."

A wide patch of dark-brown fur ran along the dog's back. He had his chin propped on the edge of my knee. As I looked down on his big, sad eyes, I thought of the word "lonesome," and I'm not sure if I was thinking it for him or for myself.

I knew from then on that's what I'd call him. So I rubbed his droopy ears a little and said it out loud, just to see how it felt.

"That whatcha gonna call him?" Daddy asked.

"I never said I was gonna keep him." I frowned.

"You keep that dawg, Bean. He'll do ya some good."

Chapter 5
The Woman with the Hoe

DADDY STAYED HOME FROM WORK his first two weeks out of the hospital. Before his accident, he'd help out with the dishes every once in a while or run the vacuum. But the only thing he was able to get done around the house now was sit in his recliner and watch TV. I was starting to feel more like his hired hand than his daughter. Maybe I wouldn't have minded so much if he'd treated me like his equal, talking to me about the things going on in his head, like who'd beat him up and why he had such a grudge against Mansfield. But instead, he seemed to keep putting his thumb on top of me every time I ventured into his mind of business.

With Daddy at home, I helped out at the store each day, ringing up groceries and counting inventory. One afternoon Mr. Tucker took an empty box from the back room and began filling it with different staple items from the shelves: coffee, dry milk, flour, canned soups, oatmeal.

Daddy and Mr. Tucker often made home deliveries to some of the older people who had trouble getting out. "Who's all that for?" I asked him.

"Just somebody that doesn't like to come around a whole lot," he told me.

"If you need to take those groceries to someone, I can watch the store," I offered.

But he shook his head as he carried the box to the back room. The door was open, letting in a stream of light and the smallest bit of a breeze. Mr. Tucker stepped out and set the box in the gravel against the wall of the building, then went back inside to help a customer.

Ever so often I checked to see if the box was still there. It wasn't until around four-thirty that someone finally came for it. The bathroom at the store was off the back room. I had just come out when I heard footsteps approaching in the gravel. I kept myself hidden and listened as someone picked up the box and began to walk away. As I stepped near the open door, I saw Earnest, the boy I'd noticed at Ruthie's house. He was tall and lean, with thick, wavy hair barely brushing the collar of his white T-shirt; his jeans hung slightly off his narrow hips and his feet were bare. I wondered how he could stand the hot rocks.

Mr. Tucker was at the cash register.

"I'm going to go ahead and leave," I told him. "I'll see you in the morning."

He nodded to me, and I left out the back door. It took a few minutes before I spotted Earnest, the box cradled in his arms against his chest, his legs moving briskly. He was walking down the side street from town, an old washboard road that looped around the outskirts of Spring Gap like a fishhook, bypassing Daddy's and my house. Adrenaline rushed through me like a bunch of sugar and caffeine.

The farther we got from town, the more quiet everything

became. Then Earnest turned off the road onto a small, hidden path that cut through the trees. I'd never been back this way before and wondered where he was going. I tried to stay a safe enough distance away so he wouldn't see me, but didn't want to lag too far behind on account of losing sight of him. The trees were so thick it was like pushing my way through wire mesh. I stepped as softly as possible, feeling my breath catch in my throat every time a twig snapped beneath my feet. Earnest didn't seem to notice. He began to whistle. After a short time, he started singing "Pretty Woman," his voice so terribly off tune, I had to cover my mouth to keep from laughing. Then, when he growled, trying to sound just like Roy Orbison, I thought for sure I would lose it.

The path eventually opened up onto the road that ran by the colored community. Earnest took a right, staying alongside the shoulder. The turnoff for the Taylors' house was just ahead. I thought he might be bringing the groceries to Mama Rae, but he kept walking. About a quarter of a mile past the Taylors', Earnest took another right, this time disappearing into the trees. I waited a good five minutes before going any farther. Up ahead was a patch of sandy ground, bare except for a few dandelions and the impressions of Earnest's feet. At the back of the small clearing stood a crooked mailbox with traces of black paint. On its side, white letters worn down to the metal spelled out "Malone." Slowly I followed a narrow footpath that led away from the mailbox between cedar saplings and sprawling weeds, a nervous sweat prickling every part of my skin. About fifty yards from the road was another clearing. On stacks of thin limestones laid in four corners stood a small green building, sagging in the center between the windowsills. My eyes searched for Earnest. I wanted to be sure he'd gone inside.

"May? Is that you?"

My heart bounded to my throat as I saw a strange-looking woman walking barefoot toward me from around the back of the house. She had thick frizzy hair the color of mud that stuck out like the quills of a porcupine. She was wearing baggy overalls. Her fingers gripped the long wooden handle of a hoe, propped up on her shoulder.

"It's Francie," I said. "Francie Grove."

"Francie May?" she said, stopping about ten feet in front of me and inclining her head in my direction. "If it don't be."

I thought I saw Earnest move from behind one of the windows. But when I looked more closely, there was no one there.

The woman raised the hoe high in her hand with a frightened look in her eyes. "You git on home, ya hear? Ain't safe. The demons live out in these woods. The demons will getcha. You git on outa these parts."

There was a crazed look about her that struck every nerve in my body with fear. Looking up at the hoe, I took several giant steps backward, then reeled around quickly and ran, not slowing till I had approached the turnoff for Ruthie's.

Leaning over to catch my breath, my hands on my knees, I saw Punkin stretched out in the grass in front of the Taylors' house, as if she was trying to get a suntan. There were voices inside.

I walked up to the house, my legs still shaky from the strange woman.

Before I had a chance to knock, Mama Rae saw me through the screen and waved for me to come in. The house smelled of fried chicken, mashed potatoes, and gravy. Rachel and Willie were setting the table and pestering each other.

"Ruthie, Francie's here," Mama Rae hollered down the hall, then looked at me and said, "You gonna stay and eat with us? Got plenty a food."

"I gotta check on Daddy," I told her. "I've been at the store all day."

"How's that puppy of yours?"

"I gotta check on him, too," I said.

Ruthie appeared from her bedroom off the hall and walked up beside me, giving me a playful nudge with her shoulder.

"Punkin's been hangin' around an awful lot," she said, her face grinning big.

"Yeah, I saw her, like some queen out front, lookin' all fat and lazy."

"Hmm, wonder why?" Mama Rae said, her big arms mashing up the potatoes and a chuckle written all over her face.

"You girls got five minutes, then supper's gonna be on the table," she told us.

I followed Ruthie out to the back porch. The two of us sat down, leaning our backs against the stack of wood.

"What are you thinkin'?" she asked me, since I wasn't saying anything.

I was fighting back a smile at the memory of Earnest's off-key singing. I liked the way his jeans hung on him, liked the way his feet strode easily down the road. As I remembered him growling in the back of his throat, I let out a laugh.

"I was just wondering if you've known Earnest a long time," I finally said.

Ruthie raised her eyebrows. "Most all my life. Why are you asking?"

My head was tilted back against the wood, a silly smile pressed on my lips. "Just wondering why I'd never seen him around before."

She shrugged her shoulders. "Kind of likes to keep to himself, I guess."

"Folks got to go to school," I told her. "How come I've never seen him at school?"

"He learns at home." She frowned.

Something about her voice made me think she wasn't telling me everything, as if her thoughts had suddenly gone all stiff inside.

"He's got a mom," Ruthie went on. "No one knows for sure who his daddy is."

"What's his mama like?" I asked, not sure I should admit to following Earnest to the green house, though feeling certain that was where he lived, and feeling even more certain that the woman I'd seen was his mom.

"Folks say she's crazy as a loon. Mama tells us to stay away from her. Some of the kids at school say they've run into her. Say she chased them with some sort a dagger."

Probably more like a hoe, I thought, though I didn't say it.

Mama Rae gave a big whoop from the kitchen. I started to laugh.

"What's so funny?" Ruthie asked, standing up.

"Why doesn't she just use a dinner bell?"

Ruthie smiled. "Says her voice is handier. How can she be ringing a bell and serving food and filling pitchers all at the same time? That's what she tells us, anyway."

Ruthie turned to go inside, then looked back with a grin written all over her face. "Want me to tell Earnest you were asking about him?"

"Don't you dare!" I said with alarm.

She started laughing.

"Ruthie Taylor!"

"Don't worry," she smiled, giving me a sly look from beneath her eyelashes.

Before I'd left the house that morning, I'd tied Lonesome up to the elm tree, setting his food and water bowls by the trunk. Both bowls were knocked over when I got home, and Lonesome had run enough circles around the tree that he and that great elm looked like they were joined at the hip. He gave a pitiful moan when he saw me, then barked and howled as if he couldn't decide which was more effective. I untied the rope from his collar and picked him up in my arms, his cold nose rubbing against my neck, his whole body wriggling as he wagged his tail. I wondered if Daddy had ever checked on him and why he'd let Lonesome get all wrapped up like he was.

Daddy had said that Lonesome was to stay outside, but Daddy wasn't home, so I let the puppy follow me into the kitchen. There was a note on the table. "Had to drive to Mayville on business. Be back late."

"What kind of business?" I said out loud. "You run a grocery store. What do you need in Mayville?"

I picked up Lonesome and put him on top of the dryer. Then I sorted Daddy's and my laundry into three different piles on the kitchen floor. With one leap, Lonesome bounded off the dryer into a pile of whites, emerging with a pair of Daddy's boxers over his head. I sat back into the pile of clothes, wrapping my warm dog all up in my arms and hugging him tight, realizing for the first time since Mama died that maybe life wasn't going to feel so lonesome after all. That maybe with Ruthie and my new puppy, Mama was still looking after me in her own sort of way.

Chapter 6
The Color of Skin

IT WAS A STICKY, HOT DAY. Ruthie and Lonesome and I were walking along the creek, passing the time and just being lazy.

"Anybody you know have to go to Vietnam?" I asked her.

Ruthie was trying to get Lonesome to fetch a stick. She'd hold it in front of his nose, then toss it a little ways ahead of us. He'd give the piece of oak a quick sniff, and trot on off ahead.

"Mac Story. You know him?" Ruthie looked over at me.

"Un-uh."

"Mama and Daddy always thought he'd go to college. He can shoot hoops better than anyone you've ever seen. And the muscles on that boy . . ."

"What happened?"

"Got drafted. Same thing that's gonna happen to all the other boys if the war goes on."

"Is that what your daddy says?"

"It's what everybody says. Tom's sixteen. Could be him in a couple a years."

Suddenly I was glad I didn't have a brother or a boyfriend who had to go off and fight. Here I was worrying about my daddy drinking, while other folks were worrying about their boys getting killed in a war.

Ruthie picked up the stick and tossed it into the creek.

Lonesome took off down the bank and bounded into the water. "Go get it, boy!" she hollered after him. "Go get it!" He bit down on the wood. Kicking mud and water up behind him, he leaped onto the shore and dropped his prize at Ruthie's feet. Ruthie and I both made a fuss over him, telling him what a good boy he was. He gave his coat a good shake, sending a fine spray of water all over us, making us laugh and cover our faces with our arms.

It was then that we heard what sounded like a bunch of guns going off, sending us to the ground with fright. I looked over at Ruthie lying in the grass. She had her hands pressed over her ears, same as me. Phinny, Sheriff McGee's youngest boy, walked up to us laughing his head off, a Dragon Fireworks bag in his hand.

"Ya ain't only a nigger lover, Francie Grove, but ya scare like one, too." He spat on the ground ncxt to Ruthie's face. She jerked her head back; her eyes flinched shut.

I didn't hesitate. I leaped off the ground and dove headfirst into Phinny, knocking him down on his back, the bag of fireworks spilling out beside him. I grabbed a wad of Phinny's curly black hair, my body sprawled on top of him.

"Take it back!" I yelled.

He slid his knee up into my gut and kicked me off him.

I fell backwards, hitting my head on the ground. That's when I saw Ruthie pick up the scattered firecrackers and start chucking them into the creek. I leaped forward again, lunging into Phinny and knocking him to the ground.

Phinny jammed his fist into my stomach. I fell back, my knees drawn to my chest and my mouth gasping for air.

"Francie!" Ruthie yelled, running over to me.

Phinny was now storming his way down the creek's sloping bank.

"Stupid nigger!" he yelled, wading into the water up to his knees. He scooped up a couple of the firecrackers now floating on the creek's surface.

"You all right, Francie?" Ruthie asked me.

"I'm okay," I said, catching my breath.

Phinny was still standing in the water, holding up the soggy firecrackers in one of his fists, then threw them down in a raging fit and started kicking his feet, making a big splash and acting like a downright fool.

"You're gonna pay for this, Francie! You and that nigger friend of yours!"

"Shut up, Phinny!" I yelled.

He tramped out of the creek, still kicking his legs as if he was trying to get water all in our faces. I jumped to my feet, ready for another fight, but he just raged past us. I swore I could hear him grumbling like some kind of wild boar. I imagined chucking a bunch of rocks at him, but knew it was better to just leave him alone.

Ruthie and I sank into the grass. I was still catching my breath.

"Where's Lonesome?" I asked, looking all around us. "Lonesome! Here, boy!"

Ruthie started calling for him, too. Both of us jumped up and trotted along the creek, whistling and hollering his name.

"Those fireworks must have scared him off," Ruthie said.

About that time, we heard the half-bark, half-howl sound Lonesome was getting real good at making. Up ahead, we found him tied to a tree, his hips swinging back and forth as he wagged his tail, his head up in the air while he continued to moan with delight at seeing us.

We ran to him, both of us hugging his neck and telling him everything was okay.

"Who tied him up?" Ruthie asked.

We looked around but didn't see anyone.

"Kind of gives you the willies." Ruthie was still searching all around us. "Who else would have been down here?"

"I'm just glad he's all right."

I untied him from the tree and sat next to Ruthie on the bank. Lonesome stretched out on my other side, laying his head on my leg, his body still damp from his romp in the water. I stroked his rumply skin, rubbing my thumbs over the lids of his sad eyes as he fell asleep. Phinny's words about Ruthie were sitting on my head and heart like a slab of concrete. What I felt for Phinny McGee at that moment was the closest thing to hate I'd ever known. I wanted to grab Ruthie with all my might and tell her I didn't care that her skin was black. And yet Phinny's words had stuck between us, making me feel like I had to tiptoe back into Ruthie's life 'cause my skin wasn't black. No matter how hard I tried, I would never be able to know the pain she must feel.

"I wish I'd hurt Phinny," I said, my voice tight in my throat. "I wish I'd hurt him real bad. He had no right to say what he did."

Ruthie stayed quiet.

"It ain't right," I told her. "I'm sorry, Ruthie. I'm real sorry about what he said."

"Mama says my heart's the same color as yours. My blood's the same color, and it moves the same direction as everybody else's. People don't have to go to different schools on account of the color of their hair. I don't see why folks should have to go to different schools on account of the color of their skin."

"Seems like some folks got thorns in their eyes," I told her. "Maybe they got thorns in their hearts, too."

"I reckon all that hate must cause them a lot of pain," she finally said.

Ruthie pulled her legs up to herself and hugged them tightly. I knew she wasn't feeling real good inside, and I wished more than anything I could make all the ugliness in people like Phinny McGee go away. I walked down to the edge of the creek and scooped up a handful of stones. Then I sat back down beside Ruthie and dropped some in her palm.

"How come?" she asked.

"How come what?"

"How come you're my friend?"

"I guess I don't have any thorns in my eyes," I said.

One by one I tossed the stones into the water. Ruthie continued to hold hers in her hand.

"What will you do when summer's over?" she asked.

"Same thing I do every year. I'll go to school and help Daddy at the store."

She looked down at the water like she was thinking. "Can we still be friends?"

"Of course we can still be friends."

Ruthie slipped the stones into the front pocket of her overalls, and snapped it shut. She tucked her chin on top of her knees.

"You know why they call this stream Mourning Creek?" I asked her.

"Never thought about it before."

"One night when Mama and I were sitting down here, she told me there's a legend of a family that settled in Alabama from Virginia. The oldest daughter in the family was sixteen. She was engaged to a Confederate soldier. Just before the family moved, the girl's fiancé was killed at the Battle of Gettysburg. Story has it that she never stopped crying. She cried so hard, her tears left a trail all the way from Lynchburg, Virginia, to Point Clear, Alabama, where they finally emptied into the Gulf of Mexico."

Ruthie lifted her chin and stared out over the creek. "Just imagine havin' that much love rockin' back and forth inside of ya."

"You got anybody you've loved before?" I asked her.

"Not anybody that could make me cry a river clear from Virginia to the ocean."

"Me neither."

Ruthie leaned back in the grass, folding her hands behind her head, giving me a grin. "We'll see how you talkin' and feelin' once you and Earnest start gettin' up all close together."

I gave her a push, making her half roll over. "Me and Earnest nothin'," I said.

"Mmm-hmm," she said, drawing her voice out long and slow behind her lips.

I laid myself back in the grass beside her, Lonesome nuzzling his cold nose into my neck.

Ruthie started singing "Chapel of Love" real quiet.

"I ain't gonna marry Earnest!" But just saying his name and thinking about those dark eyes of his made me feel all crazy inside.

Then Ruthie laughed, and before I knew it I was laughing along with her.

Chapter 7
Fire and Pain

THE DAY FINALLY CAME when Daddy got his cast off and was back working at the store, freeing up a lot of my time. After I'd finish my chores around the house, I'd spend the rest of the day at the Taylors' or down by the creek. One afternoon, as Lonesome and I approached the creek, Ruthie was already lying easily in the long blades of grass. Lonesome raced toward her, his awkward puppy legs loping behind him. He nudged her with his nose and licked her face. She pulled him down next to her and stroked his belly, then rubbed him behind the ears. I joined her, tossing my head back and facing the sun. Our shoulders were flat against the warm earth, our knees propped up. The sun went all through me.

"Don't it feel good," she said. "Lyin' here like this, feelin' all this warmth and listenin' to the water spinnin' over them rocks."

"Sure does," I said, drooping my eyelids to the sun.

"Ruthie?"

"Yeah?"

"Whatcha gonna do once you're all through with school?"

She had her arms folded under her head and was pulling and snapping blades of grass with her bare toes.

"Thinkin' I'm gonna go to college and then get in one of them big medical schools."

"You'd make a good doctor." I took my shoes and socks off and pressed my feet against the grass.

"What about you?" Ruthie asked.

"I'll probably stay in Spring Gap. Maybe I'll have a big family one day." I started thinking about Mama and all the things we did together. If we'd be out rakin' the yard, she'd pretend she was a knight challenging me to a duel, or she'd start chasing me around the garden with the hose till I was soaking wet. We'd laugh so hard we'd cry.

"Whatcha thinkin'?" Ruthie asked as I lay quiet.

"Just rememberin' stuff. Sometimes when Daddy and I eat our dinner I feel like there's a time bomb fixin' to go off, everything's so quiet. With Mama it was different. When she'd fix supper, she'd turn the radio up loud and dance her way from the 'frigerator to the stove, or sway her hips to the music while she stirred up something in a pan. If I walked through the kitchen, she'd take me in her arms and swing me around with her. She'd keep the music playing while we ate and ask me about all the things I did during the day. And sometimes she'd hum to herself, her mouth closed over a forkful of food like she was still dancing in her head."

Ruthie burrowed her hand into the pocket of her jeans, then pulled out a folded piece of paper and handed it to me.

It was a poem written in long, slanted cursive. I sat up to read it.

When you're feelin' like the sun's gone down on your head,
I'll be there for you.

And when the cold of life bleeds into your bones,
I'll be there for you.
Like evenin' comes and day comes,
like the shoes on your feet,
I'll walk with you, I'll be there for you.

Don't matter that my skin is brown,
don't matter that your eyes are green.
Like these stones in my hand,
I'll be there for you.

My eyes felt like two wet marbles. "You wrote this?"

Ruthie was still lying back in the grass. "Mmm-hmm."

I folded the poem and slipped it into my pocket. "Nobody ever wrote me a poem before."

I lay back, shoulder to shoulder with her. "I'll be there for you, too," I said.

After a couple of minutes passed, Ruthie said, "So you want to have a bunch of kids?"

"I always wanted a big family."

"Girl, you crazy."

"Your mama's got five," I reminded her.

"Suppose you'll have to find somebody to marry with all those kids you want to have." Ruthie laughed.

"Suppose I will.

"Hey, Ruthie?"

"Hmm?"

"You ever been kissed?"

"Noooo, un-uh." She pulled her head away from me, a whole bunch of laughter on the brink of her voice.

"Come on, 'fess up."

"Girl, whatch you talkin' 'bout?"

"Tell me."

She started laughing. "Jackson," she finally said.

"Jackson who?"

"Jackson Willaby."

"Jackson Willa what?"

"Jackson Willaby. Me and him were cleaning the church one Saturday for Daddy."

"You kissed him in a church?"

"Not in the church. We went around back."

"Was he your first?" I asked.

"Mmm-hmm."

"How did you kiss?"

"Well, I certainly didn't kiss him like I kiss my mama."

"Tell me!" I tugged at her arm, trying to pull the details out of her.

Ruthie started laughing again. "I just hugged him and kissed him. Oooh, Lordy, I just kissed him."

A thrill got into my stomach like it would when I'd think about Earnest.

"How many times you been kissin' on him?" I asked her.

"Just that once. He been walkin' Sadie Purkey home from church every Sunday since." She frowned.

"You sorry you kissed him?"

Her lips pressed together in an upside-down smile. "I ain't sorry I kissed him, but I ain't gonna go kissing him again. Gonna save myself up for somebody wants to start walkin' me home from church.

"'Sides, Sadie's got big breasts." She looked down over her own flat chest.

"Well, there you have it," I said. "Who wants some boy kissing on her 'cause of the size of her boobs," I said, feeling like my own chest lay flatter than the kitchen floor.

Ruthie's frown turned into a giggle.

"If I tell you somethin', promise you won't laugh," I said.

"Promise."

"I've never been kissed."

Ruthie managed to keep quiet for about three seconds, then exploded with laughter.

I gave her a strong nudge in the side with my elbow.

"Sorry," she said, only to explode once more.

I could feel my cheeks turning red, and I started laughing with her.

"You thinkin' 'bout Earnest, aren't you?" she said.

"Nooo, un-uh."

"Oooh, girl, Francie and Earnest."

Then the laughter started up again.

"Let's run," I finally said.

"Where to?"

"It doesn't matter." I jumped to my feet, pulling Ruthie with me. We ran through the tall grass, our lungs grabbing for air. Lonesome was bounding in leaps beside us till we tumbled back to the ground, doubled over with giggles.

"Francie Grove, you done turned my innards out."

I let out a wail as I tried to catch my breath. "And my back's done started to itch from layin' on this here ground."

We were both grabbing onto our stomachs, whooping between breaths. Lonesome jumped up on his hind legs and licked our hot faces.

"They's gonna find us," Ruthie said. "They's gonna find us for sure. Gonna lock us up for making such a ruckus."

"Who's gonna find us? Them birds up in them trees?" And then we wailed some more, tears streaming down our cheeks.

I wiped my face with my sleeve, still holding onto my stomach with my other hand.

"You reckon we'd end up at the ocean if we followed this here creek?" I asked.

Ruthie lifted her shirt to her face, wiping her eyes. "I reckon we'd end up without any supper," she said, and the laughter started again.

We dropped Lonesome off at the house before walking over to Ruthie's. "Where you two been hidin' at?" Mama Rae asked when we stumbled through the door.

"Just look at ya. You look like two squirrels that's been rollin' in the hedges."

I started to laugh, but held my breath.

"You two go wash up and then come on back and set the table." Mama Rae was standing over a pot of stew and a skillet frying with cornbread and pickles. We hurried through the house to the back porch, washed our hands and faces from the cistern, and combed the grass out of each other's hair. I turned around to see Alby standing by the back door watching us.

"Don't mind him," Ruthie said, catching my eye.

Alby's eyes looked like those of an old man, his lids drooping heavily, reminding me of Lonesome. I knew he had thoughts going on behind those eyes. Sometimes I thought I could feel them just by the way he'd go on staring, and it'd give me the shivers.

When we returned to the front room, the two youngest children, Rachel and Willie, were already sitting at the table, Willie wearing a crisp white shirt and navy trousers and Rachel in a pink-and-white jumper. On Wednesday nights, the Reverend held services at the church. I'd been spending as much time as I could at the Taylors', and by now Wednesday nights had become a routine. We'd eat our supper quickly, then rinse and stack the plates, leaving them to be washed later. Afterwards we'd walk over to the church, the whitewashed Baptist building I'd pass on my way to Ruthie's if

I was coming from my house. Mama Rae would usually start singing a hymn when we'd get about halfway there, and the rest of us would join in. Even Alby would clap his hands and sway with the rhythm. Sometimes Mama Rae and Ruthie would harmonize and I'd have to stop singing and just listen, it sounded so pretty.

When we'd get to the church, automobiles and trucks would be scattered across the lawn in no particular order and others would be pulling in, all of them packed to the brim with colored faces. None of them paid me any mind. They just greeted me like all the rest of the Taylor children, the men tipping their hats to me and the ladies smiling. I knew if Ruthie came visiting at the Methodist church Daddy and I attended, folks wouldn't be treating her as kindly. Lately I'd been noticing the way a lot of those white folks walked past colored people on the streets like they weren't even there at all.

Throughout the Reverend's sermons voices would lift to the rafters, the small church shaking with the thunder of hands clapping and feet stomping. "Thank ya, Jesus!" Bodies would sway, heads tilting heavenward. The aisles would become packed with standing bodies. "Sing it, brother!"

This night's sermon was no different from the others. The Reverend's voice rose as if it would carry us all, lift us right through that small whitewashed building to someplace wonderful. "Jesus knows the trouble you're in!" he yelled. "Nobody knows but Jesus!"

Mama Rae's foot tapped on the floor. Ruthie's body rocked to and fro. The Reverend's voice bellowed. His skin perspired profusely. He mopped his face with his handkerchief.

"Lord, cleanse the sins out of all of us," came his voice. "Glory hallelujah!"

Then Mama Rae's foot stopped tapping. Her body stiffened next to me. "Good Lord Almighty."

A teenage boy was coming forward, his face swollen and bloody, his body limping. I was reminded of Daddy, of the day I found him sprawled out in the gravel behind his store, and my insides cringed.

The boy, not much older than Tom, had come to turn himself in. To offer up his soul. "Thank ya, brother." "Praise ya, sweet Jesus," came the voices around me.

I looked at Ruthie. Her eyes were brimming with tears.

"What is it?" I asked her.

"That's Jackson Willaby," her voice just a whisper.

I took her hand as I stared at the boy Ruthie had kissed.

"The day's gonna come when one of them boys ain't gonna make it," she told me.

When church was over, I pulled Ruthie aside. "You want to talk to Jackson?"

We looked behind us to where he was standing. A big-breasted girl walked over to him, laying her hand on his shoulder and leaning into him, and I knew it had to be Sadie.

"No, I don't want to," Ruthie said.

As we stepped outside the building, we saw Tom standing

alongside the road. Two white boys I'd never seen before were approaching him. They looked about Tom's age. The three boys stood together talking. Then one of the white boys slapped Tom on the shoulder and all of them laughed and walked off together, heading toward town.

"Gonna be trouble with him someday," said Ruthie. "I can feel it in my bones."

"Do you know the boys he went off with?"

"Randy and Jason, and they ain't no good. They moved up here from the southern part of the county with their dad. Been comin' around the house. Mama don't like them none neither."

Ruthie was still staring down the road in the same direction I would be heading off in.

"Daddy says life for them boys is like drinkin' straight whiskey," she said. "Full of fire and pain."

I knew she was still thinking about Jackson.

"You sure you don't want to talk to him?" I asked her.

She looked back over her shoulder. "I'm sure."

As I walked home that night, I thought about Jackson and Ruthie and about the straight whiskey. The fire and pain. My daddy had swallowed his share of fire and pain, though I knew it was his way of trying to numb the pain that was already inside him.

The wind began to pick up, tossing the branches hither and

to and creating a rustling in the trees. The stars appeared hazily from behind the charcoal clouds. I searched the sky, wondering how far off heaven must be yet feeling it intensely near, as though God was watching me.

I thought of Alby, of his eyes, always staring. There was a subtle crunching sound of my shoes against the sand and the gravel in the road. I loved that sound. A few leaves blew in circles in front of me. The pungent fragrance of evergreen stirred from the wind.

Then I heard the crunching of leaves from somewhere in the woods off the road. A branch broke. *It's just an animal*, I thought, and my feet walked faster down the dark road. Again I pinned my ears to sounds other than my own. Footsteps, I was sure. I felt eyes watching me from the black woods. My heart seized up as beads of sweat stung my face and hands. I ran. The road seemed long and endless. I ran faster, fear slapping itself hard back and forth inside me. I heard the engine of a truck. Headlights beamed around the corner. The truck slowed. A door opened.

"Hey, Bean."

It was Daddy. I climbed in, my lungs burning.

"Thought ya might be gettin' a chill," he said.

I snuggled up close to his big body. *It was only the wind*, I told myself.

"Ya say any prayers for me?" Daddy asked in a playful way.

"I always do."

Chapter 8
Earnest

IT WAS THE MIDDLE OF A SATURDAY AFTERNOON. I was in the backyard trying to reclaim Mama's flower garden. Mama could grow any flower in the world and knew all their names. She'd planted gardenias and all kinds of roses, and daisies and mums and periwinkle. Now I could hardly tell the weeds from the flowers. What had once been her piece of heaven on earth now reminded me more of a nursing home that had been neglected in a bad way, everything just shriveling up. The ground was like hot pavement, making it impossible for me to pull up the weeds. I'd brought the hose around back and was giving the garden a good soaking to soften up the dirt. Lonesome was being a royal nuisance, rolling around in the mud and looking for places to dig. Every once in a while I'd squirt him big with the hose, sending him barking and galloping off. The windows to the house were open. I could hear the television going. Daddy was in his recliner, watching a baseball game between the New York Yankees and the Boston Red Sox. Every so often I'd hear him cheering or hollering at the ump.

I turned off the water, then went inside to get a steak knife, remembering how Mama would sink a knife into the dirt next to a weed, then give her wrist a good twist so that she could get the whole root up. When Daddy heard me in the kitchen, he started yelling.

"Francie, get in here!"

"What?" I yelled back.

I went into the living room and found him standing next to the TV, messing with the antenna. White lines danced across the screen and voices faded in and out of static. He finally got the antenna in just the right spot where the picture came in clear, but when he took his fingers off and stepped away, the static came back.

"Right here," he said, holding the antenna in place again. "Come stand right here and hold this."

"You want me to hold that antenna?" I asked in disbelief, my hands wadded up in fists on my hips.

"Come on, Bean. The Red Sox are ahead."

"I'm your daughter, not your servant!"

"Right here," he said, motioning me toward the spot. He cranked his head around to look at the screen. "Yes!" he shouted, when someone had gotten a hit.

I walked over and took the antenna from him.

"Don't move," he said, walking back to his recliner. "Right there. Stay right there."

I thought about all the dandelions taking over Mama's flowers. Thought about Lonesome digging a muddy tunnel from one end of the garden to the other.

"I'm not doing it!" I dropped the antenna and stormed back outside.

That's when I saw Ruthie strolling up to the house.

"Now he wants me to spend all afternoon being an electricity conductor," I said to Ruthie when she got up to me.

I told her about the antenna and she started laughing. "All you white folks with your TVs and telephones."

She followed me around back to where I'd been working on the garden. Sure enough, Lonesome was back to digging, his paws and nose all covered in dirt.

"I'll never get it the way it was." I wanted to cry.

Ruthie gave Lonesome a stern "No!" and pushed him aside. She knelt down in the dirt and began untangling the weeds from the flowers.

I crouched beside her. Then I took the steak knife from my back pocket and began uprooting the dandelions, one right after another till I had quite a mound next to us. Lonesome had trotted off, defeated, and was stretched out in the shade next to the house.

"Remember me tellin' you about my Aunt Hazel up in Maryland?" Ruthie asked me.

"I remember you tellin' me you had relatives somewhere up north."

"She was supposed to have a baby," Ruthie went on. "We just got a letter sayin' she'd had a miscarriage. My uncle says she's got the blues real bad. Mama wants me to go stay with them for a while. Help my uncle out. See if I can lift Aunt Hazel's spirits."

"How long does she want you to stay?"

"I'm not sure, maybe a month or so."

"It's already August. You'd be missin' school." My voice

suddenly felt all choked up. "When would you leave?" I asked.

"Daddy's going to drive me over to Birmingham next week. I'll be takin' the train."

"You ever ridden on a train before?"

"About six years ago. We went to visit Uncle Roy and Aunt Hazel shortly after they moved. Course, it was different then. All the colored folks had to ride in a separate car. Now, with the new laws, coloreds and whites supposed to all ride together."

I'd never thought about coloreds and whites having to sit in different places before. I couldn't believe things had ever been that way.

"You goin' by yourself?" I asked.

"Mmm-hmm."

"You afraid?" Laws or no laws, I knew colored folks weren't always treated right, and I wasn't sure I liked the thought of Ruthie traveling alone.

"Lots of colored folks take the train. I'll just keep real quiet. Mind my own business."

"Shouldn't have to keep quiet."

Ruthie didn't say anything.

"Never ridden on a train before," I told her. "Never ridden on a bus before, either. Makes you seem all grown up, traveling up north by yourself."

Ruthie had the smallest bit of a smile on her face, her eyes wandering off. "It's nice seeing all that land pass by you. Makes the world seem really big."

"Will ya write?"

"Course I'll write." She nudged me with her arm till I fell over, landing my bottom in the wet dirt. "You gonna write back?"

"Course I'll write back," I said, trying to keep a smile on my face.

That next week, Reverend Taylor drove Ruthie by my house before taking her to the train station. I'd never said goodbye to anyone before, and I didn't much care for the way it felt.

The Reverend stayed in his truck while Ruthie and I sat on the front stoop.

Ruthie held my hand, both of us quiet, not knowing what to say.

"Who's gonna feed Punkin?" I asked her.

"Mama says she'll take care of her. Maybe you could check in on her every once in a while."

I nodded.

"I'm gonna really miss you," I said.

She circled her arms around me and the two of us sat there hugging each other till we'd squeezed big tears out of our eyes.

"I better go," she said, standing up.

I walked her to the truck, feeling like I had a giant rope wrapped around my neck.

When she got in and the Reverend drove away, she leaned her head out the window and waved. "You're my best friend, Francie. Always."

            🐌   🐌   🐌

For some reason, the house seemed quieter than ever with Ruthie gone. Every little clink of a fork on a plate, every sound of my bare feet sticking to the linoleum as I walked through the kitchen echoed. I knew it was because I didn't have all our chatter to break up the day.

One evening after supper, Lonesome and I took off for the meadow along the creek. I pulled up clover and tied the stems together. Then I slid the wreath over Lonesome's head. He trotted down the bank to lap up some water, the flowers bouncing around his neck. After a couple of gulps, he raised his nose as if a noise had caught his attention. In one bound he was up the bank and running toward the woods at the far side of the field.

"Lonesome!" I shouted, chasing after him.

He disappeared into the trees, me running behind him. I'd never ventured past the meadow before. *He must be after some critter,* I thought.

A good hundred feet into the woods, Lonesome came running back for me, wagging his tail like he was proud of himself for his jaunt. "Oh, you're feeling real good about yourself, aren't you," I said, trying to scold him. "Real proud of yourself for going off and leaving me to chase after you." I picked up a stick and tossed it a little ways in front of us for him to fetch. Dapples of colored light penetrated the branches as the sky dissolved into a pool of misty oranges and shades of pink. We kept walking, the air smelling of cedar. A clearing lay just ahead. Lonesome stopped, raised his nose again, and listened. "Oh, no, you don't. Not again," I said, wrapping my arms around his neck and holding him against me. Then I heard it, too. The gentle splashing of water. A voice. Lonesome started to bark, but I held his mouth shut with my hands. A low growl sounded from the back of his throat.

We approached the edge of the clearing, me holding onto Lonesome's collar and telling him to hush. The ground opened before us into a large, tranquil pond where a boy was swimming. I knelt behind scrub oak and cedar, still holding onto Lonesome's collar. The shadows cast by the setting sun had turned the pond into a magnificent purple. The boy dove underwater, his bare buttocks rising to the surface. Soon he emerged, his hair sparkling like drops of diamonds. I felt my breathing stop as I realized it was Earnest. Again he dove under. Again he emerged, swimming across the surface in that slow, easy way of his to the bank on the far side.

It was then that I saw a man standing about fifty feet away from the pond watching Earnest. I was sure I'd never seen him before. He was tall and lean, his frame wiry beneath his pinstriped overalls. A black beard hung a good several inches from his chin. He wore a long-sleeved army-green shirt rolled up at the cuffs.

His hands were tucked in his front pockets, his elbows bent out to the sides.

Earnest said something to him and climbed onto the bank, his back to me. His lean body was evenly tanned a beautiful golden brown; his skin glistened from the drops of water running off him. I'd never seen a boy naked before. I felt warm all over, my stomach weak. Lonesome let out a bark. I had to tackle him to keep him from bounding forward. Both Earnest and the man looked in our direction. I was lying flat on the ground with Lonesome practically smothered underneath me, but I was sure they saw us. Earnest picked his shirt up from the ground, dried himself with it, and dressed. He and the man walked up the hill just beyond the pond, the dying light of the day like a halo around them. I watched them disappear into the trees, then rolled onto my back, thinking I would surely die if I found out Earnest had seen me.

Chapter 9
The Meadow

IT WAS A FRIDAY, about a week after I'd seen Earnest at the pond. Daddy left for the store early that morning. I dressed in a pair of shorts and an old T-shirt, then finished clearing out Mama's flower bed. I stood back, looking at the garden, feeling a whole bunch of satisfaction. One of the yellow rose bushes was in bloom.

In the far corner of the backyard was a small shed where Daddy kept the gasoline can and the mower. Ever since Daddy had gotten beat up, I'd been the one cutting the grass, even after his arm and ribs were all healed.

I took the mower out of the shed and filled it with gasoline. When I went to return the can, I noticed a red blanket folded up in the corner on the dirt floor. *What's a blanket doing out here?* I wondered. *We don't have any red blankets.* I picked it up and brought it inside to wash, racking my brain over why Mama or Daddy would've brought a blanket out to the shed.

After I cut the back lawn, I moved around to the front of the house, the mower still running. That's when I saw Mama Rae strolling up the driveway toward me, her arms swinging from side to side. Lonesome, who had been sleeping underneath the elm tree, ran up to greet her, his tail wagging.

"Francie, where you been hidin' at, child?" she hollered after I shut off the motor.

I grinned, surprised to see her. "Been around," I told her.

"I've come to see if you want to help me make some jam. You should see my fruit trees. I got a whole bushel of plums sittin' by my back door just waitin' for us."

About that time, Daddy's truck pulled up to the house, his brow pinned forward and his lips rolled in like he had something serious on his mind. He stopped just in front of us and got out. "Afternoon, Rae," he said, nodding his head politely. Then he looked at me.

"I got to be headin' over to Mayville," he said.

"How come all of a sudden you're goin' over to Mayville so much?"

"Just an ole friend I'm checkin' up on."

I was dying to get out of the house. Dying to go anywhere. "Can I come?"

"Not this time, Bean."

I wondered if Daddy had a girl he was going to see. That idea twisted itself around in my stomach like a bad ache. But then I thought if he was going to see a girl, he would've changed his shirt or at least combed his hair.

Mama Rae laid a hand over my shoulder. "I'd just come by to see if Francie wanted to help me make some jam."

Daddy had his hands hanging off his hips and was looking away. "Looks like Francie's got a yard to finish up."

I'm not believing this. I let out a loud sigh, folding my arms over my chest.

"Why don't Francie spend the night at our place. That way you won't have to worry about gettin' back so soon," Mama Rae said.

He wouldn't be worrying about getting back anyway. She knows that, I thought.

Daddy looked like he was eager to get going. "I guess that'd be all right. Soon as you finish up the yard," he told me.

"Yessir." I smiled at Mama Rae.

As he opened the door to get back in the truck, Lonesome ran over to him, jumping on his leg and whimpering up a big fuss.

"Wants to go for a ride," I said.

Daddy lifted Lonesome in his arms and set him on the seat beside him.

"I reckon I could stand his company," he said, the worry on his face relaxing just a bit.

After I finished cutting the grass, I took a bath and dressed in a pair of jeans and a clean shirt. By the time I got to the Taylors', Mama Rae was already in the kitchen cooking down a pot of plums.

"Come on in, Francie," she hollered from behind the big iron stove. She set me up at the butcher's block with a knife and showed me how she wanted the plums pitted.

"Where is everybody?" I asked her.

"The Reverend and Tom went fishing. Took Alby and the twins along for a swim."

I wondered if they were swimming in the pond where I'd seen Earnest.

"Mama Rae, what do you reckon Daddy's got goin' on in Mayville?"

She was heating up jars in a big pan of water. "Child, I haven't the faintest idea." Then she looked over at me. "The two of you gettin' along all right?"

I shrugged. "If that's what you call it. I think he's got the notion in his head that bein' a daddy's like a piece of clothing he can put on whenever he feels up to it."

"It ain't easy bein' a daddy," Mama Rae said.

It ain't easy bein' his daughter either, I wanted to tell her, but I didn't say it.

Mama Rae stood beside me and laid a hand on my shoulder. "Seems to me you got a lot of tired luggage under your skin. Need some place to set it all down."

I thought about what she said as I finished pitting the plums. "You hear from Ruthie yet?" I asked her.

"Got a telegram from Roy sayin' she was just fine. Haven't had a letter from her yet."

"I guess the mail can take a while," I said.

"We'll be hearin' something from her soon."

"You think it's going to take a long time for your sister to get well?"

Mama Rae smiled. "Sounds like somebody else needin' my little girl just as bad as my sister."

My throat suddenly felt like it had shrunk two sizes, and I knew if I didn't change the subject soon, I'd sure enough start crying.

Then it was as if Mama Rae could read my mind. She started telling me all about her sister and Roy and how the two of them had met and moved up north.

We made six jars of plum jam all the while we were talking. While the jars were cooling, we started on supper. I washed a bucket of collards and greens while Mama Rae fixed a skillet of cornbread. When we'd finished, she poured us each a glass of iced tea and we rested in a couple of aluminum lawn chairs under a large poplar in the front yard. Mama Rae wiped her face from time to time with the handkerchief she kept tucked in her apron. Punkin sauntered up to us from the side of the house and stretched out underneath my chair.

"She's pregnant, you know," Mama Rae said.

"You're kidding." I leaned over the chair and rubbed a hand over Punkin's fat belly.

"How long till the kittens'll be born?"

"Maybe a couple of weeks."

I sat back in the chair and sipped my tea. For no apparent reason at all the thought of Earnest and his naked body swimming in the pond crept into my head. I remembered the way the water glistened on his back and the way his thick hair fell just over his ears. No sooner had these thoughts entered my mind than he approached the house from the dirt road, one hand in his front pocket and the other holding a brown bag by his side. Just seeing him made my insides twitch.

"Earnest Malone, whatch you doin' back over here? Ya done

chopped my wood, fed my chickens. Lord have mercy, if ya ain't the workinest child," Mama Rae hollered at him.

He walked lazily toward us, kicking at the dirt with his bare feet that were soiled up to his ankles, though the rest of him looked clean.

"Came to bring you some of Mama's tomatoes." He handed her the bag.

Mama Rae reached a hand into the brown sack, then held a large, ripe tomato out in front of her. "Well now, don't they look fine."

She finished her tea and stood up to take the tomatoes inside. "I best take something out of the icebox in case the boys come home empty-handed." Earnest was still standing by the tree.

"Boy, go on and sit a spell," Mama Rae said, pointing to her chair.

Earnest sat down, crossing his dirty feet in front of him, but quickly tucked them under the chair when he saw I was looking at them.

"Want some tea?" I said, offering him my glass.

"Naw, I ain't thirsty."

"Ruthie says you've lived in Spring Gap a long time."

"All my life."

"How come I've never seen you before?"

"Never seen you before either," he said, a big swoop of his chestnut hair falling over his right eye.

"Daddy says Spring Gap's no bigger than a walnut in the big

scheme of things. Everybody knows everybody. Just wonderin' how come I've never seen you around town."

"I'm around."

I thought a moment, then said, "You always so hard to talk to?"

He removed a cap from his back pocket and twisted it in his hands. "You and that dawg of yours always go spyin' on people?" He cast his eyes over at me with a big, slow smile on his face, making his jaw slide forward.

I know my cheeks turned as red as those tomatoes. I lifted the glass of iced tea to my mouth and held it there a second or two, never having felt so mortified in all my life.

"I gotta be gettin' home," he said. He slipped the cap on his head and stood to go. After a second or two he swung his eyes back at me and I felt my face blush even more.

"Next time, why don't you join me?" he said. "Nothin' like a cool swim on a hot night like that." He turned back around, smiling big like he knew he'd done a good number on me. Then he walked down the driveway to the road, tucking his hands in the front pockets of his jeans and tilting his head forward, reminding me of the man I'd seen with him at the pond. At the road, he turned right and disappeared into the sloping woods.

My face felt hot with embarrassment. Unable to sit still, I headed back into the kitchen, where I found Mama Rae bent over the baker's table, rolling out a pie crust.

"Had some plums left over. Don't want 'em to go to waste."

I'd never had plum pie before, and tasted an instant sweetness and tartness in my mouth.

"Earnest didn't stay very long," she said.

"No, ma'am."

I pinched off a piece of the dough for myself, trying to settle a bit of my appetite.

"How come he doesn't go to school?" I asked her.

Mama Rae patted the dough in the pie pan before she spoke, waiting long enough to choose her words carefully.

"Francie, Earnest Malone's one of the finest boys there is, and don't let no one ever make you think different."

I slept in Ruthie's bed that night, wearing one of her gowns. The window at my feet was open to a warm breeze gently playing in the trees. A layer of clouds covered the stars. The kind of friendly clouds that pass through by sunup. Rachel was asleep across the room, breathing deeply.

On the table next to Ruthie's bed was a cigar box where she kept the stones I'd given her the day Phinny scared the bejesus out of us. I took them out, rubbing my fingers over their smooth surface. Underneath the box was a notebook where Ruthie wrote her poems. She had shown it to me before. I wondered why she hadn't brought it with her to Maryland. I took Ruthie's flashlight out of the nightstand drawer and began to read. Each poem carried Ruthie's voice, as if she was talking right to me. Then I came up on a poem she'd titled "Song of the Creek," and it was like the same blood was in both of us, her finding words for all those feelings inside me.

Goin' down to the creek today
Gonna swing myself silly in its song
My heart start skippin', my head so warm
The roots of my hair feelin' good.

Goin' down to the creek today
My toes slow dancin', soft blades of grass
Smooth whispers up my spine
Real gentle like my mama's voice.
Goin' down to the creek today
My thoughts start strollin', cool water flows
God's peace pourin' over me.

I closed the book of poems, the stones still in my hand, and burrowed down in the bed.

Sometime in the night I was awakened. The room was empty except for myself and Rachel, who was still sound asleep. But there was someone, a presence. Suddenly, a figure appeared in the window. It was dark like a shadow, about the size of a man. My breath seized itself in my chest. My body went stiff with fear. I lay still, too scared to move. The shadow vanished before me, like the night at home when I thought I'd seen someone along the woods. I listened for footsteps but only heard the sound of the wind, the tree branches rustling. My breathing was short. I felt like I couldn't get enough air into my lungs.

It was then that I heard him, as if he had called my name. I turned toward the doorway and saw Alby standing in the hallway, his body turned toward the room.

"Alby, are you awake?" I whispered to him.

Even in the dark I could see his eyes and the silhouette of his face.

"Did you see the shadow?" I asked.

But he only stared back at me, and I thought he must be sleepwalking.

"Go back to bed," I said, reaching for his arm to steer him away. Again, a sound from the window. I searched for the shadow, heat smothering my chest and climbing up my throat. *It's only the trees*, I told myself. I turned back toward Alby, but he wasn't there.

I crawled into bed, my heart still running fast. Each creak in the floor sounded like footsteps coming for me. I realized I still held the rocks from the creek in my left fist. I clutched them to my chest and pulled the blanket up over my eyes till my breathing slowed and I fell back to sleep.

At the crack of dawn a rooster crowed. Rachel stirred, though she was still asleep. I rose out of bed, put the stones back in the cigar box, and dressed in the jeans and blouse I'd worn the day before.

When I entered the front room, Mama Rae and the Reverend

were sipping coffee across from each other at the table. Their elbows were propped up in front of them, the mugs held close to their mouths. I smelled biscuits in the oven. Plum jam and butter were already on the table.

"Mornin', Francie," said the Reverend.

Mama Rae turned around. "Got some biscuits in the oven. Come on over here and let me get ya somethin' to eat."

Mama Rae stood to check on the biscuits, but my stomach was turning inside like a swarm of pent-up bees.

"I'm not feelin' very hungry," I told her.

Mama Rae was bent over the oven and turned her head sideways to look at me. "You're not feelin' hungry for one of Mama Rae's biscuits?"

"No, ma'am," I said.

"What is it then you're feelin' hungry for? A child's got to eat."

"Just not feelin' hungry, that's all," I said.

Mama Rae and the Reverend were both looking at me with their eyes all bunched up like they weren't real convinced by what I was sayin'.

"Didn't sleep real good," I told them.

"Come on over here and sit down." The Reverend patted the seat beside him. I was about to tell them about the shadow when Tom walked in, the screen door slamming behind him, causing my heart to jump.

"Tom, if I hadn't told you a thousand times!"

"Sorry, Mama." He joined us at the table, lifting the collar of his T-shirt to wipe off his face as if he'd already worked up a good sweat.

Mama Rae reached her arm across the table and laid her hand over mine. "What is it, child?" she said.

"Somethin' woke me up last night," I told her. "There was somebody outside the window."

Tom, who was sitting next to Mama Rae, leaned in over the table toward me. "Maybe it was the moon man." Then he started to laugh.

"Tom, get those biscuits out of the oven for me and hush your mouth," Mama Rae said sternly, giving him a shove on the arm. He got up, laughing out loud again.

The Reverend put his arm around me and looked at me kindly. "Next time you find trouble in the night, you come get me or Mama. Don't you lay there all by yourself."

"Yessir," I said.

"How 'bout I fix you up somethin' to eat?" Mama Rae said.

"I'm still not feelin' real hungry. Thinkin' I'm gonna head on home. Check on Daddy and Lonesome."

She wrapped up some biscuits for me to bring with me. "Just in case you start feelin' hungry along the way," she said.

Outside the sun was low in the sky and the ground damp. Alongside the road, wild ferns scattered so rich and green you'd think they would bloom. And behind them were spotted orange amanitas, a name I had learned from Mama.

Just as I turned a corner in the road, Earnest came up on me, scaring the wind right out of me.

"Whatch you doin' over here?" he asked.

"Ain't a woman got a right to go for a walk?" I said.

"Reckon so."

I kept walking.

He changed the direction he was heading in and started walking beside me, his hands shoved in his pockets.

"How old are you?" I asked him.

"I'm gonna be seventeen."

"I'm gonna be fifteen," I told him.

"I know."

I stopped, planting a hand on my straight hips. "How come you know so much?" I smiled up at him.

He didn't answer. The two of us just stood there looking at each other. I felt my heart beating fast, and my stomach start turning like I had fire ants crawling around inside. Then the corners of his face started creeping up, and he was smiling right back at me.

Next thing I knew we were both walking again, not saying anything.

"Ya ever been on the other side of the creek?" Earnest asked.

"No. Daddy told me it was private land."

His feet shuffled in the dirt as he walked, kicking at a few loose stones. "I got a place I go to," he said. "I'll show ya if ya want."

"How come you're bein' so nice to me all of a sudden?"

"I ain't bein' nice. Just thought you'd like to see it." He walked on ahead, then swung his eyes back at me like he'd done the day before, his face smiling easy. "Ya don't have to come."

I followed him.

We walked through the tall grasses just before the creek. I liked Earnest's voice. It had already changed, making him sound a lot older than me. He was wearing khaki trousers and a white T-shirt, and as we walked I could smell a trace of his sweat, making me want to walk close to him, so I did.

We stopped just short of the creek. I set the biscuits on the ground. Then we both rolled our pants up to our knees. I hadn't waded in the creek since getting bit by the snake. All of a sudden, I froze.

"What's the matter?" Earnest asked.

He was hunched over with his hands on the cuffs of his trousers, his big brown eyes looking up at me.

"Nothin'," I said, picking up the biscuits.

He grabbed hold of my hand without any thought to it. I was glad I didn't have to say anything more.

We crossed the creek, the water chilling my feet and ankles. After he helped me up the bank onto the other side, he let go and again slipped his hands into his pockets. We began climbing the gradually sloping hill where trees scattered in patches. At the top of the hill a meadow opened up, covered with rich lavender, native violets, and wild strawberries. Moosewood splashed the edges with white bunches of flowers. I breathed deeply, wanting to take it all in. Earnest stopped and looked back, watching me.

"It's so peaceful up here." I smiled at him.

"I thought you'd like it."

He walked to the middle of the open space, sunlight pouring over him. Then he climbed an exposed rock, draped his long legs over its side, and planted his hands behind him on the flat surface. I climbed up beside him. The creek chanted behind us. A cow lowed in the distance. I looked at Earnest, his face to the sky, and thought he was beautiful.

Chapter 10
This Too Shall Pass

THE NIGHT BEFORE SCHOOL WAS TO START, I baked pork chops and potatoes for Daddy and me. We were sitting at the table, neither one of us saying a whole lot. Ruthie had been gone for a total of fourteen days. I'd gotten her address from Mama Rae and had already written her twice, but still hadn't heard from her. The mail was delivered to Daddy at the store. Every day I'd ask him if I'd gotten anything, but he'd just shake his head.

Sometimes I wondered if Ruthie was having such a good time that she'd forgotten about me, but I knew that didn't sound like Ruthie. Other times I wondered if she'd written and the letter had gotten lost somewhere. I wished more than ever I had someone to talk to. Mama used to take me shopping over in Mayville every year before school started, buying me new clothes and taking me to lunch. My skirts were getting too tight around the waist and my feet had practically outgrown my shoes. And though I was sure my chest was the flattest one in that school, I'd convinced myself I'd graduated from a training bra to at least a double-A. Mama would have known that sort of thing without me having to say it.

Just as I'd worked up the courage to talk to Daddy about the things I was needing, he looked at me and said, "Think it's time you start finding some other girls your age."

I had a mouthful of potatoes about to get stuck in my throat. I washed them down with a gulp of milk.

"Just what are you sayin'?" I was looking at him straight on.

"Start spending time with the girls at your school. Make some other friends."

"Other than what?" I knew what he was getting at. I just wanted him to say it.

"I know you and the Taylor girl have gotten to be friends. But she ain't like you. She ain't one of us."

And what exactly are we? I wanted to say. *An alcoholic dad and a fourteen-year-old, stuck together like a couple of burrs getting under each other's skin.*

"Doesn't look right, a colored girl and a white girl spending so much time together. That's just how it is."

For cryin' out loud, Mama used to say when she'd had enough of Daddy's cockamamie. Then she'd usually toss her napkin next to her plate and excuse herself from the table. Instead, I looked Daddy in the eye, thinking his brain was about as narrow as a piece of cardboard. He wasn't going to walk his ideas all over me like they were the Ten Commandments.

"You sayin' I can't see Ruthie?"

"I'm not sayin' you can't see her. I'm just sayin' you need to start hangin' around with some of the other kids, that's all. Especially now with school startin' back and Ruthie gone."

"Since when did you care so much what other people think?"

"Damnit, Francie. Don't make this any harder on me than it already is." He looked like he'd just stepped onto a stage and wasn't sure what his next line should be.

I stood up and carried my dishes to the sink. "Ruthie's the

best friend I've ever had," I said. Then I turned back around. "That's just how it is."

☙   ☙   ☙

That first day of school, I missed Ruthie more than ever. Though I'd known the kids I went to school with all my life, it was as if I was a stranger walking into that building. Two things were different about me in the other kids' eyes: I was motherless, and I was friends with a colored girl.

"Nigger lover!" Phinny McGee yelled at me just as soon as he saw me walking up the sidewalk to the school. He was standing with a group of rowdy boys who had gotten suspended the year before for flushing a roll of toilet paper down a commode in the boys' bathroom and flooding the entire hallway.

I tried to ignore him, though could feel the blood boiling in my cheeks. I kept my books tucked close to me and walked quickly into the building.

"You say, 'Yes, Sir' when I'm talking to you, Francie Grove," he yelled to my back. Then all those boys let out a bunch of guffawing and snickering like they thought they were something special.

I remembered the tantrum Phinny had thrown at the creek. I knew Phinny was only acting like a big shot because he had his friends with him. "*There's strength in numbers*," Reverend Taylor had once said.

"Eat dirt!" I shouted at Phinny, then hurried into the building before he had the chance to say anything else.

As the week went on, I found things weren't any better with the girls. I couldn't believe I used to hang out with some of them, eating lunch with them or sometimes going over to their houses after school. Daddy still wanted me to be friends with these kids. He didn't have a clue. One day while I was in Mr. Franklin's biology class, Laurie Peppers and Essie Blalock were sitting in the row beside me passing a note back and forth. They let the piece of paper fall by my feet. I knew I shouldn't pick it up, but I did.

"Too bad you got stuck sitting next to her."

"I know. Mr. F stuck me here. Can you believe she's friends with that nigger girl?"

"I can't believe we used to hang out with her. What if she shows up at one of our houses with that colored girl? My mom would just die!"

"She's crazy enough to. Everyone says she plain lost her mind after her mama died."

"She's such low class."

I wadded up the piece of paper, my heart thundering in my chest, my fists clenched so tight I thought my fingernails might draw blood. I wanted to cream the daylights out of those girls and everyone else in that school. I stared down at the desk, my ears ringing with all the anger that was pounding inside of me. *God, don't let me cry. God, please don't let me cry.*

I knew Laurie and Essie were watching me, chalking up a victory. The bell rang. They stood, each of them brushing their hips against my shoulder as they walked past me. I didn't move. Stayed in my seat like stone, my eyes boring into the desktop in front of me. DJ + CL = *love*, someone had carved.

Slowly I raised my eyes from the desk and looked around the room. A few kids remained, gathering their books and cracking jokes. It was then that I realized there wasn't a single soul I could talk to at that school. Not one person. *Don't let them get to you. They're nothing.* The words in my head took on the rhythm of my feet as I stood and walked toward the door. On the way out I dropped the note in the trash can.

My legs felt like jelly the rest of the afternoon, moving me from one classroom to the next, where I sat with my head buried in a notebook, not talking to anyone.

When the final bell rang, I left the building with my books clutched against my chest, my feet walking at a quickened pace and my eyes staring forward.

Halfway home, about a hundred yards outside of town, something nipped my shoulder from behind. Something hard like a rock. I glanced back but didn't see anyone. Another rock whirled past me, intended for my head. I took off running. "Get her!" somebody shouted, and I knew it was Phinny. Footsteps started up behind me. They came up on me so fast I could hardly catch my breath. A group of boys circled around me, their hands seizing my arms and yanking me off the sidewalk into a patch of trees, my books spilling onto the ground. I kicked one of them good in the shin, sounds erupting out of me. A sweaty palm covered my mouth. The boys pulled me farther away from the road, deeper into a spread of woods, my feet dragging and kicking until I toppled onto the ground. The tears finally came. I couldn't stop them.

"Cryin' like a nigger," one of them shouted.

Boone Porter and Bradley Arnold were holding my shoulders to the ground. "We'll show you who to mess with! We'll show you who's gonna eat dirt!" they yelled in my face, flinging their spit in my eyes. The more I squirmed, the more they spat in my face.

Phinny stepped away from the group and reached for a pail hanging from a branch on one of the nearby trees. *He planned this*, I thought. *He had this notion in his head all day. Oh God, make them all stop!* Phinny took long, slow strides toward me, the pail in his hand, an evil grin lurking on his face, the kind that pulls the mouth straight back. He scooped his other hand into the pail and brought out a fistful of cow manure the consistency of grainy dough. He set the pail down by my feet. As I turned my face from side to side, Boone held his hand over my forehead, pinning my head to the ground. I started to scream, but just as I did, Phinny shoved the fistful of cow pie into my mouth. "Eat shit," he said, digging his palm into my teeth and lips. I gagged and spit. The other boys laughed. I heard Phinny's fingers scrape the side of the metal pail. I knew another fistful was coming. But then Boone and Bradley seemed to freeze, their eyes on something behind me. Phinny saw it too. He dropped the pail, and all three of the boys took off running. My stomach churned with nausea; grit covered the back of my throat and teeth. I struggled for breath. Manure had gotten into my nose.

I rolled over, lifting myself on all fours, spitting the manure from my mouth and wiping my eyes. I looked around me but no one was there. My throat felt like sandpaper. I untucked the tail of my shirt from my skirt, lifted it to my mouth, then rubbed it against my teeth and down my tongue in scraping motions. I had stopped crying, the tears drying in tight rivulets on my face. I was wearing my leather saddle oxfords and a pair of navy knee socks. I stood, then kicked the pail as hard as I could, my voice making the sound between a moan and a growl.

I knew I had to get home. Had to get away from anyone who could see me. I thought of the shortcut that ran by Mansfield's backyard but decided I couldn't go there. I would have to stay on the road. I walked out of the woods, fifty yards or so to the sidewalk. I kept my eyes on the ground and pulled my hair down along the sides of my face so that if any cars or people passed by they wouldn't see the dirt smeared over my mouth and clothes. My legs felt like sponges. Just ahead I spotted my books. Someone had picked them up and stacked them in a neat pile in the grass just off the sidewalk. I gathered them in my arms and kept walking.

Once the house was in sight, I saw Lonesome lying on the front stoop. He heard me and came running down the driveway toward me.

"Hey, boy." I kept walking, my arms folded tightly over the books I held to my chest, while he wagged his tail and trotted beside me.

He followed me into the house. Daddy still didn't like

Lonesome inside, but Lonesome and I had gotten real good at breaking that rule whenever Daddy wasn't there. I set my books on the counter, then turned on the kitchen faucet full-blast. I filled my mouth full of water, rinsed, and spat at least twenty times. I scrubbed my face with my hands till my skin felt raw.

Once in my bedroom, I pulled off my shoes. In one angry gust, I heaved them against the wall, slightly nicking the plaster where I had once colored in the face of a moon. Lonesome retrieved one of them and cautiously walked over to me. I sank onto the bed. He leaped beside me and dropped the shoe in my lap.

"I hate every one of them," I said, knocking the shoe onto the floor. Lonesome lay his head on my legs, looking up at me with the saddest eyes I'd ever seen. I pressed my face down against him and ran a hand along his back, tears burning my cheeks. I looked at the boat Mama had colored on the wall next to the window, the sea full of waves, the bright sun in the sky. "I want to run away," I told Lonesome. "I want to be that boat out on the sea." I rocked my body from side to side, still stroking Lonesome's fur, still crying. Lonesome's eyes were closing.

I gently moved his head from my lap, and reached over and turned on the radio on my nightstand. Some car salesman was advertising Chevrolets. I stood and walked over to my bureau. In the back of the top drawer was a pack of crayons. I sat Indian-style on the floor, the pack of crayons beside me. I pulled out green and brown and blue. Herman's Hermits were now singing "Can't You Hear My Heartbeat." I drew two wavy, parallel lines with the blue for the creek and colored it in. Then I made long strokes with the green along the creek's edges. *I wish I was an artist,* I thought. *I would draw Ruthie and me sitting in the grass. If Mama was here, she could do it. She knew how to draw.*

I heard the back door open. Daddy was home. He didn't call for me like he usually did. Instead, I heard his keys clink on the counter and his footsteps approach my room. Lonesome jumped onto the floor and quickly scooted underneath the bed, though his tail was sticking out. I wiped the tears from my eyes and continued coloring in the grass. I added yellow to lighten up the green.

"Bean?"

Daddy was standing in the doorway. I didn't answer him.

"Bean, Mr. Franklin came by to see me at the store this afternoon. Said you were having some trouble at school. Told me about a note he found that some girls had written, and said he'd seen some boys giving you a hard time earlier in the week. He thought maybe I should talk to you."

"I'm okay," I said. I was peeling the paper off one of the crayons, tears stinging my eyes like soap.

"He told me he wants to talk to you tomorrow. Wants you to come by and see him before school starts."

I wondered if it was Mr. Franklin who had scared Phinny and his friends off, who had gathered my books, but if it was, I couldn't imagine why he wouldn't have said anything.

Daddy reached in his back pocket and pulled something out. He took a couple of steps toward me and dropped it in my lap.

Before I'd looked at it, he'd already turned and left the room.

I recognized Ruthie's slanted cursive writing, real elegant looking. The envelope was postmarked August 18, which I knew was the day after Ruthie should have arrived in Maryland. I carefully tore open one of the long ends of the envelope, then pulled the folded letter from its sleeve. She'd written the letter on a piece of notebook paper.

Dear Francie,

How's my best friend doing? Miss me already? You'd better. I kept thinking on my way up here how much fun we would have had if we could have ridden the train together. Mama gave me a new notebook for my poetry before I left. I wrote five poems on my way here, all about the countryside and the different towns we passed through, and a poem about all the snoring people sitting around me, one with his jaw half open and drool dripping down his chin.

Girl, you better write me back quick, cause there ain't nobody around here my age. Uncle Roy picked me up at the train station. He's done grown a beard and gained a barrel around his middle, making him look a whole lot different than I remembered him. And Aunt Hazel's got the blues so bad, she just keeps calling me "Honey child," and hadn't once even said my name. Their house has two floors. The kitchen and living room are on the first floor, and a bathroom, just like all you white folks. Upstairs are two bedrooms. I'm sleeping in the room that was going to be the baby's, which makes me feel real sad. It's got wallpaper with pictures of Noah's ark. There's a twin bed and a dresser (they hadn't bought a crib yet), and a rocking chair next to the window, which I don't think I'm going to ever want to sit in.

I read to Aunt Hazel for a whole hour last night from the Bible, about Moses and the children of Egypt. She cried the whole time. I asked her if she wanted me to stop, but she just shook her head, so I kept on. Until I got to the part about the spirit of God killing the firstborn child of all the Egyptians. I saw that part coming and skipped a good ways past it. Aunt Hazel didn't seem to notice. I kissed her good-night and she took my hand and held it real close to her face for the longest time. Reminded me of that story you told me about Mourning Creek. Would hate to bear a sadness that deep in my heart.

You better write me back real soon and tell me all about Earnest and Punkin and anything else going on. I bet you got your Mama's garden looking real pretty by now. Hope so.

Write soon!

Love,

Ruthie

I'm sure I read Ruthie's letter at least three times before tucking it back into the envelope. Then I looked at the postmark again. Lonesome had come out from hiding underneath the bed and was now lying beside me on the floor. "Didn't know the mail could take so long," I said to him. All of a sudden, my stomach gave a queer lurch. Part of me was madder than a bull, but a bigger part of me was just plumb wore out and tired of all the wrong in the world. Tired of people not doing what they should. Tired of hurting so bad. I walked down the hallway to where Daddy was sitting in his recliner, smoking a cigarette.

"How long have you had this letter?"

Daddy let the smoke escape out the side of his mouth. He stood up slowly from the recliner, not saying anything, and planted himself in front of the bookshelf like he was looking for something. After a long thirty seconds he pulled out a book on Babe Ruth, opened the cover, and handed me another letter. This one was postmarked August 27.

"People can make mistakes," he said, his voice sounding like gravel crackling under car tires.

I'm not believing this. My own Daddy. I just stood there shaking my head. Daddy wouldn't look at me, no matter how badly I wanted him to. But I was going to make him say something. Was going to make him apologize. He had no right to do what he did.

"Ruthie's the only friend I have, and she cares a lot more about me than any other person in this whole world."

"I'm sorry," he finally said. He still wasn't looking at me. His hands were hanging off his hips, his head cowered down.

I shook my head and walked back to the bedroom, closing the door behind me. I didn't feel like slamming it anymore or throwing my shoes against the wall. I just felt sad all over. I sat on the end of the bed. The Supremes were singing over the radio. I once told Ruthie she looked like Diana Ross. She let out a loud whoop, sounding like Mama Rae at suppertime, then she started laughing. "Girl, you like one of those feel-good potions. Nice to have around."

"Mmm-hmm, Francie and Earnest," was the first thing Ruthie wrote in her next letter. I had written Ruthie about seeing Earnest at the pond and him walking me to the glen on the other side of the creek. "Girl, you got to slow down a bit till I get home or I'm gonna be missing all the action!"

Reading Ruthie's letter was just like sitting with her at the creek. "Don't you go kissin' him till I get home, but if you can't help yourself you better write me real fast and tell me all about it."

Already Ruthie had me laughing. She signed her letter, "Love and all that sweet stuff, Your Best Friend."

When I awoke the next morning, I smelled the coffee and knew Daddy was already up. I dreaded school more than ever and thought about staying in bed, playing sick for the rest of my life. Then Daddy appeared in the doorway in his sock feet, a cup of coffee in his hand.

"Time for school," he said.

I rolled over. "I'm not going."

"Oh, you're going," he said. "You're better than the rest of them, Francie. You put on one of your best outfits and you hold your head up. Don't you let them get to you. 'Sides, Mr. Franklin's wantin' to talk to you."

I knew Daddy was right. Somehow I had to find the steel inside of me to keep going. But as I lay in bed, I wasn't sure how much steel I had left. Then I thought of Ruthie, and I knew I had to do it for her. I had to show the kids at school they were wrong to say what they had about Ruthie or me.

I got ready in a hurry and left the house early. I didn't see Phinny or any of his group of friends. Inside the biology class-room, Mr. Franklin was sitting behind his desk. Most of the kids had always been afraid of him. He looked like an ex-marine, with his black hair cut close to his head. His shoulders were large and square and he must have stood at least six feet four inches.

"Francie, come in," he said when he saw me. He pulled up a chair beside his desk. I wasn't in the mood for any long-winded conversation. I just wanted to thank him for running Phinny and his friends off.

"I wanted to talk to you about yesterday." He was motioning me to the chair.

"I saw the note Essie and Laurie were passing back and forth," he told me. "And I've seen how some of the other kids have been treating you."

I sat down in the chair, my books held in my lap.

"I'm real sorry some of the kids are giving you a hard time."

I didn't say anything.

"I just wanted you to know you shouldn't have any more trouble. I spoke with the girls and will be talking with Phinny and his friends. If they want to stay on the football team, they're going to have to keep their grades up in biology."

His face suddenly had a bit of a smirk on it, and I could tell he liked Phinny McGee just about as much as I did.

"If you do have trouble, I want you to talk to me."

I wasn't sure I wanted a teacher for a friend, but I had to admit to myself I was glad I had one person in that school who wasn't against me.

"I guess you were the one after school," I finally said.

His chin pulled down and his eyebrows raised, as if asking me to go on.

"The one who ran Phinny and his friends off."

"I talked to Laurie and Essie after school. And I stopped by your father's store. Francie, what are you talking about? What happened?"

Somebody had come up on Phinny and his friends. Somebody had gathered my books. I just shook my head. "Nothing."

"Do you want to talk about something?"

"No." I looked down at the books in my lap. "Thanks," I said. I stood to go.

"One more thing, Francie. Something my dad used to always say to me when I was growing up: 'This too shall pass.'"

Chapter 11
When the Sun Stood Still

ABOUT THE TIME RUTHIE LEFT FOR MARYLAND, one of the hottest campaigns in the history of our county began. Clem McGee had been sheriff of Tallapoosa County since 1959. He was finishing up his second four-year term and was soon to run for his third. In the last election, he'd run unopposed. But that September of 1966, a young man from Mayville stepped forward, announcing himself as a candidate.

Shortly after, Daddy put a "Phil Lawson for Sheriff" sign up in the storefront window, and Sheriff McGee came to visit. "How can you, Hank? After all these years? After all we've been through?" Sheriff McGee asked Daddy one Saturday afternoon.

"That's just it, Clem. Some things ain't easy to forget."

The two of them were standing at the back of the store. I was at the cash register, and though I couldn't see their faces, I could hear them well enough. Sheriff McGee was a big man with a big voice, as was my dad.

"When have I ever done you wrong?" the sheriff asked.

"This ain't about you," Daddy said.

"You got nerve, Hank. You got real nerve."

"Why don't you go tell that to Mansfield," Daddy's voice boomed.

"You're gonna regret this, Hank," Sheriff McGee said, then stormed out of the store in a big way.

Later that night, over supper, I asked Daddy if he was going to be voting for Mr. Lawson come fall.

"Me and Lawson go way back," Daddy said between bites. "He's a good man."

"A better man than Sheriff McGee?" I asked him.

Daddy just stared at his plate, not saying anything, then got up from the table and carried his dishes to the sink. My eyes followed him as he took a cigarette from his shirt pocket and went outside for a smoke.

I felt like all the questions I ever asked Daddy fell into some hole inside of him, where they festered and stewed. Getting an answer out of him was like pushing a big ox who'd already made up his mind he wasn't going to move. I wondered what Daddy meant about him and Mr. Lawson going way back. After I cleared the table, I opened the screen door and joined him on the back stoop. His hands were resting on his knees and the cigarette, wedged between his fingers, pointed to the sky, sending up smoke around his face.

"You know Mr. Lawson?" I asked him.

He put the cigarette to his mouth and inhaled deeply. "Yeah," he said, the smoke crawling out between his lips. "We used to play against each other in football. I was a linebacker. He was quarterback." Then Daddy looked over at me. "It was a long time ago."

"Wasn't so long, Daddy."

"No, I guess you're right." He put a hand on my shoulder and stared out toward the road. "Not to folks around here, anyways.

"My senior year we played Mayville in the state finals. Lawson was a junior. He had an arm like a pro and had all the scouts after him. It was the last quarter. Mayville was ahead."

Daddy pulled in on his cigarette again, as if drawing his thoughts into himself.

"The coach told me to put Lawson out. Said it was the only way we had any chance to win. In the next play, after Lawson threw the ball, I tackled him hard. We got penalized, but I'd done what the coach said. He didn't play again. Not that year, or the next. Got his knee torn up pretty bad."

Daddy put his cigarette out on the step. "In the last seconds of the game, Mayville scored again."

"So they won anyway," I said.

"Yeah."

"Daddy, you worried about somethin'?" I asked him.

He took out another cigarette from his front pocket. "Let's just say Lawson's a better man than McGee."

Late that Wednesday, Daddy made another trip to Mayville, and I had a feeling it had something to do with the man whose knee he'd hurt. He drove me over to the Taylors' on his way out of town, Lonesome sitting up in the seat beside him.

"You gonna see Mr. Lawson?" I asked him before I got out of the truck.

"I may see Lawson," he said, then, laying a hand on my shoulder, "but don't you concern yourself with that none."

"Yessir," I said.

"Best not to say anything neither," he told me.

      🦪   🦪   🦪

That evening I walked to church with the Taylors, as I always did if I was at their house on a Wednesday night. When I entered the whitewashed building, I immediately noticed a sun suspended from the ceiling above the congregation. It had been crafted from plywood. Rays of brilliant oranges and yellows stretched from its center and glitter sparkled along its edges. It was magnificent, large in scale, and I couldn't help but fear it would fall on my head, though that fear quickly dissolved once the Reverend began to speak.

"This is the day the sun stood still," he declared. "The day Joshua called upon the Lord, and the Lord heard his cry. A day when the sun stopped in the middle of the sky. There has never been a day like it before or since, says the book of the Lord.

"'Do not be discouraged. Be strong and courageous,' spoke Joshua to his soldiers. You are the soldiers of today," the Reverend said. "Do not be discouraged. Be strong."

"Amen, Reverend!" shouted one of the men behind me.

The Reverend continued, "Later on, the Lord spoke to Jeremiah. 'They have returned to the sins of their forefathers who refused to listen to my words. They have followed other gods.'"

"Yes, brother!" came the voices.

"There are enemies among us!" the Reverend shouted, his voice holding the attention of all those in the room. All those sitting beneath the great sun.

"Their sin is greed! Their god is money! Their Jerusalem is here!" The Reverend's hands slammed on the pulpit. His voice rose louder, and I could feel my own body shudder from the excitement. "And what does the Lord say?" he yelled. "The Lord says: 'I will bring on them a disaster they cannot escape. Although they cry out to me, I will not listen to them.'"

"Amen, brother!"

Bodies moved, heads leaned forward as if to hear the Reverend's words more clearly. I found my own body on the edge of my seat.

"Our sun will stand still!" shouted the Reverend. "The Lord will hear our cry!" His body rose with each word and tilted forward. His face was sweating. "Our sun will stand still till we are avenged!" he yelled.

Then his eyes searched a group of boys who liked to sit together in the back row. At least half of them looked like they'd been in a bad fight, faces bruised, eyes and lips swollen. "You are the young soldiers of today," the Reverend said. "But you must choose whose side you're on. Resist the enemy!" Again the Reverend's voice rose with power.

"Boys from this town, this congregation even, are fighting

North Vietnam, fighting on foreign soil. And yet our worst war is that in our own backyard. Brother against brother. I say, resist the devil. Resist the evil that abides in your hearts."

"What's wrong with those boys? Who beat them up?" I whispered to Mama Rae.

Her head, like the others, was pointed forward, her eyes wide with attention. "The one who brings ruin to our boys," she said. "The one who corrupts their thinkin'."

Shouts of "Amen!" filled the room. Several different choruses started up all at once. Mama Rae was on her feet. Hands clapped. Bodies moved with the music. I stood too, joining in with the others. Emotions churned inside me. I didn't know how or why, but I, too, wanted revenge.

There was an excitement as people left the church that night. As though we were all on a war path. We returned to the Taylors' house later than usual. Many people had gathered outside the church in rumbles of conversation with the Reverend and Mama Rae. I saw Tom standing in the middle of a group of excited boys, their voices charged.

On the way home Mama Rae's voice broke into song, as did the others', even Tom's.

All except Alby's. He walked closely by my side, his presence clinging to my skin, his footsteps matching my own.

I was lying in Ruthie's bed trying to sleep when Alby appeared in the doorway. The light from the moon shone through the window on his face, giving him a pale glow.

"It's okay," I whispered to him.

He walked slowly over to the bed and knelt beside me, his eyes big and wild. I took his hands. They were shaking and cold.

"It's okay," I told him again. I wrapped my arms around him and held him close.

Across the room, Rachel stirred. After a few minutes, she crawled out of her bed, then quickly ran over to us and climbed in beside me.

"Is the enemy going to hurt us?" she said.

I remembered the Reverend's words, that the Lord heard the cries of his people.

"The enemy isn't going to hurt you," I said, with one arm around Rachel and the other around Alby. And I believed what I said.

After a while, Alby went back to his room. Rachel stayed in bed with me. I searched the window before falling asleep, looking for the man I had seen in the darkness a few weeks before. My heart felt like a hammer, but he wasn't there.

I woke early in the morning, the sun just beginning to rise. Rachel was still asleep.

In the front room, Mama Rae was getting breakfast on the table. Tom and the Reverend were sitting next to each other, each holding a mug of coffee.

"How'd ya sleep, Francie?" Mama Rae asked when she saw me.

"Real good," I told her.

I could see Tom's smile from where I stood.

"No shadows in the window this time?" he laughed.

"That's enough, Tom," said the Reverend.

Through the screen door I saw Alby sitting on the front steps with Punkin in his arms, stroking her gently. Alby's face lay sideways on Punkin's soft fur. His eyes were closed, and I knew he had left us again. His thoughts had carried him somewhere far away. A place where he couldn't be reached.

After breakfast I gathered my few belongings, deciding I would drop them off at the house before walking the rest of the way to school. Alby followed me up to the driveway, and I knew something was troubling him bad and wished more than anything he could talk to me about it.

Turning onto the road, I saw Earnest walking toward me. He had his arm cradled around a stack of books held to his side.

"Whatch ya doin' with all them books?" I asked him as he got closer. Then I noticed the pencil stuck behind his ear.

"Carryin' these over to Mrs. Taylor." He stopped about five feet in front of me. "How come ya over here so early?" he asked.

I told him about Daddy going to Mayville. About the church service and the sun. About the Reverend's sermon. "Who's beating up these boys?"

"You really don't know, do ya?" He looked around like he was thinking. "I guess I could show you, but it'd have to be late at night."

"When?" I asked.

"I'll let you know."

He walked on down the driveway to the Taylors' house. I saw Alby standing behind a tree, his hands covering his ears. I wanted to cry for him, cry for his fears, cry for the voice that had left him.

Chapter 12
Potter's Field

NOT LONG AFTER I'D SPENT THE NIGHT AT RUTHIE'S, Punkin's kittens were born. Mama Rae stopped in at the store to tell me. She'd found them behind the chicken shed and moved them up to the house beside the back steps. They were in a box underneath a tent the Reverend had made from a tarp. There were six of them in all. Four black, one calico, and one orange like its mom.

I began visiting the Taylors' house every day, holding the kittens in my lap and stroking their soft fur. Daddy and Mama Rae agreed I could bring one home once they were six weeks old. I decided on the orange one and named him Fireball, after the tabby my grandmaw once had.

One morning, while I was sitting on the Taylors' back steps watching the kittens play, Earnest stopped by.

"I've been wonderin' when I'd get to see you again," I said.

"Been around," he told me.

I gave him one of the kittens to hold and showed him which one was going to be mine.

"He's gonna be a strong fella," Earnest said. "Got them big paws on his feet."

Then he sat up next to me, holding the kitten in his lap.

"When are you gonna show me what's been goin' on with all the colored boys?" I asked him.

"Been thinkin' that maybe it's not such a good idea."

"Why?"

"It ain't safe."

"I ain't afraid."

He let out a laugh and slid those big brown eyes my way. "I had a feelin' that's what you'd say."

"So when are you gonna show me?"

He was still smiling. "Like I said, been thinkin' that's not such a good idea."

"Earnest Malone!"

He just kept grinning like he was enjoying watching me get all mad. I gave him a shove on the shoulder with my hand, almost knocking him off the steps. But all he did was laugh.

"Okay, you win," he said. "I'll show you."

"When?"

"I'll let you know."

"When'll you let me know? How do I know I won't be hearing from you till next year?" Earnest frustrated me just about as much as Daddy.

"You'll be hearin' from me." He set the kitten in my lap and stood, still looking at me and grinning in that teasing way of his.

"I'm not holding my breath."

Then he let out another laugh. Tucking his hands in his pockets, he strolled off like he didn't have a care in the world.

It was a Saturday afternoon, the third week in September. The air was hot, smiting my face like a steamy furnace. I had spent the afternoon at the store and was on my way to see the kittens. Sweat dripped down my sides from underneath my arms and stuck to my forehead.

If I was walking to the Taylors' from town, I'd take the side street by Daddy's store, then turn onto the path where I'd once followed Earnest. I liked walking through the woods and thinking about the day I'd caught him singing to himself. Liked thinking about the way his hair swooped over his eyes. Sometimes it was hard to follow the trail, everything was so overgrown. I had to be careful not to make a wrong turn and wind up lost. There were all kinds of birds tucked back in those trees: pileated woodpeckers and an occasional whippoorwill as well as a host of wrens and sparrows. I'd usually enjoy the walk, whistling some tune to myself. But that day mosquitoes were everywhere. Clouds of them clustered above me, sometimes becoming so dense I thought I could feel them in my throat. I started to turn back, when I heard a mower in the distance.

The sound was strange. It wasn't the easy putter of a mower on someone's lawn, but a revving and stalling, and then voices. I knew I was a good mile or more from any cars or houses. As I looked around me, all I could see were woods, thick with foliage. I left the trail and started to follow the hum of voices, pushing my way through the brush, leaves and branches tangling in my hair and clothes. Deeper into the woods I heard a sound like the crying of a baby. I kept pushing my way through the dense trees, the ground so quiet underneath my feet it was as though I'd stepped onto a mattress. Again boys' voices. Again a cry.

The noises finally drew close. Hidden in the brush, I strained my neck warily around the trunk of a wide tree until the images became hauntingly clear, sucking the air out of me into a gasp. The mower still revved. There were three of them. One tall colored boy and two white ones, all about the same age. Perspiration stuck to their skin like thick oil. Their voices were full of laughter. Two small heads were left. Not babies, but kittens—one black, one orange—buried in the ground up to their necks. Tiny heads on bloodstained ground. The motor revved again. I tried to cry out, my arms pressed against my stomach. Nausea churned inside of me. I leaned over, for the first time noticing the dark soil, as black as tar. The sounds didn't stop. I covered my ears, a sudden spray of blood splattering across the white canvas of my sneakers. I looked up. The tiny heads were gone. Then I saw Tom's face. His eyes pinned mine for a long split second. A darkness struck the very pit of me and grabbed hold of my gut like a wrench. I turned and ran to the road's edge, the crying now silenced.

Clouds moved sluggishly across the sky. My heart felt lodged somewhere in my throat. My eyes stung. A soft muting sensation came over me, as if the whole thing was a nightmare. I looked at my shoes splattered with blood. I took off running, my feet catching themselves in the gullies as my body stumbled forward. Within minutes I was at the Taylors', hidden in the trees and wild thicket, watching the house from a distance. I knew I could never share with Ruthie what I'd seen in the woods. Never share with her the darkness I saw in Tom's eyes. Blood is as thick as black oil in rural Alabama. Tom was Ruthie's brother. No matter how much I loved the Taylors, I was the stranger now.

Except for the lazy buzzing of a fly near my face, there was quiet. The house appeared vacant. I crawled to the back stoop. With one hand in the dirt and the fingers of the other holding onto the edge of the kittens' box, I lifted my head.

The tarp was gone. The box was empty. I walked to the road, down to the trail Ruthie and I had made to the creek. Walked toward the spilling water. Walked through the meadow to the sloping bank where Ruthie and I always met. My legs crumpled below me. I buried my face in my hands, wanting to cry. Then a pulsing rage rose up inside me, seething in my blood. Anger and one screaming question: "Why?" My voice erupted across the hills. I took off my shoes, stained with the kittens' blood and the black soil, and threw them against the deepening pink sky. They landed in the creek below.

A warm breeze touched my face. I lay back in the grass and sobbed quietly, my eyes closed against the sun. I could still see the tiny heads in my mind. Could still hear the mower. The voices. Tom's voice. The cries. I grabbed my stomach. Once more, nausea swayed over me. The breeze stirred, warm and gentle. And for a moment I smelled the heavy starch of an apron. Starch and powder and sweet perfume. I smelled it as clearly as if someone had passed right next to me, yet I lay there alone. My hands left my stomach and I wrapped my arms around myself and hugged my body tightly, my fingers digging into my arms. Everything inside me felt stuck in my throat, trying to get out. And then I saw her. For a second I saw Mama standing in bare feet on yellowed linoleum. The sun cast its golden rays over her from the window above our kitchen sink. The sounds of steam and fabric and the iron she held in her hand. Her hips swayed to and fro as she worked. Her red hair pinned up above her slightly freckled shoulders. Her white slip hemmed with lace hanging just above her knees. The powder lightly coating her chest. The smallness of her waist. The image had been with me before, though this time more clearly. I felt the sway of my mother's body as if it was my own.

❧　　❧　　❧

When I finally left the creek that night, the sky was almost dark, with streaks of deep pink and lavender shining through. Once I was on the road and nearly home, a small shape stood a short distance in front of me, its green eyes watching me. It sat still as I approached, and I knew it was Punkin. I knelt on the ground. Her green eyes stared forward. "I'm sorry," I said. Wells of tears filled my eyes and rolled down my face. She turned and disappeared into the darkness. I never saw her again.

Chapter 13
Ruthie Comes Home

DADDY AND I DROVE TO MAYVILLE the day before Ruthie was to come home. I'd told him I needed a new pair of sneakers, saying the other pair had gotten too small.

We stopped at Woolworth's, where I was fitted for a new pair of shoes, and indeed, my feet had grown to a larger size. I tried on a couple of bras, too, and found out my feet weren't the only thing that had grown. Then Daddy picked out a long-sleeved pink shirt he thought I'd look pretty in, made of soft cotton with satin ribbon around its scooped neck. He told me to go put it on and see how it fit.

"You look like your Mama," he said as I stepped out of the dressing room. He shook his head slowly back and forth. "Growin' up too fast."

Quiet settled over us on the way back to Spring Gap. The wind blew the smell of summer across our faces as the truck carried us rhythmically over the bumpy county road. I leaned back against the sun-warmed vinyl, listening to Daddy whistle. Halfway home, he began to sing tunes out of Nashville: "King of the Road," "Green, Green Grass of Home," "Truck Drivin' Son-of-a-Gun," his voice growing stronger with each song. By the time we pulled onto the driveway, I'd joined in, leaning my head into his, till we finally burst into honest laughter and dragged ourselves into the house.

It had been a long time since Daddy and I had laughed together. I lay in bed that night humming all those songs to myself in my head and feeling for the first time that me and Daddy were going to be okay.

The next evening, while Daddy was still at the store, I turned the radio up in the kitchen and danced around the house like Mama used to do. Reverend Taylor had already left for Birmingham to pick Ruthie up. I was to be at the Taylors' at five o'clock. I laid out a pair of jeans, the shirt Daddy had bought me, and my new pair of sneakers. Before getting in the shower, I turned toward the mirror, my red hair growing long and wild with summer humidity, my narrow hips beginning to curve. "You look like your Mama," Daddy had said just the day before. As I stared back at my reflection, I knew he was right.

I took a long, hot shower, singing to myself. When I stepped out of the tub, I could hear the radio still playing from the kitchen: "Wooly Bully" by Sam the Sham and the Pharaohs. I combed the tangles out of my hair, rocking my hips back and forth to the beat of the song. From the corner of my eye I noticed Mama's talcum powder that had sat on the shelf above the toilet ever since she had died. I sprinkled some on my shoulders and dabbed a little behind my ears as if it was perfume. Then I dressed in the clothes I had laid out on my bed. The music suddenly stopped, and after a couple of minutes I heard the TV on in the living room and knew Daddy was home.

I finished getting ready, combing my hair away from my face

and tying it back with a pink ribbon. As I walked through the living room on my way to the kitchen and out the back door, I found Daddy in his recliner, drinking a beer and watching the news. I stopped for just a minute, catching a glimpse of footage from Vietnam. I thought of Mac Story, the boy Ruthie had told me about, and hoped he was okay. Then I turned around, and on a whim, bent down and gave Daddy a peck on the cheek. He grabbed me by the arm and pushed me back a ways.

"Just what do you think you're doing?"

"What?" I blinked at him, not believing the anger in his voice.

He had his lips pressed together, his face still and serious-like. He let go of my arm and looked back at the TV, taking a swig of his beer. "Who said you could go using that powder?"

I just stood there, not sure why he was getting so worked up.

"Go on," he finally said.

"What did I do wrong?"

"Go on," he said again, his voice loud and sharp.

My throat tightened up. I didn't understand what was going on in his head. Didn't understand why he was talking and acting this way. I swallowed hard, trying not to cry, and left the house, Lonesome following at my heels. I was determined not to let Daddy get to me. Ruthie was coming home. I was going to the Taylors'. Everything was going to be all right.

Mama Rae was sitting in a lawn chair by the front door shucking corn when Lonesome and I walked up to the house.

"Gonna be a fine day when our Ruthie comes home. Gonna

be a fine day indeed," she said, a smile all over her face.

I sat on the steps next to her with Lonesome lying by my feet. "Been a long time," I said, watching the road. I could hear shrieks of laughter coming from the twins, who were playing around back.

"They's chasing a chicken," Mama Rae said with a chuckle. "Got itself outa the coop. They been goin' at it for an hour now."

Mama Rae was watching me out of the corner of her eyes. "Missed having you and Ruthie around the house," she said. "Missed all that silly chatter you two make."

"You and the Reverend ever get mad at Ruthie?" I asked her.

"Course we get mad at Ruthie. Get mad at all of them from time to time." She held an ear of corn in her lap and was looking down at me. "Whatch you got on your mind?" she asked.

"One minute Daddy's laughin', the next he's hollerin' at me about this or that for no reason at all. Sometimes I get so sore inside just trying to figure him out."

"Got the weather inside of him," Mama Rae said. "Could probably use a good dry spell."

I didn't know what she was talking about.

"I had a grandaddy," Mama Rae went on to tell me. "When he'd get to drinking, that's what my grandmama would say. 'Got the weather in him.' One minute he'd be hanging around the house with a mind as heavy as lead. The next he'd be kicking up a storm. 'Could use a good dry spell around here,' I'd hear her say."

"Did that dry spell ever come?" I asked.

Mama Rae started shucking the corn again, avoiding my eyes.

"No, but my grandaddy didn't have him a sweet girl like you to look after. Had himself a bunch of ornery boys."

As I sat there, I hoped Daddy would find himself a dry spell soon. I wrapped my arms tightly around my knees, trying to settle myself. I tried to think only of Ruthie coming home, of laying side by side with her in the grass by the creek and talking and laughing. Then I heard Tom's voice from inside the house, and a cold fear shot through me. I hadn't gotten so much as a glimpse of him since that day in the woods. The more I thought of Tom and those kittens, the more that fear grew into an awful loneliness, making me feel like I didn't belong. I knew something the others would never know. The Taylors had decided a fox or an owl must have gotten the kittens, and Mama Rae wished she'd brought them inside. But Tom knew, and so did I. I also knew I could never tell Ruthie or Mama Rae or the Reverend what I saw Tom do to those kittens. Tom was their flesh and blood. *I'm just the white girl*, I thought, and I hated the way that notion settled over me like a suffocating blanket on the hottest of nights.

A loud clatter sounded from the kitchen, startling me from my thoughts. "Alby, you get on outa there," Mama Rae hollered. She gathered up the corn husks in her apron and went inside, the door banging behind her.

The smell of cornbread and collards and sweet potato pie crept through the screen door. I wanted to go in, to bury myself next to Mama Rae's side, but I held still, as if Tom was standing between me and the door, his big eyes watching me. I just prayed nothing had come between me and Ruthie. Not Tom. Not her month up north. Not the color of my skin.

Again came shrieks of laughter. I walked around the house to find the twins. But as I approached the backyard, a tall figure swung out from the side of the house. I caught my breath. It was Tom.

When he saw me, he stopped in his tracks. I screwed my green eyes up at him. "What'd you go and do a thing like that for?" I said, my feet planted so firmly into the ground they might have dug themselves each a hole.

"Whatch you doin' puttin' yourself where ya ain't got no business?"

"Them kittens was cryin' like babies." I could taste the anger in my voice like a sheet of cold metal.

"Maybe they were." He shrugged and continued his walk to the front of the house, his back now toward me.

I watched him go till I thought I could stand it no longer. Sticking out my head like a chicken on the run, I lurched toward him, my arms swinging stiffly by my sides, my hands still in fists.

"He was gonna be mine," I said desperately.

Tom stopped walking, and turned around to face me. His eyes shifted toward the house, then back to me. "You best keep hush." He turned sharply and went inside.

At that moment, every part of me was shaking, and yet I knew I had to hold it together. I couldn't go getting my face all red. I couldn't let anyone know what had happened. Besides, Tom would deny it. He would say I was making it all up. I held my fingertips over my eyes, pressing them shut. I took a deep breath.

Someone called my name. When I turned around, I saw Earnest. He was wearing a long-sleeved white shirt with a button-down collar, the kind Daddy wore to church. It was tucked into a pair of clean khaki trousers. As he strolled toward me, his hands in his pockets, I could see he had shoes on. Polished brown shoes like folks wore on Sundays. His golden-streaked chestnut hair was longer than the other boys wore theirs, with thick waves combed away from his face. His big brown eyes were looking at me, and I felt goosebumps settle all over my warm skin, soothing the anger inside me.

"Earnest Malone, don't you look fine," I said, smiling.

I slid my hands in my back pockets, not knowing what to do with myself. Then I heard the truck. Earnest heard it too, both of us inclining our heads toward the road as the Reverend turned onto the path to the house. Ruthie's head was leaning out the passenger window of the truck, her arm waving big.

The truck stopped just in front of the house, where the rest of the family was now gathered. Earnest put a hand on my shoulder and nudged me forward. But as I watched Ruthie climb down from the truck, something stopped me from rushing ahead. She was wearing a navy pleated skirt and navy shoes that I knew I'd never seen. I also knew I'd never seen her look so grown-up before, either. Even her neck looked longer to me, held straight and tall, supporting her beautiful face.

As I watched the family close in around her, Earnest's face

came close to mine. "You sure look pretty," he said in my ear.

At first I thought I hadn't heard him right, but when he smiled his slight grin, I knew I'd heard him just fine.

Then Ruthie saw me. "Francie!" she yelled, her eyes opening wide. She ran over to me and threw her arms around my shoulders.

"'Bout time you got home," I said, giving her a bear hug.

"I knew you couldn't live without me," she laughed.

Same ole Ruthie, I thought to myself, and I laughed with her, feeling a huge sense of relief.

Tom didn't stay for supper. As we were all going in the house, I saw him climb into the truck and drive off. Mama Rae stood on the front steps watching him, her mouth pulled in and the lids of her eyes folded over in a worrisome kind of way. The Reverend walked up to her and, putting an arm around her, led her inside.

The rest of the evening was about as happy as any evening could be. I'm not sure I'd ever seen such a feast: barbecue, cornbread, sweet potatoes, collards, corn, and one of Mama Rae's pecan pies. Everyone was chattering at once and laughing and smiling big. Even Alby, sitting up close to Ruthie, had grins running up and down his face, and I realized how much she meant to him.

"Did you meet anybody?" Rachel wanted to know.

"Any boys?" Willie asked, batting his eyelashes in a teasing way. Ruthie swatted at him lightly.

"What was your favorite thing you saw while you were there?" asked the Reverend.

Ruthie tilted her chin up and smiled slowly. "The water," she said. "And all those tall boats."

Her aunt and uncle had taken her to see the Chesapeake Bay. I'd never seen the ocean before, and listening to her talk made me long for it.

After the dishes were put away, Mama Rae sent the twins and Alby off to bed. Ruthie and Earnest and I sat on the front steps with Ruthie in the middle and Lonesome lying at our feet.

"Bet you thinkin' 'bout movin' up there," Earnest teased Ruthie. "Leavin' all us country folk behind."

"Well, I guess if I did that, I'd just have to go takin' Francie with me," Ruthie said. She slid her eyes over at Earnest, as if saying, "I'm onto you two."

I felt my face blush. Earnest let out one quick laugh like he wasn't sure what to say.

"I better turn in," Ruthie said. "Been a long day." She leaned her shoulder into me, and I knew her saying she was tired was her way of letting Earnest and me be alone. I also knew she'd want to hear all about it the next day.

We hugged each other again and said good-night. Then Earnest said he'd walk me home.

As he and I strolled toward the road, Lonesome ran off ahead of us, though keeping himself in sight.

Earnest and I were quiet as we walked. I liked the sounds his shoes made against the rocks along the way. His stride was different that night. More confident. His feet didn't drag in the dirt, but instead lifted and fell.

The road was clearly lit from the night sky—a deep, rich layer of midnight blue, splattered with brilliant stars. From a distance, music from one of the shanties across the way swelled into harmony, then simmered into the night as we moved on.

Halfway home, a car passed by slowly. As the sound of its engine disappeared, Earnest stopped and touched my arm. I turned toward him, and for the first time that night I saw the moon, a crescent of white light gleaming against the sky. His face came close to mine. The smell of clean soap clung to his skin and stirred my stomach with a wonderful burning. Again his face moved closer till his lips pressed gently on mine, sending a wave of warmth all over my body. I reached for his hand to hold onto. Nothing in me felt solid. It was as if my whole being was one fluid wave following Earnest. Slowly we pulled away from each other. Again we walked, not saying anything until we got to the driveway of my house.

"I ain't never done that before," Earnest said.

I wanted to speak, but felt like my voice had fallen somewhere in the well of my stomach and was unable to get out.

"I just wanted you to know," he said.

He turned around and walked back down the road. I stood still, watching him: the starlight canopy over him, his clean trousers and polished shoes, his shoulders squared back, his head tilted toward the ground.

As I started up the driveway, I was startled to a halt by Daddy's voice, coming from the front steps.

"A friend of mine stopped by a minute ago. Said he seen ya tonight." His voice was loud and raspy. He held a bottle of whiskey in one of his hands.

As I walked closer, the thick smell of liquor hit me in a sickening way.

"I didn't see no one."

"Who's that boy I seen bringin' ya home?"

He emphasized "boy" when he said it, rolling up his thick lips, making my body feel limp and my skin sting with sweat. Lonesome, standing beside me, started whimpering from the back of his throat like he knew something was out of place.

"Answer me, Francie!"

Daddy was yelling now, his words slurred together, his voice stabbing a hole right through me, letting all that warmth Earnest had given me spill out.

He pushed himself to his feet, his body swaying back and forth like he was about to topple over. My eyes stared forward, level with his stomach and the white T-shirt he wore. The smell of sweat and liquor and cigarette smoke was so strong I had to breathe through my mouth. He raised his empty hand and swung it across my face like a ball of fire, knocking my body to the ground. A scream escaped me, sharp and loud. I bit down on my bottom lip, trying not to cry, till my mouth filled with blood. Lonesome started running circles around me, barking wildly. Then he lunged forward at Daddy, his bark turning into a growl, his lips raised and pulled back.

"It's okay, Lonesome," I said, my voice shaking like the rest of me. I pulled myself back up, swallowing hard, the taste of iron from the blood going through me.

Daddy turned around on the step and stumbled heavily inside, the door slamming behind him. It was then that I finally cried, the tears stinging my face and lip.

I lay awake in bed a long time, pressing my fingers to my mouth, aware all the while of the pain in my face, aware of the gully Daddy had cut through my heart, as if he was saying I had to choose sides. But I knew it wasn't my daddy I'd choose, and that knowing gave me a terrible ache.

The next morning, as I was washing my face, I noticed the talcum powder, the same powder that had sat on the bathroom shelf ever since Mama died, was gone. My fingers traced the empty space. "You look like your Mama," Daddy had said. I let my breath out in a deep way. I don't want to hurt anymore, God. I don't want Daddy to hurt anymore either.

Chapter 14
The Debate

A LATTICEWORK OF BLUE AND PINK covered the sky: the beginning of daybreak. It was the second week in October. I was sitting on the back steps when Daddy pulled up in his truck.

"You were out awful late," I said as he approached the house.

He sat beside me, his elbows propped up on his knees, then let out a slight chuckle from the back of his throat.

"Ain't the first time you've had to wait up for me."

"First time you've come home smellin' like perfume instead of whiskey," I said.

"Well now, which do you want, me smellin' like whiskey or smellin' like perfume?"

"Don't want neither."

Again the laugh, as if he didn't know what to say.

I stood to go inside.

"Gonna be a debate tonight between Sheriff McGee and Mr. Lawson," Daddy said.

I'd already heard about the debate. Everybody had. "You going?" I asked him.

Daddy took out a cigarette from his shirt pocket. "I'm going." Then, staring off down the driveway, he added, "I thought you might like to come along."

That night Daddy drove us down to Town Hall, a large brick building next to the post office. He parked the truck alongside the curb a couple of blocks away. As we walked toward the building, several people stopped Daddy to say hello.

A side door led into the back of a large classroom where the debate was to be held. The metal folding chairs, set up in rows with an aisle between them, were already two-thirds full.

"Hey, Francie!"

I recognized Ruthie's voice. In the far right-hand corner of the room was a group of colored folks from the Taylors' church. I spotted Ruthie sitting between the Reverend and Mama Rae and waved back to her.

Daddy spoke to a few people, then led us to a couple of empty chairs toward the middle of the left side. As I looked around us, I recognized a handful of kids from school scattered around the room with their parents. Debates and town meetings were about the most exciting things to ever happen in Spring Gap other than the home games at the high school.

Daddy patted my leg and stared forward at the two lecterns situated about ten feet apart in front of the double chalkboard, his legs bouncing slightly up and down on the floor. People filled the seats in front of us. Others remained standing alongside the walls.

As I continued to look around the room, I wondered if

Earnest might show. I hadn't seen him since the night he kissed me, the night Daddy was drunk. I'd been hanging around the Taylors' as much as I could, thinking one of these days he might show up. I'd even wandered up the road to where the path turned off to his house, but I hadn't caught even a glimpse of him. Ruthie said she hadn't seen him either.

One day I walked up to the meadow Earnest had shown me. I'd been thinking that if I sat on that rock and thought about him hard enough, he just might appear. I waited a couple of hours, reliving the night he kissed me over and over in my head. "*You sure look pretty*," he'd said. Now, almost four weeks later, I felt as though my heart had been sprained and wasn't ever going to heal.

Daddy draped his arm over the back of my chair, and cleared his throat, something he'd do every once in a while if he was feeling nervous. A man from the town council stood in front of one of the two lecterns and began to speak.

"Welcome to the debate between Sheriff Clem McGee of Spring Gap . . ." The classroom reverberated with claps and whistles as Sheriff McGee approached the lectern on my left. "And Mr. Phil Lawson." Again cheers rose from the crowd, this time for Mr. Lawson, who walked over to the lectern on my right. He looked small compared to Sheriff McGee. I guessed he was about Daddy's age, late thirties, with dark brown hair neatly cut. I looked over at Daddy. His hands were planted on his legs, his eyes fixed forward, his face and body still.

The town councilman explained how the debate would

work: The audience would ask questions, and each candidate would have three minutes to respond.

Immediately, arms shot up. "Wayne, I'll let you have the first question," said the town councilman, now standing to the left side of the lecterns and pointing to Wayne Foster, who was sitting a couple of rows in front of Daddy and me. Mr. Foster owned the feed barn on the outskirts of town. He wore a wool plaid shirt, as did many of the other men there that night.

"One evenin' last month after I closed up, I had a bag of chicken feed and several bales of hay stolen from the back of my shop. And just last week, someone came in and smuggled a harness right out from under me. And ain't no one caught for neither one of these incidents. I wanna ask these men what they plan to do to protect the businesses of this community."

Rumbles of voices stirred around me. Sheriff McGee was asked to speak first.

"Now, Wayne, I told ya, we're workin' it. Had two of my deputies out questionin' folks today, askin' them if they'd seen anything. Stolen feed's a hard thing to find, especially once it's all eaten up."

There were a couple of laughs in the room. Mr. Foster had his hands on his hips and shifted his weight. "What about the harness? It was a hunderd-and-fifty-dollar piece of equipment."

"Like I said, Wayne, we're workin' on it."

Again, voices.

"Phil, you wanna answer Mr. Foster's question?"

Mr. Lawson leaned forward slightly, holding onto the lectern in front of him. "No doubt there's been an increase in crimes around our county," he began. "I propose addin' another deputy trained in criminology, and then trainin' the other ones we already have. There's a good school over in Birmingham. It runs about a month. We could send our deputies over there one at a time. Within three months we'd have them all trained. I've seen it done in some of the counties in the eastern part of the state. It seems to have worked out real good. There's been a significant drop in crimes within the first six months of the new program's implementation."

Heads around the room nodded with approval. People appeared impressed with what Mr. Lawson was saying.

Without being called upon, a loud voice came from in back of me: "And who's gonna pay for this new deputy and all this educatin'?"

Sheriff McGee chuckled under his breath. I turned to see who had spoken, but wasn't sure.

"The money would come from a state grant," Mr. Lawson said. "We'd have to apply for it, submittin' statements from people in the county, such as Mr. Foster and other folks who have experienced losses."

Daddy nodded his head stiffly, his hands still planted on his legs.

"How about another question," came the town councilman. Again, arms shot up in the air. Daddy's eyes shifted uneasily to our left, then back toward the lecterns. I could almost smell the tension on his body, which set me on the edge of my seat. I searched the faces alongside the wall, so many of them crowded together. Someone else asked a question. Sheriff McGee was responding.

I saw Daddy's hands grip his legs tightly, reminding me of his hands on the steering wheel that first time he'd brought me home from Ruthie's—the time we came up on Mansfield leaning against his truck. Again his eyes moved over toward the wall on the left side of us, and as they did, I saw a man with eyes pinning Daddy like the point of a knife.

The man stood at the end of the row where we were sitting, a couple of heads taller than the people next to him, his arms folded over his chest. His hair was thick and grizzly and the color of rusted steel, his face red and bloodshot, his eyes narrow slits in bunchy flesh. His chest was large, almost fat, with rolls of flesh revealed through the tight beige T-shirt he wore.

More arms went up around us. Another name was called. A colored man stood, one of the men from Ruthie's church. "What about our boys?" he asked. "What about Harvey Mansfield?"

Immediately the room fell silent. The squeaking of chairs and coughing stopped. It seemed that everybody was holding their breath.

There was a noise from the back of the room. A chair against the floor. The sound of someone standing. "What about Harvey Mansfield?" came Mansfield's smoky voice.

Heads turned. Bodies shifted. I didn't want to look at him.

Instead, I watched in front of me. Then I saw Ruthie all turned around, her fingers grasping the metal arch of her chair. I followed her eyes to Mansfield. Her eyes didn't blink; they just stared. Her body didn't move.

People shifted again in their seats. Eyes returned to the front of the room. Ruthie slouched forward in her chair. I strained my neck higher to see her.

The town councilman cleared his throat. Mr. Lawson began to speak.

"I'd like to answer that question," he said.

"If Mr. Mansfield commits a crime in this county while I'm sheriff, he'll be arrested. It's that simple."

Faces once more looked for Mansfield, before focusing again on the two men behind the lecterns. Uneasiness crawled all over the room like a giant spider.

"What about you, Sheriff? What are you going to do?" came Reverend Taylor's voice above the tension.

The sheriff crossed his arms over his broad chest, his head tilted down. "Well, now, Jeremiah, seems to me your boy's just as eager to make a buck as the rest of them down there. Seems to me Harvey ain't doin' nothin' them boys don't wanna do."

A few men laughed to themselves. I tried to see the Reverend's face, but it was hidden by the bodies around him. It seemed to me the Reverend and the sheriff had their own conversation going on. I wondered why Tom would want to have anything to do with someone like Mansfield.

"If I's to arrest Mr. Mansfield, which I ain't, why, I'd have to arrest all them boys down there, including yours."

Rumbles of conversation erupted, heads leaning in together. I looked for Tom but couldn't find him, and wondered if he'd come. Then I saw Alby sitting on the other side of Mama Rae. She had an arm wrapped around his shoulders. His head suddenly jerked forward. There was a splattering sound against the floor followed by a second thrust of splattering. Within seconds, bodies moved away from him. The odor of sickness quickly spread over the classroom. Mama Rae led Alby out the back door where we had entered. Ruthie and the twins followed her. Others left as well. I saw the Reverend make his way toward the door at the front of the room that led into the hallway to the restrooms. I was instantly reminded of the strong smell of Lysol used when someone at school got sick.

Daddy took my hand. "Let's go," he said. Within minutes the building had emptied and groups of people huddled together alongside the street.

A couple of men who had businesses in town approached Daddy and started a conversation. I stood behind him looking for Ruthie, but couldn't find her.

It was then that I saw the large man who'd been staring at Daddy. He was walking across the street to his truck, a white Ford splashed with mud and painted gray in spots where rust had eaten through.

I felt an arm drape over my shoulder gently, and looked up to see Mr. Lampley's blue eyes and lean face.

"One of Mansfield's buddies," he said, inclining his head toward the man. "Comes into the fillin' station ever once in a while. Name's Rolan. I seen him watchin' you and your daddy tonight."

Mr. Lampley patted my shoulder as the man started his truck and drove away. "Too bad that boy got sick," he said.

"That was Alby Taylor," I told him. "He's Ruthie's little brother."

Mr. Lampley pulled out a mint from his pocket and offered it to me. I took it and thanked him for it.

"You come see me soon, Francie. Got some bacon and sausage for ya."

I told him I would. Then he patted my shoulder again and walked away.

Sheriff McGee and Mr. Lawson were now mingling with the people outside, campaigning and answering questions. Mr. Lawson didn't look so small next to some of the townspeople. In fact, he stood over six feet tall, I was sure. His eyes were dark brown and deep set, his face young and honest looking, almost that of a boy's—unlike the sheriff's with his sagging jowls.

I searched the crowd for Daddy, until I spotted his blue shirt in a small circle of people. Sylvia from the diner was standing next to him. I was instantly reminded of the scent of perfume on him early that morning, and wondered if it was her whose presence I'd smelled. I liked Sylvia, liked her easy way, and decided him smelling like perfume might be better than him smelling like whiskey after all.

I walked down the sidewalk toward the truck, knowing Daddy would find me when he was ready. As I approached the alley that ran along the far side of the post office, I heard a voice.

"Francie, it's Earnest. Over here."

I could see his shadow from the streetlight. He was squatting down with his back against the red brick of the hardware store as if he had been waiting for me. I looked behind me to see if anyone was watching, then slipped around the corner.

He stood up against the wall, his hands tucked into the front pockets of his jeans that were worn to a thin, smooth cotton. The cuffs of his green sweater were pushed up below his elbows.

"Whatch you doin' back here?" I asked. The ache inside me magnified tenfold when I saw him.

He looked at me for a couple of seconds before he spoke, looked at me from under his thick eyelashes, making my body feel strange to me.

"I needed to see you," he finally said.

"How come now?" I asked. "How come you can just kiss me and tell me ya ain't never done that before, then just walk away and never see me again?" My eyes started to sting, and I fought back the urge to cry.

"It ain't what you think, Francie. I ain't allowed to see you."

The blood in my face sank.

"Listen, we don't have much time. We'll talk about that later.

Do you still want me to show you why the boys is gettin' beat up?"

I nodded my head slowly, looking for answers in his face. Answers to what he was feeling. What he was saying. And why he wasn't allowed to see me.

"Tomorrow night," he said. "Meet me at the creek. Wait till your dad's asleep. It'll have to be late."

"Okay," I told him.

He reached out and touched my arm briefly, then turned and hurried down the alley, disappearing into the darkness.

I walked to the truck, my head swimming, and climbed in. Daddy was now on the edge of the crowd, which was beginning to disperse. I rolled down my window and waved. He patted a man on the back and shook another man's hand. Sylvia wasn't there.

Within minutes he was in the truck, starting the engine. "Hope the Taylor boy's okay," he said.

"I guess the evenin' ended kinda early," I told him.

We pulled out from the curb and away from the remaining cars. "Folks got what they needed," he said.

"You think Mr. Lawson's gonna win?"

"I don't know, Bean. Let's hope so."

"Daddy?"

"Yeah?"

"That man standin' next to the wall. The one lookin' at you. Mr. Lampley says his name's Rolan. You know him?"

The streetlights from the town were now behind us as we drove into the blackness toward home. There were no stars; the cloud cover was thick. The only light shone from the truck's headlights on the road.

Daddy took his time answering me. "No."

"Mr. Lampley says he's one of Mansfield's buddies."

"I don't know."

"You've never seen him before?"

"I already told you, 'no!'"

"Sorry," I mumbled under my breath, looking away. Once again, Daddy had closed the door on me. I wondered if there'd ever come a day when he'd let me know his mind of thought.

An eerie silence filled every space of the truck. Daddy drove up the driveway and turned off the engine.

As I climbed out, Lonesome ran up to greet me, wagging his tail. We walked up to the back steps, and as I waited for Daddy to open the door, I saw the sneakers I had thrown into the creek after spying Tom with the kittens lined up neatly on the edge of the bottom step. The blood was gone. Every trace of it. The stains from the black mud were gone, too. I picked them up and followed Daddy inside.

As I crawled into bed, Lonesome trotted into my room, his paws tapping against the floor. Not long after school started, Daddy had stopped making Lonesome stay outside. I hugged him to me as he jumped onto the bed. I stared at the sneakers that I'd set on the floor. I knew the creek couldn't have washed the blood out of them.

"You know," I told Lonesome. "You know who brought my

shoes." I thought about the day after school when someone had scared Phinny and his friends off. Thought about the time Ruthie and I found Lonesome tied up to the tree.

"Someone's out there," I said, not knowing whether or not to be afraid.

Chapter 15
Ruthie and the Dragon

IT WAS EARLY FRIDAY MORNING, the day after the debate. I hadn't slept well, tossing and turning most of the night. I kept thinking of the man staring at Daddy and me. Thought of him being one of Mansfield's friends. The Taylors didn't care for Mansfield. Willie and Rachel called him the dragon. Ruthie didn't care for Mansfield, either. I remembered the way she had twisted around in her chair as Mansfield's voice carried a creepy stillness over the room, remembered the wide-eyed look of fear on her face. I knew I had to talk to her and make sure she was okay.

I dressed quickly, packed my lunch, and hurried out the door, not taking time for breakfast. It was almost seven-thirty. School started at eight. Holding the few books I'd brought home and my sack lunch in my arms, I ran down the driveway. Instead of taking a left toward town, I turned right and headed toward Ruthie's.

As I approached the turnoff for her house, I saw the Reverend's truck pulling toward me onto the road. He waved when he saw me, then slowed to a stop and rolled down the passenger window.

"Has Ruthie left yet?" I asked, leaning up against the door.

"Just left," he said. "If ya hurry, you can catch her."

I took off again, running in the direction of the school, a small brick building where the colored children attended, almost a mile from Ruthie's house. Just ahead of me, I could see a group of kids walking in the middle of the road. As I drew closer, I recognized Willie and Rachel.

"Where's Ruthie?" I asked, all out of breath.

Willie pointed in front of them to another group farther down the road.

"What are you doin' over here?" Rachel said.

"I have to talk to Ruthie." I took off again running.

A few yards ahead I spotted her. She was wearing a plaid skirt and a cream-colored sweater, her hair pulled back in a French braid.

"Ruthie!" I yelled.

She stopped abruptly and turned around. The other kids looked at me, giving me the rundown with their eyes, as if saying, "What's a white girl doin' over here?" A stack of books was held to Ruthie's chest with one arm. A sack lunch hung by her side in her hand. She told the others to go on. They turned reluctantly, still staring at me over their shoulders, before finally moving on.

"We have to talk," I told her.

She glanced back at the twins, who were walking toward us. "I can't. Not now. I'll be late."

"Ruthie, what's wrong?" I said. But she shook her head and looked away.

The twins approached us with their friends.

"You okay, Ruthie?" Rachel asked.

Ruthie nodded her head. "I'm okay. You go on," she said.

I grabbed hold of Ruthie's arm and led her off the road, then took her books and lunch and set them with mine on the ground. "Talk to me, Ruthie. I know something's wrong." I grasped onto her arms, trying to make her look at me.

She turned away. "It was Mansfield," she said. "Last night when he got up to speak."

She closed her eyes for a couple of seconds. Her lips started to quiver.

I was still holding onto her arm. "Ruthie, what is it?"

"He's bad, Francie. He's real bad." Her voice was choking up like a big knot. Still she wouldn't look at me.

"Please talk to me. He did something to you, didn't he?"

"I've seen him around town, but not like that. Not like last night. There he was standing up so plainly, and that voice. I hadn't heard that voice since . . ." Her voice trailed off and again she closed her eyes, tears now running down her cheeks.

"Since when?" I said as gently as I could. But she just shook her head.

And then something came back to me. Something Ruthie had said, and for a split instant I hated myself for having brushed her words aside, for not having really believed her.

"You were almost killed once." I remembered what she had told me my first night at the Taylors'. "Was it him?"

She nodded her head. "I'm scared of him."

"Oh, Ruthie." My eyes cringed as I hugged her to me, a mixture of anxiety and anger curling like a snake in the pit of my stomach. *He's not a dragon*, I thought. *He's the devil.* How could anyone hurt Ruthie? And as I thought those words, an awful battle was raging inside me between the hate I was feeling for Mansfield and the need to comfort my friend and make her okay.

I held her out in front of me, both hands on her shoulders. "Don't go to school today," I said. "Let's take the day off. We can play hooky."

A smile spread across her face. "Never played hooky before."

"We can spend the day at the creek," I told her. "Eat our lunch on the bank."

Slowly, she nodded. "Okay."

We walked through the stretch of trees alongside the road until we found our trail to the creek. Soon we could hear the water rushing ahead of us. We hurried through the meadow, soaking our shoes and ankles in its tall, wet grasses.

Once at the creek bank, I took off my jacket and laid it on the ground. Then I walked down to the water and scooped up some small stones into my hands. Ruthie sat down in the grass above me, taking up one half of the jacket, her feet planted on the ground in front of her. Her tears were gone, but the corners of her mouth were pressed down and I knew she was still thinking of Mansfield.

I sat next to her, handing her some stones. Her fingers tightened around them into a fist. I looked at her face. I had never seen it in such a way: her jaw clenched, her lips pressed together, her breathing heavy like something monstrous was about to explode. In one abrupt motion, she pulled her arm back and hurled all the stones into the creek as hard as she could, a loud sound erupting from the back of her throat.

"What is it, Ruthie?"

She hugged her knees to herself, her body rocking back and forth.

"Ruthie, please talk to me!"

She was staring down at the creek. "It was before I met you this past spring," she finally said. "Tom was sneakin' out at night. I could see him from my window. I'd ask him where he was goin' off to, but he wouldn't tell me. Just said to mind my own business."

She stopped, her eyes watching the water below us.

"What happened?" I asked.

"I wanted to see what he was up to, so one night I followed him to a big wood house, kind of like a barn. There wasn't any road. Just woods. Everywhere there was trees. And lots of voices. I was gonna go in the place. Try and find Tom. I was scared and wasn't sure how to get back home. Then I saw Mansfield. He was standin' there lookin' at me. I asked him if he could take me to my brother. But he just stood there lookin' at me funny. Said what a pretty thing I was. I told him I wanted to go home."

Again she stopped. Again I waited, each second like an eternity.

"He came over to me and told me to keep quiet. With one arm he pushed me to the ground and climbed over me. His whole body was on top of me and he was grabbin' at me like he was gonna hurt me.

"'I wanna go home,' I told him. He told me to shut up and raised his hand up over my face like he was gonna hit me hard. That's when I saw the angel," she said.

"Do you remember what she looked like?"

She nodded her head. "Like an angel," she said. "With red hair like you."

My heart suddenly froze, suspended in my chest. A stab-wound feeling of fear seemed to twist itself in my lungs, my throat. *Oh, God, it can't be*, I thought, and yet I had to know.

"When? When did all this happen, Ruthie?" My voice was frantic.

Ruthie held her breath in at my urgency. "Not long before I met you. Maybe a couple of months." Her voice was shaky.

Then her face suddenly became as still as the air. She knew what I was thinking.

"It was my mom, wasn't it?" I said.

She was now looking at me, tears trailing down her dark cheeks. "Oh, Francie, I didn't know you then! I didn't know who your mom was! Everything happened so fast, and it was dark. I'm not sure."

The ache inside of me was snowballing into this huge and horrible knot of rage, grief, hurt, terror. I wrapped my arms around her, hugging her hard.

"I think she saved my life, Francie." Ruthie's voice was raspy.

"Do you remember what happened?" I asked. "Did you see anything? Did you see what happened to her?"

Her crying eased as she continued to speak. "She came at him out of the trees and told me to run. I didn't see anything else. I swear, I never looked back. And there were so many voices comin' from inside the big building. I ran through the woods looking for Tom's trail, and all I could think about was gettin' home. I never told anyone, Francie. Not till now."

"Why didn't you say something?" There was so much noise inside my head, one thread after another weaving together into this giant web. And Mansfield was in the center, catching all of us. I felt like no matter how hard we pushed or tore, we could never get free of him.

"I wasn't supposed to be there," Ruthie said. "If I hadn't been there, it wouldn't have happened. What would anyone do, anyway? Who would believe me?"

She buried her face in her hands. "Do you think she died on account a me? Do you think he killed her?" Her breathing turned into gasping breaths as the tears tore out of her. "What if it's all my fault?" A high-pitched sound wrenched out of her throat. "Oh, Francie, I'm so sorry."

My body rocked in short, quick movements. Ruthie's words felt like buckshot, charring and burning holes all through me. "No, Ruthie. It wasn't your fault. We don't know anything." My words were calm, but inside I was wild with rage and grief and fear.

"You could show me a picture. I'll know if I saw her. I'd know for sure."

"Daddy got rid of all her pictures," I told her. "Sent them to one of my uncles in Georgia."

Ruthie touched my arm. "You could write him. You could ask him to send one."

There was a splatter of heat across my chest. Ever since Mama died I hadn't seen any pictures of her. Why hadn't I thought of asking for a picture before?

Then Ruthie's eyes brightened. "The high school would have a picture," she said. "What about a yearbook?"

I shook my head. "I don't know. We'd have to sneak in. And if we go now, they'll know we're skippin' school."

Ruthie laid her palms over her eyes, rubbing the tears away. Across the creek, lines of cypress and pines stood almost black against the deep blue sky.

"Not if you go by yourself," Ruthie finally said.

"What are you sayin'?"

"If I go, the high school's sure to know somethin's up. But if you go by yourself, you could say your teacher sent you over to find something. You could go over at lunchtime so no one will suspect you're missin' classes."

I turned the idea over in my head. "Where will you be?"

"I could wait here."

"But what if I get caught? What if Daddy sees me on the way over or someone tells? How will you know?"

"If someone sees you, just tell them you're on your way home. Say you aren't feelin' good. If you don't come back, I'll know somethin' went wrong."

"What'll I say if someone sees the yearbook?"

"Put it inside your jacket," she told me. "No one will know."

"Ya sure you wanna do this?" I asked her, remembering the pain in her face and the tears she'd cried just minutes before, yet knowing I had to do something. We had to be sure.

"How else will we know?" Ruthie was now looking at me with steady eyes.

"You think she was killed, don't you?" And as I spoke those words, I heard Daddy's voice as sure as I was sitting there. Heard him saying those same words while I had watched him and Mansfield from the truck. And I knew what Ruthie knew. Knew it in my heart like it had always been there, only I was too afraid to listen. But it was there. Had been there all along, only I didn't want to believe it.

"Ruthie?"

"Yeah?"

"I still miss her."

"I know."

I looked at the watch Daddy had given me for Christmas the year before. A red band to match my red hair, he had said. It was only nine o'clock. We had at least two hours until I could leave for the high school.

"I'm goin' there tonight," I told her.

"Where?"

"The big house," I said. "He's got something goin' on there. Why else would all those boys be gettin' hurt?" And from then on, that's what we called it. Others may have called it Mansfield's place, or the barn. But for us it became the big house, where just outside an angel had once saved Ruthie's life.

Ruthie jerked her head back and forth. "No, don't go. Why would you want to? What will it tell you?" Her voice grew louder.

"I have to, Ruthie. I'm not sure I can explain it. Kind of like if I go there and I see where Mama was hurt, I'll be able to help her. I'll be able to understand what happened."

"You can't go by yourself. How do you even know where it is?"

"Somebody's taking me," I told her.

Her face turned quickly toward me. "Who?"

"Earnest."

I could feel the anger off her body as if it was heat. "He has no right to take you there. He knows better. You shouldn't go. What if Mansfield sees you?"

"It'll be okay."

My mind was set like concrete. There was no way she was going to change it. I had to know everything that had happened to Mama. I had to see where she was killed, and not Ruthie, or Daddy, not even Mansfield, could stop me.

I scooped up a few of the leaves scattered around us, then crunched them in my fist. This was the closest Ruthie and I had ever come to a fight, and I hated the way it felt.

"Let's go swimmin'," I finally said.

She turned toward me, shielding her eyes. "Where at? The creek isn't deep enough."

"There's a pond," I said. "I'll show you." I scrambled to my feet and took off running through the grass.

Ruthie picked my jacket up off the ground and followed.

"We're gonna freeze," I heard her say. "Francie May, ya ain't got sense."

But I kept running, and she kept following.

We entered the stretch of woods before the pond where I had seen Earnest and the man with the dark beard.

"Where you takin' me?" Ruthie hollered, coming up behind me.

"There's a pond in here somewhere," I told her as I searched for a trail.

We spotted a ditch just ahead of us with a steady stream of water and followed it for almost a quarter of a mile to the pond, a hole in the middle of the woods where the sun poured in.

Ruthie took her shoes and socks off, then slowly dipped her toes into the green water. I stripped out of my clothes, leaving them in a pile on the ground, and sat on the bank, edging my legs into the cold water. Ruthie ran from behind me and plunged in, sending an icy spray over me. Her head sank below the surface, then emerged with a jolt. She bobbed up and down several times before diving under again. Slowly, I slid off the bank, feeling the cold water rise up to my chest, sending sharp prickles all over my skin. Ruthie surfaced and swam over to me.

"It's not so bad once you move around," she said.

I jumped up and down, splashing water. The two of us swam

to the other side, laughing and talking and diving to the bottom.

I stopped to push my hair out of my eyes, and that's when I saw him. I let out a gasp. About fifty yards away, the tall man with the black beard stood watching us. Within a second he was gone, disappearing into the thickness of the woods.

"What is it?" Ruthie asked. She hadn't seen him.

"Let's go." I swam back to the bank. "We have to get dressed."

Ruthie quickly followed. We climbed out, dried ourselves with our clothes, and dressed, shivering all over.

I grabbed Ruthie's hand. "Come on," I said, pulling her with me.

"Was someone there?"

I told her to hush and led her to the other side of the pond and into the trees where I had seen the man, but there was no trace of him.

"Francie, tell me. What's goin' on?"

"There was a man, standin' right here." I pointed at the ground, my breathing vibrating in my chest. "I've seen him before, with Earnest. He was watchin' us."

Ruthie grabbed hold of my arm. "Maybe he's one of Mansfield's people."

"I don't think so."

"How do ya know?"

"If he was bad, why would he have been with Earnest?"

I was talking rapidly. Ruthie just stood watching me, her face frightened.

"I don't know, Francie. I say we get outa here."

"Okay." My breathing slowed. "You're right."

We began to walk the rest of the way around the pond when I spotted something at a distance. At first I thought it was the man and I felt my breath stop short. Ruthie saw it, too.

"It looks like somebody's shirt." Ruthie started to turn back. "Come on, Francie. Let's go."

Instead of following her, I walked toward the green object. Ruthie was right. It was a long-sleeved green shirt, like the one the man was wearing when I saw him with Earnest. A large piece of cardboard lay on the ground next to a pile of burnt wood.

"Someone's been stayin' here," I said.

The leaves crackled behind us.

"You girls best be careful."

Everything inside me lurched to my throat. Ruthie let out a scream and ran in the direction from which we had come. I followed, hearing the voice ringing in my head, deep and low.

We passed the pond and kept on running, never looking back. Branches broke under my feet; leaves caught in my hair. Ruthie was a good twenty yards ahead of me. Then we were out of the woods: the sun in our faces; the meadow thick under our feet; the creek. Ruthie fell on her hands and knees on the bank. I followed and knelt beside her, my lungs burning, and a stitch under my ribs.

"Who do you reckon he is?" she finally said.

I shook my head.

"I ain't ever goin' back there again. It's too weird."

"Okay," I said.

We both just sat there, catching our breath.

"Ya still want me to go up to the school?" I asked her.

Slowly, she sat back, planting her hands behind her.

"Yeah. I just don't wanna go back to that pond, that's all." She hesitated. "Maybe I'll go with you. I don't have to go in the library. I can wait outside."

I put my jacket back on and we began our walk to town.

Chapter 16
Fay

RUTHIE AND I WERE BOTH QUIET as we walked to the high school. I thought about the Reverend talking about forgiveness. *I won't ever forgive Mansfield. How could I?* I thought of Mama, of Mansfield trying to hurt Ruthie.

"You still scared?" I asked her.

"Aren't you?"

I kept picturing Mansfield on top of her, which sent a scorching rage all through me. I knew the big house where Mansfield had found Ruthie was somewhere off in the woods. I thought about the thick woods around the pond. "I'm sorry," I said. "I shouldn't have taken you swimming there."

"You didn't know he was gonna be there. Besides, just cause ya said he was watchin' us and just cause he told us to be careful doesn't mean he's bad. I just think it's kinda weird, that's all. Don't like people sneakin' up on me."

I thought about the time I was at the green house and the woman with the hoe snuck up on me.

"Ruthie?"

"Yeah?"

"The woman in the woods, the one in the green house close to where you live, is she Earnest's mom?"

We were now on the road that led into town, not far from

Daddy's and my house. Ruthie kicked at a couple of stones in the sandy gravel. "How do you know about that place? You always goin' places you shouldn't!"

I told her about following Earnest home from the store, about seeing the house and the name on the mailbox, about what the woman had said to me.

"I told you she was crazy," Ruthie said. "That's Earnest's mom all right. Mama tells us not to go over there. I've only seen her a couple of times. Once when she was sick, Mama and I brought her some food."

"Have you ever talked to Earnest about who his dad is?" I asked.

"Mama told us not to ask him. He told Tom once that his daddy left before he was born. I don't think he knows who his daddy is. That's how come he doesn't go to school."

"What does any of this have to do with him not goin' to school?"

"Everybody sayin' his mama's crazy, and him bein' raised off in the woods and all."

"Doesn't mean he shouldn't go to school. It's not right." I frowned.

"Mama's always looked after him. Don't reckon he'd really wanna go to school anyhow. Folks always sayin' stuff."

I remembered seeing the stack of books Earnest was carrying over to Mama Rae's, and him saying he could read and write. Then a truck drove by, startling us both.

"Maybe we shouldn't be on the road," I said. "Suppose some-one sees us and tells Daddy or somebody at one of our schools."

We climbed into the ditch just off the shoulder. A large auto-mobile came around the corner, passing us and sending exhaust over our heads.

"We could go the back way," Ruthie said. "Circle around so that we don't have to go down Main Street."

We crossed the road and headed for a field that would lead us to the back side of town and eventually the high school.

"You really like Earnest, don't ya?" Ruthie said once we were out of sight from the road.

"It doesn't matter. He isn't allowed to see me."

"What do you mean, he isn't allowed to see ya?"

"Heck if I know. 'I ain't allowed to see ya.' That's all he said. I'm gonna ask him about it tonight. Make him tell me what's going on."

"I still wish you wouldn't go."

"I have to," I said. "Mama didn't fall into a ravine and hit her head. I heard Daddy say so. If Mansfield killed her, I have to know."

"Mama says sometimes ya got to cross the bridge that carries you to the other side. I guess that's what you're doin'. I still don't like it, though."

"It'll be okay," I tried to assure her, though my voice was shaky.

Once at the high school, Ruthie crouched behind a dumpster in the back parking lot while I went in to find the library.

When I entered the building, I found that the school looked no different from mine. Long halls with commercial tile floors and painted cinder-block walls. There was a blue-and-black stripe down one of the walls—the high school's colors. A tall, lanky boy stood at one of the lockers. I approached him and said that my teacher had sent me over from the middle school to find something in the library. He led me around the corner and pointed to a door down the hall.

Unlike the halls, the library was carpeted and the walls were covered with dark paneling. I began weaving in and out of the narrow aisles between the tall shelves, looking for the yearbooks. Then I heard a couple of older people talking. "It can't be," I whispered to myself.

I edged my way around another row. Standing at the end of it was Daddy and the librarian, a lady with curly blond hair and very high heels. I ducked back behind the shelf, slumping to the floor with my knees to my chin. I could hear the two of them laughing. The lady had been holding a stack of books to her chest. Daddy had his hands in his pockets with his weight shifted to one side.

I folded my arms over my knees and buried my head.

"I'll see ya tonight, Fay." Daddy's voice drawled out slow and soft, the way he used to talk to Mama.

I could feel his footsteps as he walked away. Fay slid a few books onto the shelf opposite me. The library door opened and shut.

"May I help you?"

My head jerked up, hitting the bookshelf behind me. Standing over me was a pale face with bright red lipstick and a head of short, permed curls. I hated red lipstick.

She was a small lady, despite her high heels, the kind with tight straps across her scrunched-up toes. She wore a straight skirt that hung to just above her knees, and all I could think about was how uncomfortable she looked.

"My teacher sent me over," I finally said. "I need to look at some yearbooks."

"Any particular year?"

"I'm not sure."

"I'll show you where they are," she said politely.

I scrambled to my feet and followed her to the corner of the library. Next to the wall was a short bookshelf with a row of yearbooks that went as far back as the history of the school, somewhere in the 1930s. Next to the bookshelf was a fire exit door. She left me to myself and returned to the front desk.

I tried to count back to the years Mama would have been in high school, but I wasn't sure. I knew Mama and Daddy had been married a while before I was born. I pulled out the yearbook for 1945. I searched the class pictures, group shots, and scanned the names, but couldn't find her. Then I looked through the senior class of 1946. I searched the names and there she was. May McElhaney. The picture was black and white and the face small but I still recognized her, and felt a sharp pain in my chest at the sight of her. How I wished I could have saved her. She looked so young. Her hair was long and pulled away from her face in the picture, just as I remembered it; her smile stretched across her face. I slowly unzipped my jacket, placed the yearbook flat against my chest, my eyes throbbing and my mind more determined than ever to know what happened to her. I zipped my coat up to my neck, looking around. No one had seen me; I was sure. Supporting the yearbook with one arm, I quickly left out the back door that said "fire exit," then ran as fast as I could to the parking lot where I knew Ruthie was waiting.

She was sitting on the pavement with her back against the dumpster.

"I got it." I slumped against the cold metal next to her.

"Daddy was in there," I told her.

She leaned in close, her mouth dropping open. "What was he doing in there? Did he see you?"

"No. But he was in there to see her." I jerked my thumb back at the building. "The librarian."

"At least you didn't get caught."

"Ruthie, her name's Fay. Can you believe it?"

"Fanny Fay, fat and wide, couldn't get over to the other side."

"Ruthie, she isn't fat." I said. "She isn't much bigger than you. And she wears them high heels. Ruthie, he's seein' her. I'm sure of it."

A car door opened and slammed shut. Within seconds the engine started.

"We better get outa here," Ruthie whispered. "My daddy'll whoop me for sure."

After the car left, we ran for the field and followed it all the way to the road where we had crossed over.

Once at the creek, I unzipped my jacket, pulled out the yearbook and handed it to Ruthie. "It's on page sixteen."

I looked over Ruthie's shoulder as she flipped through the pages. Then she found the picture of Mama's senior class. She stared at it for a couple of minutes.

"I'm not sure," she finally said. "The faces are so small. And she was wearing a cap."

She handed the book back to me, still open, and pointed to the girl in the second row. The one with the hair pulled back. The one I had recognized. "I think it was her," she said, "but I'm not sure."

"Mama was wearing a cap that night," I told her. I remembered lying in bed, seeing Mama for the last time. I remembered the John Deere hat she'd worn on her head.

"I wonder if she saw me," I said.

Ruthie looked at me questioningly.

"The night she disappeared . . . I saw her leave. I was watching her from my window. She stopped at the edge of the woods and looked back. It was as though she was looking right at me. I should have yelled. I should have done something!"

I felt like one big sheet of rain was coming down, smothering out everything that was good. Ruthie wrapped both her arms around my shoulders while I cried.

"It's always gonna hurt, isn't it?" I said, the tears dripping off my cheeks. Ruthie didn't answer.

"I'll get another picture. We have to be sure. I'll write my uncle."

Ruthie let go of me and edged her way down the bank. She scooped up a handful of wet stones, then climbed back up and dropped some in my hand. One by one we tossed them into the water.

"Mansfield's not a dragon," Ruthie said. "He's a snake."

"Like the serpent in the Garden of Eden," I said.

We tossed more stones into the water.

"Like that cottonmouth that bit you on the ankle. I'll never forget comin' up on you and the way you looked, lyin' right here where we're sittin'."

I thought about the two point marks that were still on my ankle, as if someone had jabbed me with two sharp pencils. Mama Rae said they'd always be there. *I coulda died*, I thought, *but I didn't. Ruthie saved me.* I took Ruthie's hand in mine and held it for a long while, the fury inside me gone, and for that moment, I was happy.

❧   ❧   ❧

Daddy was still at the store when I got home, and the house was quiet except for Lonesome's toenails tapping softly on the linoleum. Standing on a chair, I pulled down the ladder from the attic. In the far corner was a box from Sears with the Christmas tree stand, lights, and a stack of old Christmas cards wrapped in a rubber band. Mama had kept them in their envelopes. I took them out and began thumbing through the return addresses. "Uncle George in Georgia," I said to myself.

Then I found it, a large red envelope. I put the rest of the cards away, climbed down, and within minutes was sitting at the kitchen table with a piece of paper and a pen. "Dear Uncle George . . ."

Chapter 17
The Big House

AFTER I WROTE THE LETTER to Uncle George, I hid it in one of my books to mail the next day. I had just finished feeding Lonesome when Daddy came home from the store.

"Don't bother fixin' me anything for dinner," he said. "Goin' out."

Within minutes I heard the shower running. "Gettin all cleaned up for Miss Perm Hairdo," I told Lonesome, wishing Sylvia was the one Daddy was seeing.

I heated up a leftover hamburger, but after a couple of bites, gave it to Lonesome. I was too keyed up to eat. Earnest had said to meet him at the creek late. This was one night I hoped Daddy didn't come home early.

After Daddy left, I put on a clean pair of jeans and a dark sweatshirt. I washed my face and brushed my hair, then stretched out on the sofa, counting down the seconds while I watched TV.

Around nine o'clock, Daddy still wasn't home. I put a pillow under the covers in my bed and turned out the lights. Wearing my dark blue jacket, I left the house, telling Lonesome to stay. I walked until I came to the meadow which sloped from the road-side woods to the creek. I was wide awake, my nerves wired.

Earnest approached from the weald of pine trees to my far right and walked along the bank of the creek. A silhouette of black. He turned toward the water, his elbows to his sides.

The water rippled ahead of me; the wind jouncing my hair. I walked through the grass, cool against my ankles.

Earnest turned and saw me.

"Ya sure you wanna do this?"

I burrowed my hands into my jacket for warmth. "I'm sure."

"It's gettin' cold."

"I'm all right."

He nodded his head, rolling his lips in together.

"How come you're not allowed to see me?" I asked him.

He forced a small laugh and looked away.

"Me and you, Francie, we're different," he said, still not looking at me.

"We don't seem so different to me." I shifted, trying to make eye contact. "Is it your mom who won't allow you to see me?"

His eyes fixed quickly on mine. "It ain't my mom."

And then something in him softened. He reached out and touched my arm with his fingers, holding them there for a second before they dropped back to his side.

"It's my dad, isn't it?" I demanded.

He tucked his hands into his pockets, his body pivoting toward the creek.

"What'd he say to you?" I felt my throat tighten and my eyes sting.

"What do you think he said, Francie? He told me to stay away from you."

"It ain't his right to say so."

He turned and faced me, his eyes squinting slightly. All I could do was stand there and look at him, not knowing what to say, my chest aching.

"Like I said, Francie, we're different."

My eyes burned so bad with tears, I was afraid to blink. That's when Earnest stepped closer to me. He wrapped his long arms around my shoulders, pulling me to him. He was a lot taller than me and had his chin tucked on top of my head. I closed my eyes, letting the tears fall out. My bones felt unjoined. I didn't move, and after a couple of seconds, realized I wasn't breathing, either.

Earnest leaned back and took my face in both his hands. "I wanna see you," he said, his face real close to mine. All I could do was nod my head.

His hands were long and angular and felt strong against my skin. He wiped my tears away with his thumbs and pressed his lips against mine ever so gently. A wonderful heat spread through my body, taking away the tightness in my throat. He smelled of wood smoke and the wind and trees. His lips stayed on mine for a while, touching them softly, then he pulled back, his hands still holding my face. We just stood there looking at each other and everything inside of me felt drawn to him.

"Come on," he said. I walked with him to the other side of the meadow and across the road. Earnest reached back and took my hand. We followed a narrow trail like that made by a deer. It led up a hill thick with trees that opened into an empty field.

I squeezed his hand tighter. He slowed his steps for a second and looked back. "Not too much farther," he said. "Actually, it's only about a mile from where you live. Through the woods behind your house and along the back side of Mr. Lampley's property. There's a gorge across the way. Mansfield's place is about a quarter-mile stretch down from the other side of it. We're making a circle around to the back of the place. Less chance of bein' seen."

I nodded my head slowly, though not moving forward. "Earnest?"

"Yeah?"

"Do ya ever feel like the past is real close? Almost like you could look right over your shoulder and there it'd be?"

He turned back, taking my other hand in his. "You're thinkin' about your mom, aren't you?"

"It's just that sometimes when I go places, it's as though she's right there with me. And then everything comes back, almost like she'd never left. But I know she's gone. And there's this empty spot inside me. Sometimes I feel like it's staring at me and will swallow me up."

"Do you feel that way now?"

I nodded my head.

"I know," he said. "But it won't always be there."

"How do you know?"

"That's what a friend of mine tells me."

"Do you ever feel that way?"

"Sometimes."

"I bet it's hard not going to school and living off with your mom."

"No different than you living with your dad."

"Earnest?"

"Yeah?"

"Who's the man I saw you with at the pond?"

"He's just somebody looks after me and my mom once in a while."

"So he's okay?" I asked.

"Of course he's okay."

At first I thought he was angry, but then he grinned small at the corners of his mouth.

I thought about Ruthie and me running into that man at the pond the day we cut school, and remembered the cardboard we'd seen, laid out on the ground like a bed.

"Where does he live?" I asked.

"What's with all the questions?" he teased, tugging at my hands, making my body lean into him. "He lives around. No place in particular."

Standing close to him like I was, I got this strong urge to reach up and touch his face, so I did, my fingertips brushing against the edge of his jaw. "Is he the friend you were talking about? The one who told you about that empty place inside of you going away?" The man in the woods was the only person I'd ever seen Earnest with, other than the Taylors.

Earnest was staring back at me, making me want to hold him

close. The smile on his face was gone. He gave an easy nod of his head. "Yeah, he's my friend," he said.

"Kind of like me and Ruthie," I said.

"How's that?"

"Kids at school always talking. They don't like that I'm friends with a colored girl, and here you are friends with a man who lives off by himself in the woods."

"People in this town talk too much. You can't listen to them. What do any of them know about anything?"

Earnest turned around. "We better get goin'," he said. Still holding one of my hands, he led me through the field. Clouds had thickened over the sky, and I wondered if it would rain.

On the other side of the field, there was a dark sweep of woods. Again we were in the midst of trees, with only the sounds of our footsteps racking inside my head. Farther ahead we heard an engine and music.

Earnest tugged on my sleeve. "Crouch down."

He had one knee on the ground and the other one bent in front of him. "Over there." He pointed.

Not too far off in the distance were lit windows and head-lights from a few parked trucks. Voices drifted toward us.

Hunched over, we crept on a pelt of pine needles to a small grove of shrubs and evergreens, the voices becoming clearer. Fragments of laughter.

No more than sixty feet before us and slightly to our left was the big house. Ruthie was right. It looked like a barn painted dark brown except for the small back porch and the window on the side. From where we were, I could barely see its front corner, where a bulky man with black hair and jeans hanging off his hips stood. "Get over here!" he shouted to someone in the distance, scooping a hefty arm through the air. He turned his profile to us. The flap of his shirt stretched over his protruding gut. Then he was gone, disappearing around the house.

To the side of the building stretched a clearing full of pickup trucks parked at odd angles, reminding me somewhat of Ruthie's church. A truck door slammed. We edged closer.

I wondered where it was Mama had been killed, where Ruthie had been hurt. My skin shivered with a cold from the deepest part of me. Overgrown hedges clung to the back side of the house. "Let's go," Earnest whispered. On his hands and knees, he moved swiftly over to the thick branches, ducking underneath them. I followed till both of us had our backs pressed against the foundation of the building. We were hidden by the dense growth and surrounded by the pungent fragrance of juniper. Golden shafts of light streamed from the window above us, barely touching the ground where we sat.

My heart clapped loudly and my skin felt like gooseflesh, though my palms continued to sweat. "Someone will see us," I whispered.

Earnest put a finger to his lips. He turned toward the building and slowly stood on his knees, so that his face reached the edge of the window. He looked inside, then motioned me to him.

I rose to my knees, feeling the cool stone of the foundation against my thighs. Pressing my hands flat against the wood siding, I lifted my head to the right corner of the square pane. My chin was now on the windowsill, chips of paint sticking to my skin. The glass was filmy and the air inside the building thick with smoke, making it difficult to see.

Earnest licked his thumb and ran a small circle on the glass, wiping some of the dust and water stains away. The room was full of men and smoke and body heat. I spotted the sheriff off to one side with a couple of his deputies. I recognized other faces as well: Carl Shephard, a young man in his twenties who worked for Mr. Foster; Mr. Patterson, the custodian at my school; Mr. James from the Methodist Church—all of the men white. Then I saw Mr. Tucker from Daddy's store. I couldn't believe he was here too. A bell rang and someone hollered. The men stepped to the sides of the room, beers and cigarettes in their hands, a few nursing bottles of whiskey, all of them laughing. A tall man in a feed cap with a wad of tobacco in his bottom lip waved a bill in the air. The man I'd seen outside the building approached him, taking the money. His black hair was combed to the side, one tuft hanging in perspiration over his shiny forehead. He was thick and shorter than the others, the bulk of his forearms making his elbows stick out to his sides. Even his wrists seemed to bulge.

The backs of the men were to us, making it difficult to see. I could swear one of them was Mr. Hersh, the history teacher at my school. He lifted a beer to his mouth, then turned toward the man on his left in conversation. An opening formed in the crowd, through which we could see the center of the large room, a dirt arena fenced off by nothing more than a motley of men, drinking, smoking, and sweating out some sort of suspense.

"They're all in on it," Earnest whispered.

"Who?"

But he didn't say anything else.

A couple of colored boys appeared from the crowd, approaching the dirt clearing. I recognized one from Ruthie's church. Amos Lucas.

"Pappy's boy," Earnest whispered. "Been at it since he was fifteen."

Amos was a heavyset boy with skin as black as strong coffee. He stood several inches over six feet tall. Like a linebacker, everything about him was wide, even his neck. His jeans were tight on his hips and his feet bare, as was his chest.

The other boy was lean with skin almost the color of rich honey. He stood a good six inches below Amos. His jeans, a bleached blue, hung low, revealing the bones of his hips. Like Amos, his feet were bare to the ground.

"Is this a match?" I whispered to Earnest, alarmed at the considerable difference in size between the two boys.

"If ya wanna call it that."

Then I spotted Rolan, the man who had been watching Daddy at the debate. A blue bandanna was knotted around his head. He approached the two colored boys and said something to the men around them. More dollar bills waved in the air. More money was collected.

"Mansfield is over in the corner," Earnest whispered to me. But all I could see was a slice of silver from his hair. "He records the money, takes bets on who will win."

Again the bell rang, and the two boys faced each other, their bodies tilting backward slightly like a couple of snakes, coiled and about to strike. They slowly walked around each other, each hesitating to make the first move, their faces already beaded with sweat.

The crowd began shouting, egging the two boys on, though we couldn't make out what they were saying. It seemed strange to see these two boys against each other like a couple of roosters being forced to defend their ground. Then the smaller boy lunged at Amos, throwing his whole body at him, and the fighting began. Not fighting like that of a boxing match, the kind I'd watched with Daddy on TV. There were no boxing gloves or fancy shoes. Just bare skin pounding and meshing together.

"Anything goes." Earnest's voice was grim. "Anything. They're both in it to win."

"Who's the other one?" I asked him.

"His name's Glenwood. Works on a tobacco farm with his family outside of town."

Blood was now trickling from Amos's nose, and one of Glenwood's eyes was swollen shut. Amos had knocked Glenwood to the ground and was kicking him in the gut, making his whole body double in pain. Most of the men around them continued to whoop it up like a rowdy bunch of animals. Others stood idly pulling on cigarettes or bottles of beer.

Glenwood slowly pushed himself back up, only to be kicked down again by Amos. His body wrenched violently with that final blow, and blood spilled from his mouth into a large pool on the ground.

"Amos is gonna kill him." My eyes were fixed against the glass. "We have to do something!"

Immediately, I felt Earnest's hands on my shoulders, pressing me to the ground. "Someone'll hear ya, Francie. You have to keep quiet."

It was then that I realized how rapidly I was breathing. "Why don't they do something? Why doesn't someone stop them?"

"They choose to do what they're doin'."

"Like they got the spirits in them or somethin'," I said.

"That and next month's rent ridin' on their backs. Just like the folks bettin' on 'em. Everyone's in it to make a buck. The colored boys get paid to fight. If they win, the profit is bigger."

"It's not natural. Two boys fightin' their own kind. It just doesn't make sense."

"That's right, and the next thing ya know, Amos'll be over there nursing Glenwood's wounds and Glenwood will let him."

"Ruthie says one of these days one of 'em ain't gonna make it."

"Maybe she's right." Earnest held one of my arms in his hand. "Come on, let's get outa here."

As we started to crawl out of the hedges, we heard voices

coming around the building. Earnest held his arm out across my chest to hold me back, though I had already ducked against the wall.

Through the branches I could see Tom and Randy and Jason. They each had cigarettes in their hands and were passing around a bottle of whiskey.

"Did ya see all that blood, man? That nigger got beat up bad." Randy swallowed a mouthful of whiskey, then handed the bottle to Tom, who was now crouched on the ground with his back against a tree.

"When you gonna get out there and fight Amos?" Randy asked.

Tom held the cigarette between his thumb and finger and took a long drag, then stabbed it on the ground. "I don't fight; I just work here, remember?"

"Good thing, too," Jason said. "I'd hate to be cleaning up your blood."

The two white boys laughed. Tom took a swig of whiskey, and looked away.

From the light of the window, I could see the boys' faces about fifty feet in front of us. Randy was standing on the right side of Tom. He was tall and lanky and pale, his hair in dirty blond waves that hung down to his shoulders. Jason stood on the other side, one hand in his front pocket, the other holding a cigarette. He was heavyset and stood several inches shorter than his brother. Both wore jeans, Jason's with holes in the knees, and both had on plaid flannel shirts that hung below their hips.

"Who's up next?" Jason asked. His voice was deep—a good octave lower than Randy's.

Tom shrugged his shoulders. "What does it matter?"

"Doesn't matter. As long as they can put on a good show," said Randy. Again he laughed. The other two were quiet.

"'Bout that time," Jason said, tossing his cigarette to the ground and putting it out with one of his boots.

Randy finished the bottle of whiskey and tossed it into the brush from where Earnest and I had come. We waited as the three of them walked to the front of the building.

"Got to have some weak blood to be hangin' around with them two," Earnest whispered once they were out of sight.

"If his daddy knew . . ."

Earnest cut me off. "Maybe he does. Can't keep a tomcat on a leash. He'll break loose every time."

"I don't get it. Why would Tom want anything to do with Mansfield? Why does he hang out with these guys?"

"He's a P.K."

"What does that mean?"

"He's a preacher's kid. Maybe he doesn't want to be so good all the time. Maybe he thinks having some bad in his life will balance things out. He and his dad haven't seen eye to eye for a long time. Tension's been brewin' between those two for as long as I've known them. Mama Rae says its 'cause they're so much alike. That's the last thing Tom wants to hear. Probably him hanging out with Mansfield's kind is his way of sayin' he's different from the rest of them."

"He *is* different. Ruthie wouldn't ever be like Tom." I thought about the kittens. *What kind of person could do such a thing?*

Earnest took my hand. "We should get goin'." He led me out from the hedges. The two of us ran with our backs bent over the ground. We didn't stop till we were deep into the trees. Then we walked the rest of the way to the creek, Earnest holding my hand the whole time.

At the edge of the water, I scooped up a handful of stones. I climbed back up the bank and sat in the dry grasses, the earth cool underneath me. Earnest joined me, sitting so close that the entire length of his body touched mine. Everything inside me seemed to flutter from his warmth. His legs were stretched out in front of him, his feet crossed at the ankles. I rubbed my fingers over the smooth surface of the stones I held in my hand, thinking about all the times Ruthie and I had sat along the creek. Then, one by one, I tossed the stones into the water, listening to their *kerplunks*, feeling their circular ripples as if they were inside me, sending out little waves of peace.

"Now you know," Earnest said.

"Can't say I'm any better off for it." I tossed the last stone into the water. "Angrier, I suppose. They all looked like a bunch of animals. Didn't look like people at all."

"The Reverend tries to stop the boys from goin'. Problem is, he can't even keep his own boy at home. The only way any of those colored folks is gonna stop Mansfield is if they get the law behind them. That ain't gonna happen as long as McGee's in office."

"Maybe that will change. Maybe Mr. Lawson will get elected."

"Maybe. Now that the laws have changed and the colored folks are finally getting to vote, Lawson might just have a chance."

I hoped Earnest was right. I thought of my day with Ruthie. Mansfield had hurt Ruthie, and I felt sure he had killed Mama as well. I wanted to tell Earnest, but decided to wait until Ruthie and I had the picture. We had to be certain before telling anyone what we knew.

"You know Tom and all those guys. How come you don't work for Mansfield?" I asked.

"Reckon I'm not one of those animals. Like to think I got a little more sense in my head."

"You got a lot more sense in your head."

Earnest put his arm around my shoulder, pulling my body against him. We were quiet for a minute, then he said, "Did you have a problem sneakin' out?"

"Don't know yet."

"What do ya mean?" Earnest leaned forward, tilting his face toward mine.

"Daddy wasn't home."

"Now if that ain't real fine! Your dad's gonna have me for sure."

"Sometimes ya gotta cross the bridge that carries you to the other side."

Earnest lifted his eyebrows slightly, still looking at me.

"Just somethin' Ruthie said," I told him.

"Ain't gonna lighten the burden of your daddy's reckonin'."

"Maybe not."

The temperature was dropping, and my body shivered. Earnest hugged me closer. His other hand reached for my chin. Then his lips touched mine and our mouths pressed together, searching each other, holding on. I reached my arms around the waist of his shirt, my bones melting, my head swimming, and my blood pounding with a hunger I had never felt before.

Chapter 18
Woods Colt

THE NEXT MORNING, when I came into the kitchen, Daddy was sitting at the table with his gold glass ashtray and a cup of coffee.

"Sit down," he said, pulling out the chair next to him, the one we never used.

He knows, I thought. *He knows I snuck out.*

"That ain't my chair," I told him.

"That's right."

"So why you want me to sit there?" My voice quavered the slightest bit, which I hated.

Daddy took his hand from the chair and propped his elbows on the table, holding the cup of coffee to his mouth.

"Ya know where we got this table?"

"No, sir."

"It belonged to your grandparents. They had it from the time your mom was a little girl." He cast his eyes over at me for a second before looking back at the table. "There's a cigarette burn in that chair. Your grandpa made it before she was born. Your mom used to stick green peas into the hole, or anything else she didn't have a mind to eat."

He finished his coffee, his eyes staring across the table. "I think you've graduated to that chair," he said.

I slowly walked over to it and sat down.

"Don't worry. Your grandpa restuffed it. Kept the cigarette burn for memories, I suppose."

Daddy stood from the table and poured himself another cup of coffee. Then he took Mama's gold mug from the cupboard, filled it with the hot black liquid, and set it on the table in front of me.

"Don't usually drink coffee," I said.

He reached for an open pack of cigarettes in the center of the table. Tilting the pack to his mouth, he slid one between his lips and lit it with the green lighter he kept in the front pocket of his shirt.

"I figure if you're old enough to be sneakin' out at night, you're old enough to be drinkin' coffee with your ole man." His eyes stared at me from beneath the deep burrow of his brow. "Who ya with last night?" he asked.

I didn't answer him. Instead, I lifted the hot coffee to my mouth and sipped it slowly, feeling it scald my tongue and the roof of my mouth. Setting the mug on the table, I said, "How come you know I snuck out? You weren't even home."

His lips pulled in on the cigarette. After a couple of seconds, he slowly exhaled and tapped the ashes into the gold dish.

"I had a date last night," he finally said. "I stopped by the house so you could meet her."

I continued to stare at the table in front of me, fixing my eyes on each little gold speck.

"I think you'd like her," he said.

The air immediately escaped from my lips in a loud way. I

turned my head and looked through the screen door. I could see the blue sky from where I sat, and I tried to think of something else. Of Ruthie, the creek, Earnest. And again, the smell of starch and steam and the powder Mama wore. The way her arms felt when she'd hold me at night and we'd search for the stars.

Tears began to sting my eyes, as they'd been doing a lot lately, and I fought with all my might to push them back.

"It was that boy, wasn't it?" Daddy's voice was cold. I just kept staring out the screen door.

"I thought I'd made it clear to him he wasn't suppose to see you."

Daddy tilted the mug of coffee to his mouth. "I should of known I was tellin' the wrong person."

"He isn't the wrong person!" My head jerked back around, as if I was a rubber band that had just snapped.

"Oh, Francie." Daddy set his cup on the table and draped his big arm over the back of my chair. "It isn't that I'm against you seein' somebody. It's just that he ain't the best one for you to be seein'."

My teeth ground together as tears smoldered all through me.

"Ya know what a woods colt is?" Daddy asked me.

"No, sir."

"Francie, that boy don't come from the right people. The whole town knows him for what he is. Doesn't even go to school. It just ain't right, Bean."

I thought about what Earnest had said the night before.

"People in this town talk too much," I told Daddy, repeating Earnest's words. Again my eyes fixed on the table, the gold specks now turning into blurry images.

"Ya know what a bastard is, don't ya?"

I nodded my head.

"Same thing as a woods colt," Daddy said.

"So what if Earnest doesn't have a dad. I don't have a mom!" My voice burned from the back of my throat.

"Damnit, Francie, it ain't the same thing."

"What do you care what people in this town think?" *You didn't care all those nights you were drunk,* I wanted to say, but I bit my tongue. "I don't care what people say. What makes them right?"

Daddy's breathing was heavy. Staring down at the table, he said, "As long as you're living with me, you're gonna listen to what I have to say. The way I see it, he ain't the boy you should be hangin' around. Ya hear what I'm sayin'?"

"I hear ya," I said. I hadn't lied to him. I'd heard him just fine, but there wasn't any way I was going to obey him, either.

Daddy stabbed his cigarette into the ashtray. With a stiff nod, he stood up from the table and left the room. The discussion was over.

a   a   a

That afternoon, Ruthie met me after school at the creek. I told her about the big house. Told her about seeing Tom.

"He promised Daddy he'd stopped going. Said he was just

hanging out with a couple of friends from town at night. I knew he wasn't tellin' the truth. Where else would he be gettin' the money for his cigarettes or the gas he was usin' up each time he took Daddy's truck?"

"Maybe your daddy knows. Maybe he's more worried about stoppin' Mansfield than he is about stoppin' Tom."

Ruthie was pulling up the dried grass and tearing it into tiny pieces. "Did you write your uncle?"

"Yeah. May take a while before I hear from him, though."

"What about Earnest?" Ruthie asked.

"It was Daddy. He told Earnest not to see me anymore." Then I told her what Daddy had said that morning.

"You and Earnest gonna keep seein' each other?"

"Hope so. Don't know when. We'll have to make sure Daddy doesn't find out."

Ruthie rubbed the grass from her hands. "How much kissin' you two do last night?" Her eyes were grinning at me from under their lids.

"Enough to let me know not Daddy or anyone else is gonna keep me from seein' him."

"Feels good, don't it?"

"Good enough that I could go on kissin' him forever."

"Ooh, girl."

Then we were both laughing like always.

❧   ❧   ❧

The next two weeks, Daddy and I didn't say a whole lot to each other. We just went through the motions, not really being rude but not being overly friendly, either. I sat down by the creek more than a time or two, hoping Earnest would show, but he never did. I started worrying that maybe I'd end up obeying Daddy after all—that maybe I wouldn't have any choice in the matter. As I'd sit on the bank of the creek, I'd start praying that Earnest and me would run into each other and everything would be just fine, but so far that hadn't happened. Some days I was angry at Earnest, wishing he'd find a way to see me. But most of the time I just felt sad, each day feeling like an eternity. *What if he doesn't want to see me?* That was the thought I hated the most.

I stewed myself crazy right up to the first Tuesday in November—Election Day. Ever since the night Daddy hit me across the mouth, I hadn't seen him drinking. Hadn't seen any beer bottles laying around the house, either. I wasn't sure if it was on account of him having a remorseful heart or if it was because of the new woman he was seeing. Either way, I was glad. But that Tuesday morning he took down a bottle of whiskey from the cabinet above the refrigerator and added a shot to his coffee. "To posterity," he said when he saw me looking at him. I wasn't even sure what that word meant. Then he gulped his coffee down in a hurry and offered me a ride to school.

Cars were already lined up alongside the street when we pulled into town, and people were gathered in coveys up and down the sidewalks. Most of the folks in our county were

Democrats who rarely veered away from the party ticket. Mr. Lawson was a Republican. If he won, he would become the first Republican sheriff in our county's history.

When Daddy and I pulled up to the school, he told me he was going to be closing the store early and to meet him at the diner when I got out.

"Okay," I said, kissing him on the cheek and smelling the strong scent of aftershave mixed with tobacco.

Nothing much happened the rest of that morning until lunchtime. Most of the kids liked to go outside after they finished eating. I would usually find a spot underneath a tree and read a book so I wouldn't have to talk to anybody. After Phinny and his friends shoved cow pies in my mouth, being social with the likes of them was the last thing I wanted to do. And ever since I'd had my talk with Mr. Franklin, they'd pretty much left me alone. Sometimes I felt like I was a virus that kids didn't want to get close to. Ruthie wasn't the only reason the kids stayed away. My mama had died a little over six months before. I knew a lot of kids kept their distance from me on account of them not knowing what to say, as if just seeing me made them feel guilty 'cause their mamas were still around.

One day after biology class Mr. Franklin called me up to his desk. "They don't know you," he said after all the other kids were gone. "They don't know what's inside you. Maybe if they got to know you . . ."

"It's okay," I said.

Ruthie knew me, and Earnest knew me; I was sure of it. In one of Reverend Taylor's sermons, he had talked about not feeding your pearls to the pigs. He read those words right out of the Bible. When I'd watch the way the kids at school acted, that's how I felt. I wasn't going to let them know all the things that went on inside me. I wasn't going to feed my pearls to the pigs.

That particular day in November, I was too keyed up to read. I sat with my back against a tree, my legs stretched out in front of me, thinking if I prayed hard enough in my head, Mr. Lawson would win. Then Phinny McGee and Kevin Cook started passing a football no more than twenty feet from where I was sitting. I didn't pay them any mind until Jason McClure, one of their friends, ran between them to intercept the pass and knocked the ball right in my lap. I tossed it back to Kevin, him probably being the nicest out of the bunch.

"Hey, Francie, who you goin' to the bonfire with tonight?" Kevin asked, still standing where he was and passing the football back to Phinny.

Following an election, the town would build an enormous bonfire in the field between the middle school and high school. Hot chocolate and soft drinks would be served, compliments of the diner, and a number of people would pass around bottles of whiskey and beer.

I just sat there, not sure I'd heard him right. Kevin and I had never even said so much as "hello" to each other. He was one of those good-looking jocks who seemed to care more about sports than having a conversation with anybody.

About that time, Billy Bombeck, probably the loudest kid in the school, walked up to me, as if he'd been standing behind the tree that whole time. "I know who Francie's goin' with," he said. "That bastard who lives out in the woods with the crazy lady. Either him or that nigger girl Francie's always hangin' around with."

I'd flat out had it. I jumped up from the tree and lunged into Billy with all my might, pushing him a couple of yards backwards, directly in the line of Phinny's pass. The football hit Billy square in the face, making his nose bleed like a running faucet. Phinny started laughing at both of us. He liked Billy about as much as he liked me. "Maybe Billy ought to start hanging out with you and those friends of yours." He was still laughing.

"Shut up, Phinny," Kevin said.

Billy was holding the tail of his shirt to his nose, his bare stomach spilling over the sides of his pants. Mrs. Dale, one of the teachers, saw him and came over. "Got hit in the face with the football," Kevin told her. "It was an accident." I knew no one was going to argue with Kevin, not even Phinny.

The teacher led Billy inside the building, Billy pinching his nose shut and holding his head back. Once they were far enough away, Phinny heaved the football as hard as he could at my chest. I saw it coming and held my hands out in front of me, catching it like I'd been playing football all my life.

Though I tasted the anger in my mouth at Phinny, I also felt a wonderful victory for having caught the ball and for Billy having

gotten a bloody nose. I dropped the football where I was standing, picked up my books, and started walking, heading across the
back property of the school. The bell rang. I listened to all the
commotion as the kids clamored their way inside. I'd had enough
of Phinny and Billy and all of them. Kevin might be okay, but he
was still one of them. I kept walking, wondering if anyone would
notice I was gone. I didn't care. If a kid had three unexcused
absences, the school would contact the parents. I'd only had
one—the day I'd played hooky with Ruthie. Besides, I knew if
anyone did call Daddy, all I had to do was tell him I'd gotten
cramps real bad from my period and he'd get all embarrassed and
not say another word about it.

I walked out to the middle of the field that connected the
middle school to the high school. Benches had already been set
up for the bonfire that night, and a tall pyramid of wood had
been built. I set my books in the grass and lay down on one of the
benches, my face to the sun.

After a couple of minutes, I heard the engine of a truck
pulling toward me. An old Ford, light blue, with an enormous
white brush plate welded to the front was slowly edging its way
through the field from the road. As it drew closer, I saw the limbs
sticking out from the bed and knew someone was bringing more
wood for the celebration that night. The sun hit the windshield
with a blinding splatter of rays as the truck turned to the right
and backed up toward the pile of wood. The door to the truck
opened, then slammed shut.

"Whatch you doin' outa school so early?" came Earnest's voice as he walked around the side of the truck.

I couldn't believe it. "Decided I'd had enough for one day," I said.

Earnest began unloading the dried limbs and throwing them into a pile. "How come?" he asked, stepping on one of the limbs with his thick boots and pulling it toward him till it snapped.

I climbed into the truck bed and helped him unload the wood. "'Cause Billy Bombeck got a bloody nose." I threw a limb onto the pile. Earnest laughed.

"And you didn't have anything to do with it, I suppose."

"Not directly." I gave Earnest a nudge on the shoulder with my hand, causing him to almost lose his balance.

"What'd you do that for?"

"How come you've been such a stranger?" I said.

"Guess I was a little worried about your dad. Didn't think I should be coming around."

You could have come by the creek, or by the Taylors', or met me after school, I thought, not sure I wanted to let him off so easy.

"What happened when you got home the other night?" he asked.

I climbed out of the truck. "Daddy wasn't home yet." I decided not to tell him about the run-in I'd had the next morning. If Earnest was already fretting about Daddy, I wasn't about to go adding any more fuel to his fears.

"That's good." Earnest jumped out of the truck, landing

beside me. He tucked his hands in his pockets and leaned his head down, trying to get me to look at him. "I still wanna see you," he said. "I just didn't want to go gettin' you in trouble."

That's all Earnest had to say, his words like magic making whatever anger I had for him disappear. "Nobody's gonna go gettin' me in trouble." I smiled back at him.

"So what about that bloody nose? How come you left school so early?"

"School's the last place I belong," I said, my chest tightening with that familiar anger I felt around Phinny and his friends.

Earnest let out a laugh from the back of his throat. "Me and you both."

"Where'd ya get the truck?" I asked, changing the subject. "Is it yours?"

"Mr. Foster over at the feed barn sold it to me. He's letting me make payments to him."

"It's nice." I patted the fender, glad the subject of school had been dropped.

"Thinkin' I'm gonna paint it green once it's all paid off." He turned and looked the truck over. "Mr. Lampley says I can use his garage."

"The blue's not so bad."

Earnest walked closer to me and took my hand. He leaned his back up against the truck. "I was wonderin' how I was gonna get to see you again. Been kinda prayin' it over in my head. Then all of a sudden you just show up."

I leaned beside him, the metal warm against my back from the sun. *I've been kinda prayin' it over too*, I thought. "I wish I was older," I told him. "If I was older it wouldn't make any difference who I wanted to see."

Earnest looked away, not saying anything.

"We aren't so different," I told him, remembering what he'd told me the night we went to see the big house. "I don't care what anyone says. Maybe you ain't got a dad. Well, I ain't got a mom. So how does that make us so different?"

He dropped his eyes toward me, smiling easy. Then he lifted my hand to his mouth, held it there for a second, and kissed it lightly. "You're okay, Francie."

I tucked my forehead against his chest and rolled it back and forth in a playful way. "Don't stay such a stranger," I said, wrapping my arms around his taut waist.

He hugged me back, kissing the top of my head. "Deal," he said.

Chapter 19
The Bonfire

WHEN I GOT TO THE DINER, Fay was already there. She and Daddy were sitting next to each other in one of the booths, their backs to me as I walked in the door. The bell rang above me but was drowned out by the television and the busy chatter around the room. The diner was packed with bodies and smoke and the smell of fried food and coffee. Someone slapped me from behind, and I instantly turned my head to see Sylvia holding a coffeepot in the air. She gave me that playful grin that seemed to be fixed permanently on her face, and I watched her work herself in a maze across the room, stopping periodically to fill somebody's cup.

Daddy cranked his head toward the door and saw me, then scooped his arm through the air. I edged my way through the crowd, set my books on the table and scooted in across from him and Fay.

"It's gonna be a fine day, Bean. I can feel it." He smiled and put his arm around Fay. "Fay, this is my girl, Francie. Francie, this is Fay."

I tried to smile, but felt my face pulling sideways.

"I've seen you before." Fay lifted a finger to her chin, her bright red nail polish matching her lipstick.

Oh, no, here it goes, I thought. *Daddy's gonna find out I was skippin' school.*

Daddy raised his brow in my direction, "You two know each other?"

"Francie came by the library one day," Fay said.

I nodded my head. I couldn't help but like her voice. She spoke clear and smooth, unlike the other women from our town whose voices drawled with a small-town twang. She sipped on a glass of iced tea, and as she set it back on the table, I noticed the neat imprint of her lipstick just below the rim.

Daddy waved Sylvia over to us and asked me what I'd like.

"How's my honey doin'?" Sylvia said, smiling at me.

I smiled back at her and ordered a chocolate sundae.

Sylvia winked before turning toward the counter.

"How come Sylvia never married?" I asked.

Daddy chuckled. "Well, Bean. I don't really know."

He squeezed Fay closer to him, then reached in his pocket with his other hand and pulled out a pack of cigarettes.

Fay wasn't like the other women in our town. Most only dressed up on Sundays and rarely had time to put polish on their nails. They aged into hardworking women with round abdomens from having all their children and soft wrinkles around their eyes. As they got older, they usually turned into grandmothers who baked cookies and wore their house slippers during the day and chased dogs out of their gardens with brooms. I guessed Daddy didn't want one of them.

I remembered all the times Mama and Daddy and I would come to the diner. If she was sitting next to Daddy like Fay was that day, she would've been pretty without the perm or makeup, I thought. Mama was beautiful. A wave of hurt came over me and I stared at the table, hoping the tears wouldn't come.

Sylvia brought me my sundae. Somebody stopped to talk to Daddy, asking him questions about Mr. Lawson. Had Daddy talked to him? How was the voting going over in Mayville?

All of a sudden the door flew open in a big way, like a tornado had just rolled in. Sheriff McGee appeared, holding onto the door with an outstretched arm, letting in the cool air. A few men walked over to him, smacking him on the shoulder.

Daddy reached in his back pocket for his wallet. He slapped a five-dollar bill on the table, put his cigarette out on his plate, and asked us if we were ready to go.

I finished the last bite of my sundae, picked up my books, and followed him and Fay outside.

The sun was beginning to set over the town and the hills surrounding our valley. The old bricks of the few buildings glowed a rich garnet red. Spring Gap usually rolled up its sidewalks at sunset, but not that night.

Across the street from the diner at the hardware store, a handful of older men with tobacco in their mouths and cups in their hands for spitting sat in chairs tilted back against the brick. One of them saw me and waved. It was Mr. Lampley. I told Daddy I would be right back. He nodded his head and turned to start a conversation with some women from the school.

Mr. Lampley set his cup on the sidewalk and stood up as I approached.

"Did you vote?" I asked him.

"Yep." Then, leaning toward my ear, "Voted for that young feller for sheriff."

"Daddy's wantin' him to win real bad."

"I know he does." He paused.

"Got a friend of yours working for me now." He smiled at me.

"Who?"

"Oh, that young fella. Hard-workin' boy."

"Earnest?"

"Uh-huh."

"He didn't tell me."

"Oh, he keeps to himself, I suppose. Sure does work hard, though. I told your dad so, last time he was in. Told him what a fine boy I had workin' for me."

"How did you know me and him were friends?"

"I reckon an ole man like me has his ways." He smiled, his face deeply carved and handsome, the colors from the sun dappling on him in a soft way. A colored man passing by touched a finger to the cap on his head. Mr. Lampley nodded amiably in return.

Daddy and Fay were walking toward us from across the street, her hand in his. They spoke to Mr. Lampley, Daddy rocking on his feet as they talked, and I could tell he was eager for the results of the long day. "May the best man win," Daddy said. Mr. Lampley gave a genial nod. He picked up his cup and returned to his chair, again tilting it against the brick as he joined his comrades and watched the evening pass by.

We walked a block to Daddy's store. Fay and I followed him to the back room, where he pulled up a couple of chairs around the old black-and-chrome transistor radio he'd had for years. He clicked it on and, sitting on a wooden crate, scraped the dial across AM static until he picked up WPRO out of Birmingham, which was giving continuous coverage of the elections. He had me go get a few colas from the front of the store, and the three of us sat in that back room listening to the voices on the radio, the naked light bulb flickering above us. I looked at Fay while she sipped her cola and wondered how much she knew. Did she want Mr. Lawson to win as much as Daddy and me? Had Daddy talked to her about the night Mama died or the morning I found him all beat up? The way she sat listening to the radio, her eyes staring down at the concrete floor like she was just as nervous as the rest of us, made me think she knew a whole lot. I wasn't sure I was comfortable with that idea. Wasn't sure I liked her stepping into our business.

Daddy set his cola on the floor in front of him, then lit a cigarette and wadded the foil from the empty pack in his hand. Every move we made seemed to be amplified in the stillness. Every swallow of soft drink. Every breath. A clock above the doorway ticked quietly behind us, eating away seconds. We were in another world inside that room. Away from the crowds. And I knew that was the way Daddy wanted it. If Mr. Lawson lost, Daddy would want to be alone. It was personal for him.

The polls were closing across the state. Finally, the reports on the local elections.

"In Tallapoosa County, in the race for sheriff," came the voice over the radio, "Phil Lawson, eleven hundred and fifty-three votes. Clem McGee, eight hundred and thirty-nine."

Daddy had put his last cigarette out on the floor, and I watched his fists tighten and raise in the air. "We did it," he said. He reached for me with both his arms and lifted me off my chair, hugging me tight against him.

Fay clicked the radio off, and we gathered our things to go to the bonfire. Outside, the red of the sunset had dissolved, and the lights from the street cast shadows across the sidewalks.

We climbed into the truck and rolled down the windows, despite the cold air. Then we drove to the field next to the high school while the radio blasted a tune from the country station in Anniston. People were already gathering amid the haphazard array of vehicles. Men were sitting on coolers; teenagers were smoking away at cigarettes. Mr. Moody from the diner had his truck parked not too far off from the tall tower of limbs Earnest had built earlier that day. He was sitting in the back with kegs of beverages. A couple of girls from the high school climbed up to help him. Cups of foaming soft drinks and hot chocolate were being passed out.

Daddy stopped the truck and we climbed out, the night air smelling richly of wood and grass and cigarette smoke and occasional whiffs of booze. Daddy stood next to Fay, his arm draped over her shoulder. I wandered over to Mr. Moody's truck for a cup of hot chocolate. There was already a line, mostly teenagers and young kids. A couple of girls from my class stood in front of me.

Oh, great, I thought. *The whole school's probably heard about Kevin and Phinny and Billy Bombeck's bloody nose.* I felt my body stiffen, waiting for some remark. One of the girls glanced back, catching my eye. She looked straight through me as if I didn't even exist. Finally, the cups were handed to us. I held the warm liquid to my mouth and sipped it slowly as the two girls walked away.

The noise was beginning to mount around me as more people collected together. I found Daddy and Fay in the crowd. *At least Phinny won't be here,* I thought. As I looked around, I knew Sheriff McGee and Mansfield wouldn't show, either. Then I saw Kevin Cook leaning his head in close to Essie Blalock, one of the girls who had been passing the note about me in Mr. Franklin's class. Kevin had his head so close to hers, I was sure he was either trying to kiss her or get a whiff of her shampoo.

Not far off, I could see a group of colored families. Within seconds I spotted Ruthie, wearing jeans and a large red woolen sweater. Her hands were tucked up into the sleeves as if she was cold. Rachel and Willie took off running from the group with some of their friends. "Hey, Ruthie!" I hollered. She turned and saw me and waved. A few boys stopped to talk to her. I lay a hand over my cup and jogged over to them. Boisterous chatter surrounded us. Shoulders bumped against us. Then Mr. Lawson stepped up on a platform next to the enormous mound of wood. He gave a wave, and cheers went up around him. Someone from the crowd handed him a torch.

A group of rowdy men stood on top of a pickup cab parked

near the clearing for the bonfire and began the annual count-down: "10-9-8-7-6-5-4-3-2-1!" Mr. Lawson tossed the torch onto the mound, lighting the fire in a burst of orange flame. Cheers went up, the air buzzing with whistles and laughter and clapping hands.

As the night wore away, more bodies gathered. Lights from trucks bounced over the field. Then low, almost hushed, some-where behind us, like a soft ripple in a tranquil pond, a song rose from the colored folks, building in harmony, pouring itself over us like warm liquid. Bodies swayed. More voices joined. Ruthie and I took hold of each other's hands. Our bodies, like the others, moved with the song.

> Oh, well, I'm tired and so weary,
> but I must go along
> till the Lord he comes and calls me,
> calls me away.
> Well the mornin's so bright,
> and the Lamb is the light,
> and the night, night is as black
> as the sea.
> There will be peace in the valley
> for me, someday.
> There will be peace, peace in the valley
> for me, oh Lord I pray.

There'll be no sadness, no sorrow,

no trouble I see.

There will be peace, peace in the valley

for me.

As the song continued, I saw Earnest alone on his truck, his hands held prayerfully in front of him as his elbows rested on his knees. The golden light from the fire washed over his face. I held onto Ruthie's hand tighter. Held it for him. Held it for all of us.

Chapter 20
The Christmas Scarf

IT WAS CHRISTMAS EVE, nearly two months after the election. I had melted butter and molasses and made popcorn balls while Daddy sat in his recliner watching TV. The Christmas tree was in the corner of the living room, a Fraser Fir which Daddy bought from the Boy Scouts.

The roads through town were less traveled during the winter months, especially at Christmas when folks stayed at home. Except for the television, the house was quiet. I sat on the floor next to the tree, leaning my back against the paneled wall with Lonesome stretched out alongside me. I thought of my Grandmaw Grove, as I always did on Christmas Eve. Thought of the Christmas Eve dinners at her tiny house in the woods: the chestnut and cornbread dressing, the roasted turkey and baked ham, the stone fireplace in the small front room where we gathered, and the smell of the crackling wood. Grandmaw had died during one of the few snowstorms ever to hit Alabama. She'd ventured out in her nightgown to feed the birds, fell somewhere along the way, and wasn't able to get back up. Daddy was the one who finally found her. I was nine years old when it happened. Now, with Mama gone, I missed Grandmaw more than ever.

Miss Dorsey had invited us to spend Christmas day at her house. Her parents were coming into town from Cincinnati, she said. But I had already asked if I could go to Ruthie's, so Daddy and me would be spending Christmas apart.

I stared at the tree and its colored lights, the TV droning in the background. It was then that I saw a small stack of unopened Christmas cards underneath the branches. I figured they must have come in the mail earlier that day. I glanced over at Daddy. He had dozed off in his recliner. I picked up the cards and thumbed through them. The third one I came upon had my Uncle George's return address. I set the other cards aside, feeling my fingers tremble.

As soon as I opened the card, I saw my mother's face next to my own. The picture had been taken at the Fourth of July celebration in town the year before she died. She and I had our arms around each other, the cheeks of our faces pressed together. I instantly held a hand to my face, remembering the feel of my mother's skin against mine, the smell of her cologne. I missed the way she laughed, the way she chatted on the phone to her friends, the way she sang in the kitchen while she was fixing supper. My heart throbbed with a terrible ache as my eyes filled with tears.

I heard a truck rumbling up to the house, its headlights beaming through the drawn curtains of the living-room window. I slipped the picture and card in the envelope, then hurried to my bedroom and tucked the envelope under my mattress next to Mama's scarf.

Back in the living room, Daddy was still sleeping. I peered out from behind the curtains and saw Earnest's truck. Wiping my eyes,

I tiptoed through the kitchen and out the back door. Lonesome followed me outside, tearing off for the front of the house.

As I turned the corner, I saw Earnest stepping out of the blue Ford. The engine and lights had now been shut off. He was wearing a denim jacket and blue jeans and held a package in one of his hands.

Lonesome dropped his forelegs to the ground, his tail wagging vigorously in the air. Earnest bent over, tugging at Lonesome behind the ears. I hugged myself, feeling the cool earth underneath my sock feet. "He likes you," I said.

Earnest looked up and smiled when he saw me. "Ain't your feet cold?" The warm breath escaping from his mouth turned into a cloud of smoke.

I shook my head and walked over to him.

He stood up, holding the package out to me. "Merry Christmas," he said. He looked tall and handsome and wonderful.

The package was wrapped in white tissue paper and tied with red yarn.

"My mom made it for you."

"Thanks," I said.

"You can go ahead and open it."

I unwrapped the package. Underneath the paper was a long red scarf knitted from silky wool.

"Your mom made this?" I held it up to my face, laying my cheek against the soft yarn. "It's beautiful," I said.

"It's kind of her way of sayin' thanks."

I didn't understand.

"She wanted me to tell you that. For your mom."

"They knew each other, didn't they?" I asked, remembering the day his mother had called me May.

"Once," he said. "It was a long time ago. Your mom helped her out."

The outside light was switched on and the front door opened.

"I better be goin'," Earnest said.

I turned around to see Daddy standing in his undershirt and jeans, holding the door ajar.

"Wait. I've got something for you." I ran up the front steps and quickly ducked under Daddy's arm.

"Hello, Mr. Grove." Earnest looked calm, but I could hear a small quaver in his voice. Daddy still hadn't given his blessing to Earnest and me.

I slipped back into the house. Behind the Christmas tree was a small package I had wrapped for Earnest. I grabbed it and hurried outside. The storm door was now closed. Daddy was standing on the front stoop in his sock feet with his arms crossed over his chest. I opened the door and squeezed past him.

"You know, I've been seein' Miss Dorsey over at the high school," Daddy said.

"No, sir, I didn't know that."

I was now standing next to Earnest. Lonesome was stretched out against the back tire of Earnest's truck.

"She says you spend a lot of time in the library over there."

"Yessir."

Daddy just nodded his head, then turned to go inside, closing the front door behind him.

"What was that all about?" I said.

"At least he didn't go runnin' me off."

"Must be the spirit of the season." I rolled my eyes.

"That and Miss Dorsey." Earnest kicked his foot into the dirt.

"Merry Christmas." I handed him the package.

He looked up at me from underneath those thick lashes of his, and reached for my face, pushing my straight hair away from my eyes, his fingertips gently brushing my skin.

"Go ahead and open it," I said.

He carefully undid the ribbon and tape so as not to tear the paper, then looked at the small picture frame he held in his hands.

"I made it for you," I said.

He circled an arm around me, my neck fitting in its crook, and pulled me toward him so that my face came just below his shoulder. My nose pressed against the denim of his jacket. I inhaled the smell of crisp air, the smell of the woods, the smell of Earnest. He tucked his chin on top of my head. The picture frame with the flowers I'd pressed for him and arranged beneath the glass was held to his side in his other hand.

"I love you, Francie."

My blood felt warm and wonderful. I felt safe.

"I love you, too."

The next morning, I wrapped some of the popcorn balls in bright red cellophane and packed the others in a tin can. I baked an apple pie for Daddy to bring to Miss Dorsey's, and another for me to bring to the Taylors'. It was almost lunchtime when I finished. I put the food in a brown grocery bag along with my gift for Ruthie. Daddy offered to give me a ride, but I told him I'd just as soon walk.

I was dressed in a pair of jeans and a green sweater. After I put on my jacket, I wrapped the scarf Earnest's mom had knitted me around my neck and set off down the road with Lonesome. When I reached the driveway to Ruthie's house, I decided to keep going until I got to the tiny green house where Earnest lived with his mother.

Taking a deep breath amid the cold silence, I began down the gutted drive that led to the front door. The house appeared to be deserted. I told Lonesome to stay, then walked up the front steps. They were made of concrete and separated by at least three inches from the door frame, allowing me to see down the dark crevice to the bare ground.

I knocked a couple of times. Still there was silence. I knocked again and waited. Finally the brown curtains in the window to my right stirred, and I thought I saw a shadow. The door opened slightly, revealing the face of the woman I'd seen with the hoe.

"I just wanted to thank you for the scarf," I told her.

She nodded her head but didn't say anything.

"And I wanted to bring you something." I thought of the popcorn balls in my bag, but handed her the pie instead.

"Merry Christmas," I said.

The door widened just enough for her to take my gift.

"Earnest ain't here," she told me. "Went to take some food out to our friend."

I knew she was talking about the man who lived in the woods. "That's okay. My name's Francie." I held out my hand to her.

She looked down at it, hesitating for a second, before opening the door. "Ya wanna come in?"

"You sure?"

She nodded her head stiffly, and moved away from the door so I could enter. The house felt cold and empty.

"Ya wanna set or somethin'?" the woman asked me.

I took slow steps across the room, my eyes taking in the simple surroundings. On one side was a fireplace made out of brick which held a glowing handful of embers. Next to it was half of a whiskey barrel filled with wood and old newspaper. The room was small, with only a few items: a table painted light green with a kerosene lamp in the center, a box of matches, and a book. Except for a calendar from Daddy's store, which was thumbtacked to the wall next to the front door, the rest of the room was as bare as the wood floors, weathered and warped with age. There was a leeway off the back of the house which I assumed to be the kitchen, and I couldn't help but wonder where Earnest and this woman slept.

I took a seat at the small table, setting my bag on the floor next to me. The woman set the pie on the table, then bent over the fireplace, stuffing it with wood and paper and stoking it with a long stick. She had on men's Levi's that looked way too big for her and a gray woolen sweater. Her brown hair, thick and coarse and bushy, was as unkempt and wild as it was the day I first saw her. She wore a pair of red-and-blue striped athletic socks, all bunched at the ankles.

The fire soon became ablaze, and sent a wonderful warmth over the room. The woman turned around, pushing her sleeves up to her elbows. Her skin was tan, with a few freckles. Her eyes were a deep brown.

"My name's Laney," she said, holding out her hand.

I took her fingers in mine and smiled. Her skin was rough and her nails short and broken. She was tall and lean and mannish in her ways. As I watched her, I could only think of Earnest, they looked so similar.

"I got some coffee from this mornin'. I could warm it up if ya like," she said.

"That'd be nice," I told her.

She disappeared into the other room, which from where I sat looked like a dark closet. I heard the clinking sounds of dishes and utensils. When she returned, she took some wood from the barrel. "Ain't used to havin' company," she said, then carried the wood to the back of the house, where I assumed there was a stove.

On the table was a book by e. e. cummings from the high

school library. I picked it up, noticing the newspaper strips sticking out from the top edge.

"That belongs to Earnest," Laney said. She was now standing in the doorway with her hands in her pockets, watching me.

I laid the book back on the table.

"Coffee'll be ready in a minute." Once again, she disappeared into the other room. I watched the fire and waited, weighing each second carefully and wishing Earnest would return.

Within minutes the woman reappeared, holding two metal cups in her hands and a can of condensed milk. The coffee was hot and strong, sending up pyramids of steam.

"Ain't got no sugar," she said. "All out."

"That's all right." I took the can of milk and poured some into my coffee. Laney did the same.

"Thank you for invitin' me in," I said. "And for the coffee."

She didn't say anything. I picked up the cup, sipping from it slowly, feeling the liquid burn my tongue.

Silence hovered over the room. Laney had leaned back in her chair, her legs stretched out in front of her, the cup of coffee supported on her chest. She watched the fire, occasionally bringing the hot liquid to her mouth. I wondered whether I should have come.

Then Laney set her cup down, drew her legs up under her chair, and leaned in over the table. "They killed her," she whispered. "Our friend says so. And the boy saw."

Everything inside of me froze. I felt as though I was holding a deck of cards, and if I laid the wrong one on the table I would be out of the game, and the cards would be put away.

"What boy?" I asked cautiously.

"The Taylor boy. He was there."

"Tom?"

Laney shook her head impatiently. "Not Tom. The other one. He was there. Our friend knows. He brung him out of the woods."

Again I held the cards in front of me, carefully selecting my next move.

"You and my mom were friends, weren't you?"

Laney nodded her head stiffly and leaned back, her fingers spread over the table. "She saved my boy's life."

I drank the coffee, holding it close to my face. Laney picked up her cup and gulped down the rest of the hot liquid. Then she set the cup on the table and clasped her hands in front of her, her thumbs pressed together. She began rocking back and forth as if in a trance.

"Can you tell me what happened? How did she save your boy?" I asked.

"I promised my daddy I'd be good. I told him I would be. I never did nothin' wrong!"

Laney had slipped away. She wasn't speaking to me. It was as though I wasn't there, and suddenly I felt like an intruder. I knew she was sinking into a well of memory. Sinking deeper and deeper, and I would have to look within myself to find the rope to bring her back.

Again I drank the coffee, watching Laney. Her eyes remained transfixed on the fire, the blaze reflected in the brown pupils of her eyes.

"You miss her, don't you?" I said.

Laney looked at me, her eyes seeming to fold with curiosity, as if seeing me for the first time.

"She come in like an angel. Like God sent her to me. My friend, he'd gone to get Miss Rae. It was in the night. But instead, he brought your ma."

"Who is your friend, Laney?" I asked.

"He looks after us, me and Earnest."

"Is he the man in the woods?"

Laney nodded impatiently. "I was in the way, and the pains, they came on strong. Your ma come in with blankets and things. She held my hand and talked to me. She tell my friend what to do. And then my boy, he's born, but he ain't screamin', or breathin', or nothin'. He's all blue, and I start to hollerin', 'He's dead. My baby's dead.' But your ma, she holds that baby to her like he was her own. She puts her mouth over my boy's nose like God himself was whisperin' in her ear, tellin' her what to do. And then my boy, he starts to makin' sounds, and the blue starts to go away. And your ma, she looks down at him and says what an earnest face he has. Then she puts him in my arms and I know right then that's what I'll call him."

"Did you ever see her again?" I asked.

Again Laney looked at me as if she'd forgotten I was there.

"She come by once after that night. Come by on my boy's first birthday, bringin' him things. She stayed and talked to me a while, and that's when I know she is my friend."

Laney sat up slowly, as if hypnotized, and grasped the table with her fingers. "They killed her," she cried. "They killed my friend. Now she won't never come back."

"Who killed her?" I said, my heart quickening.

"The bad man."

"Who is the bad man, Laney? Tell me."

Again she leaned back in her chair. She lifted her hands to her face. "I told him not to do it, Daddy. I told him not to do it. I'm not a whore. I told him to stop. He wouldn't stop."

Laney began to cry.

"What is it, Laney? Talk to me."

But once more she had slipped away, and I knew she couldn't hear me.

Soon she dropped her hands onto her lap, again transfixed by the fire. The crying stopped, though I could still see the tracks the tears left on her cheeks.

I finished the coffee. My head felt foggy, as if clouds were wrestling inside of me. *The bad man? She had told him to stop. He wouldn't stop. And he killed Mama? He hurt Laney, and Mama, and Ruthie? Was Laney crazy, or did she really know what happened?*

The wind picked up outside. The naked limbs above the house made a scratching sound on the roof, like that of someone trying to get in. The fire began to die down. I picked up the long stick leaning against the brick and stoked the flame. Laney didn't move, didn't see me.

I took our empty cups to the small room off the house. It was still warm from the stove Laney had lit, which stood against the back wall. I washed the cups in a bucket of soapy water next to the stove, then dried them with one of the rags on the shelf to my left and stacked them with the other dishes and utensils. The shelf was mostly bare except for a few staples and canned goods from Daddy's store.

Underneath the shelf was a sleeping bag rolled out on the floor. On the other side of the room was a mattress and pillow covered with a wool blanket. On top of the pillow was another book from the library, a novel by William Golding. And leaning against the wall above the bed, on one of the exposed two-by-fours, was the frame I'd given Earnest. I sat on Earnest's bed, listening to the wind outside and wondering what it would be like to have a life like his. Next to his bed was a small hunting rifle and a cardboard box with some more of his belongings. Again the wind stirred and the limbs moaned.

I returned to the front room where Laney sat. "Thank you," I said. I laid a hand on her shoulder. She still didn't move. I lifted my bag and left out the front door, closing it quietly behind me.

Chapter 21
The Silent Cage

OUTSIDE LANEY'S SMALL HOUSE, Lonesome was waiting for me, his tail wagging when he saw me. I stroked him on the head, feeling peaceful inside. I thought of Mama holding Earnest. She had come in the night. She had saved Ruthie and she had saved Earnest. *Oh, Mama, why couldn't someone have saved you!* There were so many questions. Who was this man who had brought my mom to Laney and who was now friends with Earnest? How had my mom known him? Why had she come? And suddenly I felt an intense longing to be held. To feel safe.

Lonesome and I walked west along the road, the ground hard beneath our feet. The wind blew my hair, slapping it against my face. I thought of Earnest bringing food to his friend. Bringing food to a man who lived in the woods. A man isolated from the rest of the world and yet connected in some strange way.

As we turned onto the drive to Ruthie's house, I saw the smoke from the stove, smelled it as the wind now whipped around us. Two men stood next to the front door, passing conversation back and forth. One of them was smoking a cigarette, the other a cigar. A handful of cars were scattered across the lawn.

The front door opened and Willie and two of his cousins came running out, chasing each other behind the house. As the two men stepped back, one of them saw me. "Merry Christmas," he said.

"Merry Christmas," I offered back with a smile. I stepped between them and entered the house. Lonesome stayed outside. A host of family was gathered in clusters around the room. All around me was laughter and chatter and the smells of good food mixed with the strong scent of cedar from the tree the family had brought in from the woods. It stood in the center of the room, strung with popcorn and cranberries and construction-paper chains and pinecones dipped in glitter. Underneath it, amid the presents, was a wooden train set that had belonged to the Reverend as a small boy.

I set my bag on the floor and took out the popcorn balls and my present for Ruthie. Then I laid the gift under the tree and put the caramel balls on the table with the other food—a bowl of chestnuts, a basket full of pretzels, and lots of pies: chess, pumpkin, pecan. In the center of the table was a poinsettia wrapped in bright-red foil. Draped above the table were Christmas cards, taped to the ceiling with lengths of red yarn.

A group of women busied themselves in the kitchen area, laughing and talking as they worked. An older woman sat in one of the rocking chairs, her dark face a network of wrinkles, her eyes closed, her hair white and pulled in a bun behind her head. She began to rock, though she seemed to be asleep.

Alby was curled up in the recliner watching her. A knot formed in my chest and seemed to harden there as I thought of Laney and what she had said. *Had Alby watched my mother die?* He raised his hands in front of his face, his fingertips touching together, his eyes peering through the cage he had created, still watching the woman, as if he too would like to sleep, though all he could do was watch.

"Merry Christmas, Francie." Ruthie came up from behind. "I thought you'd never get here," she said, hugging me to her.

I pulled Ruthie into a corner. "I went by to see Laney," I whispered. "I talked to her for a long time. She invited me in."

Ruthie's eyes went wide. "You shouldn't have done that. Mama says never to go there." She glanced over her shoulder to make sure no one was listening.

"I know, but it was okay. Ruthie, she knitted me a scarf. She had Earnest give it to me. And she talked to me. She talked to me about my mom. Ruthie, there's so much I want to tell you. She knows so much. I can't believe it all. And Ruthie, Alby knows. He was there. He saw."

Ruthie looked long and hard at Alby across the room, then she shook her head. "She's crazy, Francie. She makes things up in her head. Everybody says so."

"But what if it's true? What if he did see? What if that's why he can't talk? Oh, Ruthie, what if it's true?"

Ruthie looked down at the floor, still holding onto my hands. "He was at the Lucases'," she said, remembering. "Him and Pappy Lucas's boy, Curtis, was friends. Then, the next mornin' when Daddy goes to get him, he isn't sayin' anything, and no one knows what's happened. Daddy talked to Mr. Lucas. He talked to all of them."

We were both speaking in whispers. "The big house," I said. "I saw Amos Lucas there. He was fighting a boy named Glenwood. Oh, Ruthie, what if Alby was there that night? What if he saw? How could Laney make up such a thing?"

"You saw Amos?" Ruthie let go of my hands and sat back on the floor. I sat down beside her.

"What is it, Ruthie?"

"I don't know," she said, shaking her head.

"Talk to me, Ruthie."

Her eyes were on the floor, searching, still remembering. "Mr. Lucas had gone out that night, Daddy said. He left Curtis and Alby with Amos, him bein' the oldest. He'd gotten a call. He's a mechanic. Works out of town a ways. A truck had broken down. Daddy talked to Amos, but he said nothin' happened. Said he was home all night."

"Ruthie, Earnest says Amos has been fightin' ever since he was fifteen."

"I don't know." Again she shook her head.

"Curtis would know. He would've been with Alby."

Ruthie's eyes now met mine. "Curtis and Amos's mom moved away over the summer. She took Curtis with her. No one's sure where they're at. Amos stayed around to work with his dad."

I slumped over and held my head in my hands. Ruthie reached out and touched my arm. "What about the picture?" she asked. "Have you heard anything from your uncle?"

I nodded my head.

"We'll know then," she said.

"I don't know, Ruthie. Maybe we shouldn't. Maybe we've gone too far. Maybe this is too big for us."

"Whatch you two girls talkin' so serious about?"

Mama Rae knelt on the floor, draping an arm over each of us.

"Nothin'." Ruthie looked away.

"Then why the blue faces?" She patted us on our backs.

"Francie, I seen all those caramel balls over on the table. Now, how is it your Daddy lets you bring all that good food over here?"

"Only thing Daddy cares about lately is that girlfriend of his," I said.

"Now, Francie." She sat down on the floor, pulling me to her. "A man's got to have somebody to share his bed with. Maybe that time's come for your Daddy. Don't mean he cares for you any less."

"Yes, ma'am." I frowned, disagreeing inside, but not wanting to cross Mama Rae.

"Your Daddy's a good man, Francie. He needs a good woman."

I nodded my head, thinking all the while about sharing my house with another woman, her lipstick in our medicine cabinet, her shirts being pressed on Mama's ironing board, her sleeping between Mama's sheets.

"You know what my mama always told me?" Mama Rae said.

"No, ma'am."

"For every sunset, there's a sunrise. You remember that, Francie."

Smiling, she hugged me with both her arms, and I wished

Daddy had him a woman like Mama Rae.

She pushed herself up off the floor. "Now it seems to me Ruthie's got a present for you hidden somewhere under that tree."

Ruthie grinned, and Mama Rae returned to the kitchen and the chatter.

"Go ahead," Ruthie told me, her face now full of smiles. "See if you can find it."

I searched every package, lifting up labels, crawling around the tree on my hands and knees. "Am I hot or cold?" I asked.

Ruthie laughed. With the tip of her finger, she pushed the wooden train around the track till one of the freight cars stopped in front of me. Inside it was a small red present. "Go ahead and open it."

I unwrapped the box, then held it to my face and slowly lifted the lid. "Oh, Ruthie," I breathed, laying the box in my lap.

"Earnest helped me make it. He drilled the holes."

Inside was a bracelet made from the stones at the creek.

"I can't believe it!" I smiled.

"I made one for me, too." She held up her wrist for me to see.

I asked Ruthie to help me put mine on. "You're my best friend, Ruthie. Always." I hugged her with all my might.

"I have something for you, too." I told her.

She searched under the tree until she found the present I had wrapped for her, then quickly tore off the paper. On one of my trips to Mayville with Daddy, I had found a book of poetry on friendship and had bought it for Ruthie.

She opened the book and began thumbing through the pages. "It's perfect," she said.

After dinner was finished, and the dishes were washed and put away, and the carols had all been sung, and the presents had been opened, and the conversations waned, I gathered my things to begin my walk home. Ruthie said she would walk with me. The two of us set off with Lonesome, turning our faces against the cool wind and the smoky black sky.

"It's a pretty scarf." Ruthie reached over to touch its soft fringe.

"She gave it to me on account of my mom," I told her. "That's what Earnest said." I wrapped the scarf up around my face and tucked my hands into the pockets of my jacket.

"Ruthie?"

"Yeah?"

"Do you believe in spirits?"

"Depends on what kind ya mean."

"Do you think people can get the spirits in 'em that make them do certain things or say things they normally wouldn't say?"

"Daddy's always preachin' about the spirits gettin' in people. The bad stuff livin' in them. So I reckon there's such a thing."

"What about good spirits? Do ya reckon there's such a thing as good ones?"

"I suppose. Why do you ask?"

"I was just thinkin', what about my mom or my grandmaw? What about their spirits? What if they got inside of me and started makin' me think certain things?"

"If they're good spirits, I don't think they'd still be wantin' to hang around here."

"You think they're up in heaven?"

"Uh-huh."

"But sometimes I feel like there's this other voice inside of me tellin' me stuff. Like goin' to Laney's. It was as though this voice inside of me was tellin' me to go, and I knew that's what I had to do. Do ya ever hear voices, Ruthie? Do ya ever feel like somethin' else is inside of you?"

"Sometimes I hear a voice," Ruthie said, her eyes staring up at the sky. "Sometimes it doesn't make a lot of sense to me, and sometimes it does. Like the day when I first found you at the creek. You was layin' off a good distance from where I was walkin'. At first I thought you was just restin' and I should leave you alone. But then there was something inside of me, almost like a nudgin', tellin' me you was hurt and it was up to me to do something. That's when I ran over to you, and when I saw you I thought for sure you were dead. Your skin was as white as any white folk I ever saw."

"Ruthie?"

"Yeah?"

"You reckon that was God's voice talkin' to you?"

"I reckon so."

"Ruthie, there was somethin' else Laney said. About Earnest. She said my mom was there when he was born. She said Mama saved his life."

Ruthie just kept walking, not saying anything. The night was quiet except for our own breathing and the sounds of our feet as they lifted and fell against the loose gravel.

"Maybe she's not so crazy," I said.

"Maybe so."

When we got to the house, Daddy wasn't home yet. I fixed Lonesome dinner, laying a Christmas cookie on top, then made Ruthie and me a pot of coffee. She sat down in Daddy's chair at the table while I set out the cups and spoons and a pitcher of milk.

"It seems so quiet," Ruthie said.

I sat across from her as we waited for the coffee. "I guess it is."

"Do you ever wonder how come your parents never had any more kids?"

"Mama said she had a hard time gettin' pregnant. Doctors told her she couldn't ever have kids. She used to say I was her miracle."

"Maybe you and Earnest'll get married and have a big family."

I smiled, my cheeks turning red.

"Ruthie?"

"Yeah?"

"Earnest told me he loved me."

"What did you say?"

"I told him I loved him too."

Ruthie nodded her head. "I'm glad. Earnest'll be good to you."

"You really think we'll get married?"

She smiled. "Yeah, I do."

"Hey, Ruthie?"

"Hmm?"

"You still wanna be a doctor?"

"I don't know. Been thinkin' I might wanna be a teacher."

"You'd make a good teacher."

I stood to get the coffee, then poured it into our cups. Ruthie stirred the milk into her mug, staring into the liquid and becoming quiet.

"Whatcha thinkin'?" I asked.

"I think I'm ready," she said.

And I knew what she meant. She wanted to see the picture. "Okay," I told her. I walked back to my bedroom and pulled the picture out from under the mattress. Before heading back to the kitchen, I stopped for a minute, holding my breath as I looked at Mama's face.

When I handed the picture to Ruthie, she simply nodded her head.

"You're sure?" A gut-shaking chill settled on my skin.

"I'm sure."

She pushed the picture to the center of the table, both of us looking at it. It was as though I was standing at the edge of an abyss and Ruthie was on the other side, both of us looking down where Mama lay.

"Ruthie, I'm afraid. Maybe we should leave it alone."

But Ruthie shook her head no, still staring at the picture. "I have to do something." Her voice was loud, breaking the quiet of the house. "Not just for me or for your mom, but for Alby. He used to laugh and sing. Now it's as though he's in a silent cage. Don't you see? If I don't set him free, there's no one else who will."

"Then you believe Laney."

"Yeah, I do."

She took a sip of the coffee, her eyes still on the picture between us.

"Should we talk to Amos? Find out if he was there that night with Curtis and Alby?" I asked her.

"I don't know. I don't think it's safe to talk to Amos. I've been thinkin' about talkin' to the new sheriff once he's in office. Maybe he'll know what to do."

"I'm still afraid," I said.

Ruthie looked up at me. "So am I."

Chapter 22
The Moon Man

I was slouched into the sofa watching *Gunsmoke* on the TV when Daddy walked into the living room and sat in his recliner. Instead of stretching out as usual, he planted his feet on the floor and glanced over at me like he had something on his mind. After about a minute, he stood, snapped off the television, and returned to his recliner.

"What?" I asked, looking back at him.

"I guess there's no other way to say it than how it is." He clasped his fingers in front of him and started twisting his thumbs around each other like he was real nervous about whatever it was he was fixing to say. Then he laid it on me.

"Bean, Fay and me are gonna get married."

"What?" My voice squeezed out of me sharp and high like breaking glass.

"We're gettin' married. Fay's wantin' a summer wedding, so we figure sometime in June after school's out."

I glared at him, stunned. "Maybe I don't want you and Miss Dorsey to get married. Maybe I don't wanna share our house with someone else. Ya could've asked me what I thought."

"Aw, Bean." Daddy stood up and walked over to the sofa.

"Fay likes you real well," he said, sitting next to me. "She'll be good to us."

"She can't cook," I shot back, not knowing where those words had come from, yet desperate to defend my ground.

"That's what I got you for." Daddy smiled and put his arm around my shoulder.

I stood up, shoving his arm away. My back was to him as I fumed toward the kitchen.

"Give it time, Bean," he hollered after me.

I reeled around and bore my eyes into him. "Give it time? Mama's not even been dead a year! How can you?"

Daddy's face dropped. I had him, and I wasn't going to let go. I'd been quiet for too long. "Mama's dead because she went looking for you! And now you're gonna bring some other woman in here?" The more I shouted at Daddy, the faster all the emotions stored up inside of me rose to the surface. "Didn't you even love Mama at all?"

Daddy looked up at me, his eyes all wet, his lips trembling. "Bean, of course I loved your Mama—"

I turned my back to him, almost running to the kitchen. My sneakers were beside the back door. I sat on the floor, my hands shaking as I tied the laces. Daddy was now standing in the doorway.

"Bean, look at me."

Lonesome was hunkered over his bowl by the table, lapping up his dinner in big sloppy gulps.

I grabbed my jacket and scarf off one of the kitchen chairs. "Come on, boy," I said. He lifted his head from his food hesitantly.

I opened the door; Lonesome trotted outside ahead of me. I

looked at Daddy. "If it had been you, Mama wouldn't have been so quick to fill your shoes." I turned and slammed the door as hard as I could, hoping it would make the whole house shake. I kicked my heels against the cold gravel as Lonesome and I walked up the drive, anger stirring in me so fierce I could feel the steam rising up the back of my throat.

It was a cold January evening. Dusk filled the hills with a purple haze. At the road, I turned toward town, Lonesome tromping alongside of me. The air smelled wet, full of the debris of winter. I passed the mayor's house. Just around the corner I could see the Methodist church, a brick building with large white doors and stained-glass windows arching to the ceiling. I stopped and took a deep breath, feeling as though heavy hands were pressing on my shoulders. Moving in slow but determined steps, I circled around to the cemetery at the back of the building. "I have to do this," I told Lonesome. I hadn't been to Mama's grave since the day she was buried. I hadn't wanted to think of her lying in the ground. And yet that night, as I thought of another woman taking Mama's place, I felt a voice inside of me telling me that's where I had to go, like God himself was nudging me on. Darkness had gradually taken over the sky, leaving only the lights from the town.

I walked past the church parking lot and climbed the hill in front of me. Looking over the vast rows of shadows from the cold tombstones, I felt as though I had been dropped into quicksand and told to breathe, as if all those slabs of marble and concrete were caving in on me. I tried to remember where Mama was buried. I walked toward the back row, passing so many markers, till I reached the woods. Then I saw it: her name carved in marble, a wreath of evergreen lying beside it. *Someone else has been here,* I thought. *Maybe Daddy.* I knelt on the ground, the tears stinging my eyes, the solid weight of reality lodged in my chest.

"Oh, Mama," I cried.

A gust of wind slapped across my face, bringing the smell of winter, of damp leaves, of dead wood.

"She knew you'd come," a voice spoke out from somewhere in the trees.

I gasped and looked around. Lonesome took off toward it, disappearing into the blackness.

"Who's there?" I yelled.

My eyes searched the edge of the woods. Footsteps against the dry earth came closer. A man appeared, tall and lean, stepping out of the dense wall of trees. He continued to approach me. My breath caught in my throat. I didn't move. "Lonesome!" I hollered. Within seconds he bounded out of the trees, running to me and almost knocking me over.

"Who are you?" I asked, my arms wrapped around Lonesome, my voice trembling.

The man continued to approach until he was about twenty feet away, allowing me to see his face. He was Earnest and Laney's friend, the same person who had spoken to Ruthie and me at the pond. Still, I was uneasy. Why was he here?

"I told her I would take care of you. I told her I wouldn't let them get you." His body stood like steel.

"What are you talking about? Who did you tell?" I could hear the nervous edge in my voice.

He tilted his head sideways. "Your mother," he said. "I promised her I'd look after you." His voice raised almost an octave, like he couldn't believe I didn't know what he was talking about.

"When did you tell her this?"

"That night," he said. "The night she was killed."

"You were there?"

He shook his head. "I was too late." He paused. "The boy knows. He was there."

"Alby?"

"Yeah."

"You know what happened that night? Tell me!" My voice was frantic, questions ripping inside my head like someone tearing a cold cotton sheet.

He sat down next to me, folding his legs Indian-style, resting his arms on his knees. His eyes were deep set. Shadows hung underneath them. I suddenly felt the urge to wipe them away, to reach up and touch his face.

He stared at the tombstone in front of him. "You're a lot like her," he said.

I followed his eyes to where Mama lay. "I miss her."

"I know. So pointless."

I remembered Mama standing at the edge of the trees, looking back. *Don't go!* I wanted to tell her. *Come back!*

"Please, you have to tell me what happened that night." My voice blurred with grief.

There was quiet, except for the wind tugging against my clothes and his.

"Each month the government gives me a check," he finally said. "Not much, but some. It helps. Helps the boy. Gives him food."

"Earnest?"

He nodded. "I pick the money up at night so no one will see me. Behind my father's house. His property runs next to yours."

"Your father? . . ." I interrupted. My hand reached out and touched his arm. He stopped talking and looked at me. The only neighbor whose property ran next to ours was Mr. Lampley. And then I remembered the pail Mr. Lampley had set over the white envelope behind the pen. I thought he was fooling with me when he said it was a bunch of money. Both of his boys had gotten drafted in the Second World War, he'd told me that day. Wade and Maurice. Wade wasn't ever coming home. "You're Maurice," I said, as if talking to myself. "You were friends with my mom."

He continued, "On one of the nights I'd gone to get my check, I saw her. She was running through the woods. That's when I followed her. I should have stopped her," Maurice said. His hands were now in tight fists, his voice strained. "I should have been there for her, but I was too far back. I was afraid for her to see me. Afraid for her to know I was watching. I kept at a safe distance, hiding behind trees, crawling in the brush. When I got there, I was too late."

"What did you see?"

"I saw your mother." He was now speaking more rapidly. "She was already on the ground. He was standing over her."

"Who?" I felt like I was pushing a giant stone out of the way, using everything I had to get answers.

"Harvey Mansfield."

My skin turned cold—the hate in Maurice's voice so strong.

Maurice went on, "He was wrenching his cap in his hands, muttering words to himself. He looked around but didn't see me or the boy. It was pitch black that night. Then he took off into the house.

"When I got to her, she was already dead, lying on her stomach, a stab wound in her back, a trail of blood down her dress. I looked up and saw the boy standing at the corner of the house. He didn't move, didn't even seem like he saw me. I led him away."

A hurt bigger than anything I had ever known rose in my chest until I was sure it would consume me. Now I knew. I covered my face with my hands. Aching sobs racked my body. Lonesome licked my hands, then leaned his cold nose against my neck. Maurice was quiet. When I finally looked up, I saw the tears in his eyes.

"I told her I would look after you," he said. "There was nothing else I could do."

"But she was already dead!"

"She knew."

My crying slowed. "There was a man along the woods one night. I saw him from my bedroom window. It was you." My voice was shaky.

"Sometimes I watch from the woods. If it's cold, I hide in the shed. But I'm always listening."

I thought of the shed behind our house. The only time I went out there was when I was working in the yard. "The red blanket. That was yours?"

"I never meant to frighten you. I just wanted to make sure you were safe." He stared at me for a few seconds. "Did you ever find your shoes?"

"You found my sneakers? You brought them to the house? Did you know about Tom? Were you there, too?"

"I saw."

"Why didn't you stop them?"

"Those boys, they work for Mansfield. It's best if no one sees me."

I thought about Phinny and his friends. The cow pies. "What about the day after school? Wasn't that you? They must've seen you!" I remembered how someone had scared everyone off and had gathered my books.

"You were on the ground." He paused. "Your mother. I kept thinking of her." His voice choked up.

My eyes focused on the tombstone, the Christmas wreath someone had brought her.

Maurice seemed to read my thoughts. "I loved her," he whispered.

I wasn't sure what he was telling me. Did he love her like I loved Ruthie? Or did he have the same feelings for her that I did for Earnest? "Did you bring the wreath?"

He nodded. "After I was sent to the war, your mom and I wrote for a while. We talked about getting married. 'Love always protects, always trusts, always hopes, always perseveres.' Your mother wrote that in her letters," Maurice said. "Always ended them with those words."

"Why didn't she wait for you?"

"She didn't love me the same way I loved her. I was only her friend."

His voice weakened as he told me this, letting me glimpse the hurt he still held onto.

"What about Laney? How do you know her? And Earnest?"

"Laney needed someone. She was young. Her parents threw her out when they found out she was pregnant."

"Has she always lived here?"

"She moved here when she was sixteen. Her parents were sharecroppers outside of town. That was before Mansfield." His voice stopped.

"What about Mansfield?" Just saying his name made my mouth taste bitter.

"The girls in this town aren't safe." His face was set in grim lines.

I knew what he was talking about. I knew the word *rape*. Immediately my mind flew to Ruthie, understanding full well what Mansfield could have done to her, and wishing he was dead. Wishing he had never lived.

"Laney's parents thought she was a whore. She wasn't a whore. It was Mansfield. He's the one who got her pregnant."

I was silent. *Mansfield got her pregnant? That was Mansfield's baby? Earnest was Mansfield's? No!*

Maurice continued. "He was the sheriff. She was poor white trash as far as anyone else was concerned. After her parents threw her out, she started living in the green house. It had been abandoned for years. I knew I had to look after her. Wasn't anyone else who would." Then, looking at me, he said, "You know, your mom helped her once. She helped Laney give birth to Earnest, and when he was born not breathing, your mom gave him breath."

I remembered what Laney had said. *Maurice went for Mama. Mama saved Earnest's life.* My heart sank. It was true. Laney was right. *Oh, dear God,* I thought. *Not Mansfield. Please, God, no!* My head rocked back and forth. I pulled my knees up to my chest, squeezed them close to me, my arms pressing against my shins till they hurt. "It can't be. It just can't."

Maurice's fingers touched the back of my head. "It's okay."

"No!" I yelled back. "It's not okay. Mansfield is his father. It will never be okay!"

He cupped his fingers around my shoulder, shook me gently. "Don't you know Earnest? Don't you know him by now?" he said, his voice firm. "When you look at that boy, who do you see? Do you see Mansfield? Or do you see your Mama and Laney and everything good?"

"I can't." I pressed my eyes into my knees. "Does Earnest know?" I asked.

Maurice let go of my shoulder. "No."

I felt his eyes on me, pleading. I knew what he was asking me—would I tell?

I rolled my head back and forth against my knees. "Why?" I said. "Why Earnest?"

"Your mama saved his life. She gave that to you. To everybody. Her own breath went into the boy's lungs. You think about that."

Maurice stretched out one of his legs. There was a long, angled pocket alongside the thigh of his pants. He pulled out an object wrapped in a strip of green tarp and handed it to me. I unwrapped the tarp. Beneath it was a knife with a black handle, the blade about four inches long. It looked dirty.

I held it closer, ran a finger over the flat side of the blade. It felt like dried dirt.

"It's blood," Maurice said.

I dropped the knife in front of me. Maurice picked it up. "It's a hunting knife. Mansfield usually kept it in a sheath on the outside of his belt. That blood doesn't belong to an animal."

He hesitated. For a moment, I didn't want him to go on. I wanted everything to be okay. I wanted to go back in time. I didn't want Mansfield to ever have been born. I wanted Earnest to have a nice father. I wanted Mama sitting beside me at the creek, tracing the freckles on my hands.

I shook my head. "No."

"I found the knife layin' on the ground next to your mom. Mansfield must have dropped it before he went back to the house. The next day he had McGee out there looking for it. They were all in on it. McGee, the coroner. They covered the whole thing up. Mansfield owns this town. The money from his gambling operation pays those guys' rent."

"Why? Why didn't you do something? You could have done something!"

He laid the knife on the ground in front of me and stood to go. "They say Laney's crazy," he said, staring off ahead into the blackness. "They say the same thing about me. But you . . ." He looked down at me.

He wanted me to stop Mansfield. He wanted me to stop all of them. "But I'm just a kid. What am I supposed to do?" I asked.

He didn't say anything.

"Talk to me." My voice was on the brink of tears. "Tell me what to do!"

"I've told you everything I know. Your dad made his choice. Now you have to make yours."

He turned and began walking away.

"You have to help me!" I cried. "You can't just leave!" I called out as he disappeared into the trees. He was gone, but I knew he would be watching, waiting.

I shook my head. This whole thing had taken on a dream quality—a nightmare—with Mama dead and all the terrible things Mansfield had done tied together to make one horrible web. Once my biggest worry had been getting through a test at school. Now I was being asked to face a murderer. I might as well have been asked to face the devil himself. Yet as I looked at the knife, I knew I had no choice. I picked it up, wrapped it back in the tarp, and carefully slid it into the pocket of my jacket.

I sat for a while longer, staring at the ground under which my mother lay. "Tell me what to do, Mama," I said out loud, but there was only silence. The wreath was leaning against the tombstone that marked her name, and I knew Maurice had been watching over her too.

A steady wind began to pick up. A drizzle fell. Lonesome stood, walked a few feet away from me, and looked back as if saying, "Let's go." The wind whipped stronger. Then the rain came, slashing through the sky in sheets. I held the jacket over my head and hurried with Lonesome around the church and down the hill to the road. We were halfway home when headlights approached from behind us. Daddy's truck pulled up. The passenger door opened. I climbed in, soaked to the skin. Lonesome jumped onto the floorboard beside my feet and laid his wet head on my knees.

"I've been lookin' for ya," Daddy said. "Not the best of nights to be out for a walk."

I didn't say anything. We rode in silence until we were in the driveway, the rain still beating down.

Daddy shut off the engine and reached for the door.

"Mama didn't hit her head," I said.

He froze, not saying anything.

"You saw the body," I pushed on. "You knew. Why didn't you do something?"

"You don't know what you're saying, Francie." Daddy breathed deeply. He let go of the door and turned toward the steering wheel. He wouldn't look at me. "I had no choice," he finally said.

I just shook my head.

"You don't understand, Bean. I owed him a lot of money from the gambling. It would've ruined us." His voice choked. "Bean, I'm sorry."

"How can you say you're sorry? Mansfield killed Mama, and you let him get away with it!"

Daddy reached for my hand. I flung it away.

"You don't know them," he said. "You don't know what they can do. The day you found me behind the store, that was Mansfield's people—one of the deputies that used to work for him, and Rolan, and a couple other men he's got shoveling his manure and doing all his dirty work. You seen what they did to me. Francie, if I had turned Mansfield in, no tellin' what they would've done to you or to me. I couldn't let that happen. Where would you be? Who would look after you?"

I knew how to look after myself, but I didn't say so. "So you knew! When Mama died, you knew it was Mansfield?"

He shook his head slowly, back and forth. The corners of his mouth pulled down; his chin began to tremble, his jaw tightened. He covered his face with his hands and dropped his head against the steering wheel. His shoulders lifted and fell and his voice tore out of him in moans with each breath he took. I thought I would die listening to him cry. *Oh, God, make him stop!* I thought. I reached my hand toward him, laid my palm over his back. I thought I should hold him, tell him everything would be okay, but I couldn't. Laying my hand there was all I could do. Why hadn't he done something? Why had he let Mansfield go?

Daddy leaned back against the seat. His crying slowed, though his breathing was still uneven. He wrapped his arms around me, cupping the back of my head in the palm of his hand, stroking my hair. "I would never do anything to hurt you," he said.

I closed my eyes, held them tightly shut, wanting so badly to believe everything from here on out would be okay.

Once in my bedroom, I slid the knife under my mattress, next to Mama's scarf and the picture my uncle had sent me. It had been a long time since I'd dreamed about the night Mama died. Ever since Daddy had brought Lonesome home, it was as though I had an angel guarding my sleep. But that night the dream returned.

Again I was following Mama into the woods. I was screaming,

shouting, trying to make her stop, but she kept going, moving faster and faster through the trees. There was a clearing just ahead where the big house stood. Finally I had caught up to her, but she was already dead, lying face down in the dirt, her dress soaked with blood.

The sheets were coated in sweat and tangled around my legs when I awoke. My clothes lay on the floor next to me in a pile. I rose, planting my feet on the cool wood. The house was quiet except for Lonesome's breathing. He was stretched out, using my clothes as a pillow. His eyes were open, watching me. I pulled my gown off over my head and quickly dressed. A dim light shone through the window of my room, casting a glow across the floor. I wondered if Maurice was watching.

It was as though I had brought Mansfield into my room with that knife. I had slept over my mother's murder. I didn't want any part of him in my room, in the house. I lifted the mattress part-way and pulled the knife out from under it.

Then I walked quietly to the kitchen, listening all the while for Daddy, wondering if he was awake, if he had heard me, but the house remained quiet. I slipped the knife into the pocket of my jacket. After wrapping the red scarf around my neck and face, I quietly left, letting Lonesome follow.

The rain had stopped. The sky was still smoky black, though beginning to clear, revealing the white light from a crescent moon. I turned toward town, walking hypnotically, as if in a dream. The night air was cold, my breath like smoke though my body perspired. When I got to the bend, I took a right off the road, a route I had not taken for years. Trees lined the sides of the broken pavement with blackness. Soon, I caught the thick smell of pine as the road carved its way through a grove of cedar.

I wished I had brought my flashlight. It had been a long time. Lonesome and I walked about another mile, when I recognized the driveway to my right. The gravel had eroded. In the distance I saw the shadow of Grandmaw Grove's house, and as I drew closer, the boards Daddy had nailed across the door and windows. It looked much smaller to me now. The wood steps were hollow underneath and sagged in the middle. They moaned and shifted as I sat on them. I remembered the way it had felt running up these steps, the door banging behind me. I could hear my grandmaw's voice in my head, the sounds of the cupboards and dishes. For a second, I thought I could still smell the stove heat.

I took the knife, wrapped in its piece of tarp, out from my pocket. Leaning over the steps, I laid it on the ground underneath them. I searched the trees around me before leaving, but saw no one.

When Lonesome and I returned home, the house was still quiet. I looked at the clock on the kitchen wall. It was already three in the morning. I laid my jacket and scarf on the table, then sat in Daddy's recliner in the living room, too restless to go back to bed.

The curtains were drawn. The room was dark. I switched on the lamp next to the chair, the one Daddy used when he read the paper. The bookshelf to my left was filled with stacks of *National Geographics*, newspapers, and some old textbooks from when Daddy was in school. All of a sudden, I noticed a black Bible which neither Daddy nor I had ever opened on the end of one of the shelves.

I stood from the chair and walked over to it. A layer of dust coated its edges. As I blew the dust away, I wondered if the Bible had belonged to Mama. But Daddy had gotten rid of all her things. I sat back in the chair, holding the book in my lap. Just inside the cover was written, "Presented to May McElhaney." I thumbed through the pages. There was an envelope tucked toward the back. I opened the letter, the paper crisp and fine, and set the envelope aside.

Dear May,

It's 1:15 in the morning and I can't sleep. I read your letter like a bad dream. I have loved you for as long as I can remember, and now you're telling me you love someone else. I'm supposed to be fighting a war. Instead I want to die. You promised to wait for me. I saw a man die yesterday. I wished it was me. How can you love someone else? If I wasn't so far away, would you still love him? You say I've changed. Who wouldn't in this Godforsaken war? God, how I pray I could travel back in time, just to see you, to hold you.

You asked me if I believe in marriage, if I believe in love, if I believe in God. You say these things are important. But how can I believe in anything when I'm at war? I believe in death. It's all around me. How can I know anything else? I've already lost my brother. Will I be next? You don't feel this way, I know. But you're not here.

Don't do it, May. Don't marry Hank. How can you? Wait. The war will end. It has to. "Love always protects, always trusts, always hopes, always perseveres." I love you, May.

Maurice

I read the letter several times, then carefully returned it to its envelope, closed the Bible and held it to my chest. "Love always protects, always trusts, always hopes, always perseveres." I thought of Mama, Maurice, Earnest. "Love always protects . . ." I knew at that moment I could never tell Earnest that Mansfield was his father. No matter what happened, I would always keep that secret to myself.

Chapter 23
The Knife

THE DAY AFTER I TALKED TO MAURICE, I met Ruthie at the creek. I told her everything Maurice had said except for the part about Mansfield being Earnest's father.

"We were right," Ruthie said.

We sat so still, it was as if we were both experiencing some sort of shell shock. Maurice had given us the certainty we needed to go forward.

"I think it's time I talked to the sheriff," Ruthie told me.

"You want me to go with you?"

She shook her head. "I'm going to tell Mama and Daddy first. They need to know. I'll see what they say after I tell them."

         ❧   ❧   ❧

A couple of days after Ruthie and I talked, I went by the filling station to see Earnest just as he was getting off work.

"You all right?" he asked when he saw me.

"Wanted to see you about something," I said. "Thinking you could drive me out to my Grandmaw's house. Maybe we could talk there."

"Me and you okay?" he asked, alarmed.

I reached out and squeezed his arm. "We're fine," I said.

"Just got some things I need to get off my chest."

"Okay, sure." His eyes narrowed with concern. He walked with me over to his truck and opened the door for me to climb in.

Earnest rolled his window down against the sun that was beginning to set over the hills while I gave him directions. The road curved around to the right. "Over there," I told him, pointing just ahead of us. Earnest slowed the truck and turned onto the small driveway, then stopped just in front of the tiny clapboard house. Everything looked much different in daylight—more overgrown, more deserted. I realized how badly the place needed work.

"I bet it wasn't a bad piece of property in its time. Could still be a nice place," Earnest said.

I frowned. "Just look at it. All boarded up and overgrown like it is. There used to be flowers, and a stone path up to the front steps, and a garden in the back."

"Could still be flowers and a garden. Just needs a little attention, that's all. And a little paint."

"Earnest?"

"Yeah?"

"I'm gonna fix this place up one day. I'm gonna make it a real nice place to live."

"Ya might need somebody to help ya." He smiled, casting his eyes over at me.

I grinned back. "Suppose I will."

His face moved toward me, and his lips touched mine. I reached my arms up around his neck, tangling my fingers in his thick hair. He held me close, running his hands up and down my spine, making me feel like I'd just crawled within the walls of a mighty safe place.

Slowly, I pulled back. "There's somethin' I want to show you." I slid over to the passenger door and got out.

He followed me up to the front steps. I knelt on the ground and reached for the knife. As I wrapped my fingers around the tarp, I let out a sigh of relief, thankful that it was still there.

"What is it?" Earnest asked.

I sat next to him on the steps and unrolled the knife from the tarp. "It belonged to Mansfield," I told him.

My voice trembled and my eyes burned with tears as I told him how Mansfield had killed Mama. Earnest's whole body tensed. "That bastard!" he yelled through his clenched teeth.

Neither of us said anything for a couple more minutes. Then Earnest looked at me. "Francie, I'm so sorry. I knew he was bad. I didn't know he was that bad."

I wrapped the knife back in the tarp.

"What are you going to do with it?" Earnest asked.

"I don't know yet." I reached down, returning the knife under the steps.

"There's something else I think you should know," I said. I took his hand in mine, clasping my fingers between his. "The night Mama was killed, Ruthie was there. Mansfield was trying to hurt Ruthie. Mama made him stop. That's why he killed her. Ruthie got away."

Earnest drew his breath in long and deep. "That son of a bitch!" His face wound itself tighter than I'd ever seen it. "That son of a bitch!" he yelled again. His fingers gripped mine so hard, both our hands started turning white.

"Ruthie wants to talk to the sheriff," I told him.

Earnest looked away, his fingers still bearing against mine. "The law didn't do a lot of good when your mama was killed."

"Yeah, but this time the law's in different hands. Daddy says Mr. Lawson's a good man."

"Forget Lawson—what about Mansfield? No tellin' what he'll do to Ruthie or you once he knows Ruthie's talked. I don't like it."

"He killed Mama, Earnest. He tried to hurt Ruthie. Someone has to stop him."

"Why Ruthie, or you?"

Earnest loosened his grip, though still held on. He reached for my face with his other hand, his eyes looking straight back at me. "I'm worried about you. I'm worried about both of you."

"I know," I whispered. "But we have to do this. We're the only ones."

He looked away, rubbing his thumb back and forth over my hand. "I'm sorry about your mom," he said again. "I don't know what to say."

I leaned my head into his shoulder. "Not long after Mama died, I kept having this dream that I was following her into the woods the night she died. I was trying to save her, but I kept losing sight of her among all the trees. I couldn't catch up to her," I told him.

"A few nights ago, the dream came back. Only this time I followed Mama to the big house. By the time I got to her, she was already dead. I couldn't help her. I was too late. I have to do something. Don't you see? It's as if the dream is trying to tell me something. I can't bring Mama back, but I can still do something. I can put Mansfield away. I can make sure Mama didn't die for nothing."

Earnest raised my hand to his mouth and held it there. "Be careful," he said, his breath against my skin.

Not long after I'd met up with Earnest, Ruthie said she'd told her parents everything and that they were going to take her to see Sheriff Lawson. That's why I wasn't surprised to find the sheriff's car parked in our driveway one cold February evening when I was on my way back from town.

Inside, Sheriff Lawson and Daddy were sitting across from each other at the kitchen table, Daddy with an ashtray out in front of him and a cigarette hanging from his mouth, Sheriff Lawson holding a cup of coffee.

Sheriff Lawson set the cup of coffee down. "A friend of yours came by to see me today," he said.

Daddy tapped his cigarette into the glass ashtray, then raised it to his mouth again.

My hands went clammy. *There is no going back now.*

Sheriff Lawson pulled out the chair next to him for me to sit down.

I set my books on the counter and joined him and Daddy at the table.

"Her parents brought her over," the sheriff said.

I tucked my hands under my legs and planted my feet on the floor.

The sheriff gave me a long look. "I guess you know about her and Mr. Mansfield?"

"Yessir. I know."

"And your mother?"

"Yessir."

"Can you tell me about it?"

"I know my mother was killed." I looked at Daddy. He had now stabbed his cigarette out and crossed his arms over his chest. I thought about the knife. Thought about telling the sheriff about it, yet something inside of me held those words in. Having the knife made me feel like I had power over Mansfield. I wasn't ready to give that power away, not yet. "Ruthie saw a picture of my mom. She recognized her as the woman who saved her, who stopped Mansfield from . . . We know Ruthie was there the same night Mama died."

Sheriff Lawson took a deep breath, then let it out slowly. "We're going to reopen the case," he said.

"You can do that?"

"That's what I came to talk to you and your daddy about.

Wasn't ever a case to begin with. Between the gambling debts everyone owes him and the bribes, it seems Mansfield's got half the town in his back pocket."

Daddy hung his head over his chest, avoiding my stare.

"Gonna have to start askin' questions," the sheriff went on. "Folks aren't gonna like it real well."

I met his eyes. "Alby saw. Alby Taylor. He was there."

He nodded his head. "I know. Francie, I don't want you walkin' alone. You or the Taylor girl. Till we know how this thing's gonna all come out. Maybe you and Ruthie ought'n be together either. For the time bein'. Be safer that way. Don't want you drawing any attention to yourselves."

"I have to talk to Ruthie."

Mr. Lawson and Daddy looked at each other. "Can you call her?" the sheriff asked.

"They don't have a phone," Daddy said. He uncrossed his arms and reached for his carton of cigarettes. "You can see her tonight. I'll drive ya over."

"You really think they would hurt us, don't you?" I asked Mr. Lawson.

Again, the deep breath. "I don't know."

●   ●   ●

Daddy made us both a sandwich for dinner, but all I could do was stare at the table.

"I'll wrap it up. You can eat it tomorrow," Daddy said. He put the dishes in the sink, then grabbed his keys and jacket. "Gonna be all right, Bean. You and your friend did the right thing. I wish I could've done it months ago."

When we got in the truck Daddy was quiet, his jaw set. His face looked tired, like he'd been through the wringer. I guess he had. Only it was the guilt that had been doing the wringing.

"It'll all be over soon," I told him.

He reached over, taking my hand, holding it tightly. "Sometimes I'm not sure if I'm talkin' to you or to your mom."

The sky was pitch black when we pulled up to Ruthie's. Daddy stopped the truck just in front of the house. Mama Rae and the Reverend met us at the door.

"Come on in." She waved us inside. "Got some coffee on the stove."

The house was unusually quiet. Alby was curled up in the recliner. Tom was sitting at the table. Ruthie appeared in her sock feet from the back of the house, wearing jeans and an oversized T-shirt. I wrapped my arms around her and hugged her for a long while.

"I talked to the sheriff," she told me.

"I know."

We walked back to her room and crawled up on the bed, facing each other. Rachel was studying on the floor, her books spread out in front of her.

"Hey, Francie, got some baby chick eggs in the barn fixin' to hatch. Wanna see?"

"Maybe some other time, Rachel," Ruthie said.

"It's for Ruthie's school," Rachel told me.

I looked at Ruthie.

She shrugged. "It's my science project. Rachel, we can show Francie later."

Rachel closed her books and left the room.

"How are you?" I asked.

"The truth?" Ruthie sighed. "Scared out of my wits. But I know I've done the right thing."

"What all did you tell him?"

"Everything. Just like I said I would. And Mama and Daddy, they were sittin' right there. And I told him about Alby." Ruthie reached out and clasped my fingers in hers. "Francie, there's been others. The sheriff told me so. Mansfield's bad, Francie."

"What do you mean others?"

"Others he's tried to hurt. Other girls like me. Young girls. Some younger than Rachel."

"I'm scared for you," I told her. "If there were others, then maybe you didn't need to talk to him! Maybe the sheriff already had enough to put Mansfield down."

"They're just as scared as we are, Francie. And the sheriff, he wants to get Mansfield on murder. Wants to put him away for good. You see, Francie, I had to talk to him. Not just for me and Alby, or you, but for all of them."

"I don't understand. If there's been others, why haven't they arrested him?"

"Sheriff Lawson says there's two other girls that came to talk to him with their parents. Says they talked to Sheriff McGee when it happened, but he didn't do anything. Told the girls they were makin' it up. Sheriff McGee was probably gettin' paid. Paid off by Mansfield. And there's probably other girls, only they're too afraid to talk."

I shook my head. "Wouldn't have done any good anyway."

"But things are different now," Ruthie said.

"Mr. Lawson says we have to be careful. Says we can't see each other anymore."

"I know. It's just for now, though."

I looked at Ruthie, so sure, so strong. And suddenly I felt as though I had a watermelon lodged in my throat. "I love you," I said, my eyes burning with tears.

She laid the back of her hand against my face, then hugged me to her. "You're my best friend, Francie. Always."

Chapter 24
The Day the Chickens Hatched

IT WAS SUNDAY, MARCH ELEVENTH. Daddy and I had just gotten home from church. I had changed into jeans and a sweatshirt and was sitting at the kitchen table, about to eat lunch, when I heard a truck drive up to the house. Outside, the sun was hazy, the air wet. I went to the front door. Reverend Taylor's Chevy was in the driveway. He climbed out, leaving the engine running, and walked toward me, wringing his hands. Lonesome darted out the door to greet him.

"Francie, have you seen Ruthie? She disappeared this mornin'."

Daddy was standing behind me now. He laid a hand on my shoulder. "Dear God," he said, his voice barely audible.

I ran inside and grabbed my shoes, a sudden quickening in my blood. I stumbled past Daddy and down the steps toward the Reverend's truck. Lonesome was already in the bed of the truck, his head leaning out over the side. "Let's go," I said, climbing into the passenger seat and closing the door behind me. My mind felt numb, as though my head had just been submerged into ice water. I couldn't think. All I knew was I had to find Ruthie.

The Reverend drove without speaking, tapping his thumbs against the steering wheel impatiently, staring straight ahead at the road. It began to rain—no thunder, no lightning—just rain, as though it had come from nowhere.

"We'll never find her now," he said.

The windshield wipers slapped back and forth in front of us. "What happened?" I asked.

"Rachel been out to the barn. We was gettin' ready for church. Then she come runnin' in sayin' the chicks had hatched. Ruthie went out to check on 'em. More than two hours ago. That was the last we seen her." His voice stopped abruptly as his throat tightened around his words.

My fingers dug into my jeans. "We'll find her," I said.

The Reverend didn't say anything else. He just drove, the tires speeding through the wet gravel road, the engine pushing. We turned onto the driveway for Ruthie's house, the rain slowing down. As we climbed out of the truck, Mama Rae approached us. Her face was drawn, the apron over her dress wrung up in her hands. Lonesome leaped out beside me.

"The sheriff's on his way," she said. "Any minute now."

A host of colored faces stood around her.

"We've scoped everywhere," Tom said, his hands hanging on his hips, his face dripping from the rain. "There's no sign of her. Amos is bringin' his dog. We'll keep lookin', Dad."

"The rain's gotta stop. My God, let the rain stop." The Reverend's eyes were to the sky. The weight of his pain pulled on his face in a terrible way. "Dear God, this is my Ruthie!" His fists went to his face, covering his eyes. Mama Rae laid a hand over his shoulder.

I looked around for the others, for Rachel and Willie. Then I saw Alby sitting in the mud against the side of the house, hugging himself with his arms, his face tucked into his knees, his feet bare. Lonesome jumped out of the bed and trotted toward him. I watched as he nuzzled Alby's neck.

Within minutes another truck pulled up, Amos's dog barking in the back. Tom jogged toward it with one of Ruthie's shirts. The Reverend took off in another direction with a group of men from the church.

A pale yellow glow began to cover the sky. A light through the mist of the rain. An arm pressed against my back. As I turned, I saw Earnest, and buried my face against his shoulder. "Let's go," he said.

Lonesome followed us to Earnest's truck and jumped into the bed. As the engine started, the sheriff's car pulled in. Earnest drove around it and onto the road.

"What have they done to her, Earnest?" My breathing was fast and shallow, my body shaking.

"We'll find her," he said, his hands gripping the steering wheel, his eyes forward.

"Dead or alive?"

He didn't say anything.

"Oh, God!" I cried, dropping my face to my knees.

"They'll pay," Earnest said. "Whatever they've done to her, they'll pay."

Earnest pulled the truck off to the side of the road, just before the creek.

"She wouldn't have come here, Earnest. Not alone. She knew better."

"Where do you wanna look?" His eyes searched the woods around the creek. "They've scoped the entire area behind the Taylors' house and barn. Maybe someone brought her here."

"Mansfield," I said. "We have to find Mansfield."

"It wouldn't do any good. He won't talk. The sheriff's probably on his way there now anyway."

"Okay, okay. We'll start here!"

Earnest and I searched the banks of the creek, the field, the woods all the way to the pond. Lonesome stayed a good fifty feet ahead of us.

"What if she's in there?" I said. "What if they drowned her? Earnest, she could be anywhere!"

"She's not in the pond. She'd still be afloat. We have to think."

He stood still for a second, his jaw pulling forward. Hours seemed to pass. Seconds ticking away. Time vanishing before us. He grabbed my hand. "Come on."

I held an arm over my stomach. "I can't. Oh, Earnest, I can't. Something's wrong. It hurts, Earnest. Oh, God, it hurts so bad!"

Earnest turned to hold me. My whole body seemed to collapse as he wrapped his arms around me.

"We've got to find her, Francie," Earnest whispered in my ear. "We've gotta go."

I took a deep breath, pulling myself together with all my might.

We climbed into the truck. The sky had turned to blue. Earnest drove back to the Taylors'. Daddy's truck was parked near the house. A tall colored man walked up to Earnest's window, shaking his head. "Still lookin'," he said. More cars and trucks were scattered across the lawn. Mama Rae was sitting on the steps, one arm around Rachel, the other around Alby who had his head tucked into her bosom, his knees still drawn up to his chest. She looked up and saw me. I wanted to run to her, to bury myself under her arms.

Earnest reached for my hand. "I'll be right back," he said. He squeezed my fingers with his, then let go and climbed out. He said something to a couple of the men. They shook their heads. He approached another. "Oh, God!" I cried. The pain racked my body with silent sobs. I buried my face in my knees so no one would see. Too many memories flooded my mind all at once.

"God is with her." The voice was strong, rich. Ruthie's voice, all grown up.

"Oh, Mama Rae!" I cried.

She was standing beside the truck. Her arms reached through the rolled-down window. Her hands held my face, her fingers warm against my skin. She cried, too, the tears streaming down her cheeks. The two of us clasped onto each other.

Earnest returned to the truck, bringing me a cup of water from the house. I drank it quickly. He touched my face, stroking it gently. "We'll find her," he told me.

Again we were on the road.

We drove toward town, past Daddy's and my house, past the hemlock and spruce, past the sidewalks. We turned the corner and pulled into the gas station. Some black men gathered around one of the trucks, talking to Mr. Lampley. I knew they were talking about Ruthie. The Taylor girl, they called her. I knew they, too, had been searching for her. Earnest filled up his tank with gas. "Oh, God, help us," I prayed.

As I got out of the truck to stretch my legs, I saw the white Ford pickup with the Rebel flag hanging in the back window. Randy and Jason got out of it and walked over to the soda machine, the cuffs of their jeans and their boots covered with black mud. Earnest saw them, too. He returned the gas cap and approached them. I walked over to their truck, telling Lonesome to stay. Cigarette packs and trash were scattered across the floor-boards. The mats were covered with the same black mud I'd seen on Randy and Jason's boots and jeans. I looked in the bed of the truck. Leaves. A couple of beer bottles. Then I saw the handful of small brown stones, like the ones at the creek. I reached over the side, held a few of them in my hand. I rubbed my fingers over them and felt the tiny holes. Sickness washed over me like ice water. Shattering screams racked inside my head: *No! Dear God, no!* I clasped my fingers shut, closed my eyes.

"What the hell are you doin'?"

I turned around abruptly. Randy and Jason were walking toward me.

The voice kept screaming in my head—*No! Please, God, no!*— hate and fear clawing my gut. I walked back to Earnest's truck, my legs stiff with rage, and that cold sickness all over me. I climbed in and slammed the door shut.

Earnest got in beside me and started the engine. "They did it," I told him. I held out my trembling hand, the stones from Ruthie's bracelet pressed into my palm. The matching bracelet Ruthie had given me still circled my own wrist. Earnest closed his eyes slowly and looked away. Jason and Randy pulled off, their tires screeching.

"Take me to my grandmaw's," I said, my voice strange to my own ears. Earnest pulled out of the gas station. At the edge of town, he turned down the county road toward my grandmother's house, neither of us saying another word.

When we pulled up to the tiny clapboard house, I looked over at Earnest before getting out. "It's Mansfield," I said.

He nodded his head. "I know."

I slipped the stones into my front pocket and climbed out, again telling Lonesome to stay. I slid my hand underneath the first step, felt for the knife, then wrapped my fingers around it. I tore off the piece of tarp, dropping it on the ground.

"You planning on doing any hunting?" Earnest asked when I climbed back in the truck.

"I want to see Mansfield," I said. "I want to see him face to face."

"We have to find her first."

I pushed the pain down as far as I could. "She's my best friend," I cried.

"I know."

Earnest reached for my hand.

"There's a bog off in the woods," I told him. "I found it one day when taking a shortcut to the Taylors'. The mud's like tar back there. It's off the same trail I've seen you take when you're coming from the store."

"What are you saying?"

The pain was rising like a fist inside me. *Oh, God, what was I saying? The mud on Randy and Jason's truck. The mud on their jeans. What had they done to her?*

"Take me there," I said.

"We need to get the sheriff," Earnest told me.

"Take me there," I insisted, my words sounding far off, as though I was speaking through a tunnel.

Earnest backed the truck onto the road, the sun low and in our eyes. He took a left onto the side street that looped around town, then pulled over a few feet from the opening of the trail, the same trail I had walked when I had seen Tom and Randy and Jason. The day Punkin's kittens were killed. I closed my eyes tightly, the tears falling down my face.

Earnest turned off the truck and started to get out. "I'm coming with you," he said.

"No!"

He grabbed my arm. "Francie, I'm not leaving you!"

He let go of me and we both jumped out of the truck, slamming the doors behind us. We took off running down the trail, Lonesome bounding a good twenty or so feet ahead of us. I felt like we couldn't run fast enough, the limbs snagging our clothes and scratching our faces. Everywhere there were trees. An awful panic took hold of me. What if I couldn't remember where I had left the trail—where I had seen Tom and his friends? Deep into the woods, I stopped.

"What is it?" Earnest was standing behind me, so close I could feel his breath on my neck.

"I don't know. I can't remember." My eyes were searching all around. New leaves had already begun filling the branches of the hardwoods; cedars were scattered everywhere. "Oh, God, why can't I remember?"

Again I moved forward. "Ruthie!" I yelled.

Earnest began to yell her name with me.

It was then that Lonesome disappeared from the trail, tearing off into the thick trees and brush.

"Let's go," I said, taking off toward him, my arms out in front of me as I held limbs aside. Ever so often we would stop to listen for Lonesome's lead.

Deeper into the woods from the trail, the soil turned black. "Ruthie!" I cried, my eyes scoping everywhere. I still held the knife in my hand, and yet I felt as if it was inside of me, twisting in my chest. We kept walking. Kept searching. The smell of woods, of wet leaves and pine needles, clung to us like a drenching sweat. My fingers were numb. My body felt like a machine—walking, moving, pulling me forward. And time, slipping away, dissolving before us. We moved faster, panicked.

The smell of fresh dirt cut through the air. *Someone has been here.* My head spun. Something was different. I heard Lonesome barking, but I couldn't see him. Earnest took my arm, holding me back. I tore myself away, stumbling forward. The smell of freshly turned dirt grew stronger. My eyes spotted an opening in the trees, a clearing. There I saw Lonesome, digging frantically. Earnest and I raced forward. I dropped the knife, my feet tripping, my blood roaring in my head. "No!" I screamed.

Earnest and I quickly fell to the ground, digging through the loose soil. Lonesome whimpered and dug beside us, the dirt piling up all around. Then I felt the touch of her shirt beneath my fingers. I let out a scream and reached my hands deeper into the ground, holding onto my friend, pulling her up with everything I had. I lifted her to me, her body, curled up as if in a womb, becoming stiff. I wrapped my arms around her, laid her head against my chest, stroked her hair, kissed her cool cheek, cried into her neck. The sound of my own sobs and Earnest's echoed through the woods.

The sky deepened around us.

Earnest laid a hand over my head as I continued to hold Ruthie, my body rocking to and fro.

"We have to get the sheriff," he finally said.

"I can't leave her."

He kissed my head.

"I can't leave her," I said again, the crying twisting itself through my body, every part of me shaking.

"I'll get the sheriff." Earnest's voice was a wreck. "I'll be right back."

He kissed me again, and stood to leave.

I kept rocking Ruthie back and forth, crying into her cool skin as the sound of Earnest's feet pulled away from us. The day was ending, though it had just begun. The hours had vanished; the life was gone. Dark pines towered above me. The sun was sinking lower. I was gasping for air, the sweat on my body beginning to dry, chilling me all the way through. I held Ruthie's wrists in my hands. The bracelet was gone. She still wore the white T-shirt she had slept in the night before. She had run out to see the chickens. Rachel said they had hatched.

Gently, I laid my friend on the ground and kissed her forehead. Then I scrambled around on my hands and knees, searching for the knife as tears dripped down my face and off my chin. I found it a few feet away, clutched the black handle tightly, and rose to my feet. Still crying, still gasping for air, I ran. Lonesome took off with me, both of us darting through the woods. I didn't feel lost anymore; it was as if everything had become clear. I kept pushing my way forward, farther and farther, my breathing grating in my lungs, my heart hammering in my chest. I stumbled, but didn't fall. Lonesome stayed within ten feet of me.

I was now on the back side of Daddy's and my house. I could barely see it through the woods, the same woods where I had watched Mama disappear from my window. I was climbing a hill, adrenaline flowing through me like a strange kind of poison, my mouth dry. I tried to spit, but nothing came out. I kept moving up another hill. From the top I could see the big house. Then the truck, the blue Chevy, parked off to the side. Hate boiled inside of me. My heart beat faster as Lonesome and I moved down the hill. *"I almost died once, but a beautiful angel came and saved me."* The house was now before me and slightly to my left. I grabbed Lonesome by the collar, making him stay. The two of us stood between the house and the truck. A door to the building opened; footsteps came toward us. Lonesome stood at attention, his eyes pinned forward. Mansfield turned the corner, his head down, not seeing us at first.

"You killed her," I said, my voice clear and strong, the knife against my side.

He stopped directly in front of us.

A grin stretched across his face. He began to laugh, his voice blasting in my ears. My body screamed with hate. "Why?"

His laugh continued. He took a few steps toward me. I felt Lonesome's body tense next to mine. A low, even growl started up inside of him.

"You killed Ruthie, and you killed Mama." My voice was steady and deep, though my chin trembled with rage. I held the knife out in front of me, tight in my fingers.

Mansfield's eyes shifted to my hand. The smile on his face dropped. "Where the hell did you get that?" He stepped toward me. I gripped the knife tighter.

"You little bitch!" His left arm raised behind him, his long strides moving quickly toward me.

Lonesome's growl exploded from the back of his throat, his body lunged forward, bounding off the ground, his teeth bared, his jaw open. He grasped Mansfield's arm, knocking him down.

"Get him off me!" Mansfield was kicking and yelling, his body sprawled out in the dirt. Lonesome was on top of him, his teeth still tearing into Mansfield's arm.

"You killed them!" I screamed.

The sound of sirens roared toward us.

"Get him off me!"

The sirens grew louder, engines coming closer from the front of the house. Within seconds, flashing lights were all around, tires screeching to a halt, my head spinning. Doors slammed. The sirens continued blaring. Voices and feet scuffled against the ground. Sheriff Lawson and his deputies surrounded Mansfield. A heavy arm circled my shoulders. It was Daddy. I dropped the knife, buried my face in his chest. My legs crumpled, my body went limp. He held me against him. Huge, gasping sobs tore out of me, mixed with a high, eerie moan that wouldn't stop. *Oh, God, bring her back! Oh, God, bring her back!*

Chapter 25
The Lion and the Lamb

A CANOPY OF STARS LAY OVER ME, splattered across the depths of the early-morning darkness. I sat upon the dew-wet ground, my arms crossed over my chest, holding the pain inside. The creek hastened before me as the cool breath of March blew in from the hills. The heat from within had left me. The adrenaline was gone. Instead, I felt cold waves of hurt wash over me as though I was sitting on the edge of an arctic ocean and the tide was rolling in.

The woods would soon be spotted with the blossoms of dogwoods like tufts of clean snow, and the flowers would begin to bloom in the grasses. The pastures would become green. And for a moment I felt Ruthie's presence around me like that of an embrace.

Slowly the darkness began to lift from the sky and the stars began to fade, as though the air had become liquid and clear, rain-washed and pure. Streaks of lavender and blue stretched before me ever so slightly. I watched the colors expand, reaching over the hills, casting a wonderful glow upon the water. The sun rose with delicate veins of gold, patiently spilling across the sky into a beautiful mosaic.

From a distance, the trees moaned as the wind stirred their branches. A body drew close.

"I knew you'd come," I said, never looking at him.

Maurice Lampley sat down beside me, tall, yet less stoic. His demeanor was gentle, defeated. His blue shirt touched my arm.

"I'm sorry," he said. "I know she was your best friend."

The tears ached in my eyes and slowly fell down my face.

"I kept having this dream," I told him. "Each time, I'd be out in the woods the night Mama died. I was trying to save her. But I couldn't get to her in time. I couldn't help her, and I couldn't help Ruthie!" Then, looking at Maurice: "Why did Ruthie have to die? Wasn't Mama enough? Why both of them?"

Maurice laid his hand on my back. "I don't know."

"I miss her so much," I cried, my eyes raw from all the tears. "I'll always miss her. . . ."

"As you would miss the beating of your own heart. I know."

It was midmorning. The great rays of fire, crafted out of plywood, had been taken down at Reverend Taylor's church as soon as word was out that Mansfield had been arrested. Yet outside the sun rose full-bodied against the deep blue sky. A crowd had clustered together on a small plot of ground behind the church. Tombstones were scattered unevenly around us. The wind had become mild and warm, almost caressing. Some of the people hummed to themselves; others talked in soft whispers. Black faces, black clothes. The only whiteness was that of the starched collars worn by the men and the handful of white faces. Daddy and Fay stood close by me, their hands held together. Fay had brought me flowers the day after Ruthie was found and had been taking care of the meals and the house, giving me the space I needed.

There were tears that morning, though different from when Mama died. Some people swayed as they cried, many holding carnations or roses. Others' arms were joined together. From a distance, I saw Mr. Lampley approach. I knew his gait and his white hair well. He was dressed in the same suit he wore to Mama's funeral. He walked slowly toward me, his shoulders slumped only slightly. He pressed his arm over my shoulders, hugging me to him. I reached around his neck and cried softly against his chest. Releasing each other, I saw the tears filling his clear blue eyes.

I looked for Earnest, then spotted him walking toward me from the back of the crowd. He was wearing his khakis and white shirt and a blazer he had borrowed from the Taylors. As he drew close, he pressed his hands gently on my shoulders from behind.

The Reverend walked in front of us and stood before the ground which had been prepared for Ruthie. His face was solemn, his body erect. Some of the humming continued softly around me.

"God gives us the grace to live each day as it comes. Not always can we see very far. But neither can we see very far at night when we are driving a car. We drive it by faith, as far down the road as we can see. Step by step.

"Today a child has been taken away. A sister. A friend. A child who loved life. A child of laughter, a child of faith."

Chants filled the space around me, quiet words spoken by others as the Reverend continued, as he spoke of Ruthie, his own flesh and blood.

"'Laughter is good for the soul,' she often said. And those who knew our Ruthie know how she made us laugh. The kind of laughter that brought tears to your eyes. And she could sing, dear brothers. Oh, how our sister could sing."

"Amen, brother."

The Reverend paused for a moment, gaining his strength, breathing in deeply. "'We are more than conquerors through him that loved us,' saith the word of the Lord."

"Yes, dear brother. Amen, brother."

"Our child is not dead, dear brothers. Our child lives!" The Reverend crossed his arms over his chest as though holding onto an unleashed power. A spirit. A strength. As the voices rose around me, again I felt the touch of Ruthie's presence.

"'Oh, Lord, you have set your glory above the heavens. From the lips of children and infants, you have ordained praise because of your enemies to silence the foe and the avenger,' says David."

The Reverend's voice suddenly became quiet. "Ruthie loved the fields. She loved the pastures. The banks of the creek where she and Francie spent so much time together. Our Ruthie is in safe pasture now, dear brothers. The avenger has been silenced." Tears streamed down the Reverend's face. His arms fell to his sides as the pain poured forth from his body. Choruses began around me. I leaned against Earnest, holding onto his hands.

Tom stepped forward. He turned to face us, standing beside his father. Then he spoke, a Bible opened in front of him.

" 'The Lord will strike the earth with the rod of his mouth; with the breath of his lips he will slay the wicked. Righteousness will be his belt and faithfulness the sash around his waist. The wolf will live with the lamb, the leopard will lie down with the goat, the calf and the lion and the yearling together; and a little child will lead them,' so says the word of the Lord."

He closed the Bible and held it to his side. A gentleness overtook him. A struggle inside him was over. The Reverend took his hand, clasped it tightly with his own. Tears beaded Tom's eyelashes. Voices rose around me, somewhat soft at first, then growing stronger. Bodies swayed in unison despite the pain.

> Oh, well, I'm tired and so weary,
> > but I must go along
> till the Lord he comes and calls me,
> > calls me away.
> Well the mornin's so bright,
> > and the Lamb is the light,
> and the night, night is as black
> > as the sea.
>
> There will be peace in the valley
> > for me, someday.
> There will be peace, peace in the valley
> > for me, oh Lord I pray.

There'll be no sadness, no sorrow,

no trouble I see.

There will be peace, peace in the valley

for me.

At that moment, Alby came forward. He turned to face us, taking Tom's hand in his. And with a force almost ethereal, he began to sing the rest of the song. "I have to do something," Ruthie had said. "Not just for me or for your mom, but for Alby." I remembered her words as clearly as if she was speaking to me through the boy's voice. "If I don't set him free, there's no one else who will."

His voice rang out, flowing over us like sweet honey.

Well, the bear will be gentle

and the wolf will be tame,

And the lion, lion will lie down

by the lamb.

And the beasts of the wild

shall be led by a child,

And I'll be changed, changed from this creature

that I am.

The chorus picked up around me, voices joining in, pouring over the valley, growing stronger.

When the singing ended I stepped forward, the poem Ruthie had given me held in my hand. In a trembling voice, I began to read.

When you're feelin' like the sun's gone down on your head,
I'll be there for you.
And when the cold of life bleeds into your bones,
I'll be there for you.
Like evenin' comes and day comes,
Like the shoes on your feet, I'll walk with you,
I'll be there for you.

Don't matter that my skin is brown,
don't matter that your eyes are green.
Like these stones in my hand,
I'll be there for you.

As I read Ruthie's words, I felt her spirit all around me, and I knew even death cannot end a friendship. Ruthie would always be with me.

People began moving forward to drop flowers on the plain pine box that held my best friend. Ruthie would soon be laid in the ground. I couldn't watch. I turned to Earnest with pleading eyes. He understood. He walked to my side, laid an arm over my shoulder, and led me away.

I reached a hand into the pocket of my jacket, wrapping my fingers around the smooth stones Ruthie had once worn.

Someone called my name. I turned to see Sheriff Lawson walking toward us.

"Alby testified this morning," he spoke softly. "Told us everything."

I nodded my head.

"Francie, I'm gonna take every one of them down."

And I knew what he meant. Sheriff McGee, Randy, Jason, Rolan. All of them. It was over.

Earnest and I continued walking, the voices fading behind us, the stones held tight in my hand.